MW01088216

Yellowstone
Heart Song

Yellowstone Romance Series
Book 1

By Peggy L Henderson

Yellowstone
Heart Song

Chapter One

Aimee Donovan raised her head a few inches off the ground and squinted into the bright light. She blinked several times, hoping to bring the blurry images into focus. The world suddenly tilted precariously, and a wave of nausea hit her. Someone must have turned off the heart monitor in the room. Things were way too quiet all of a sudden. Her hands moved, brushing against a carpet of . . . grass?

She took a deep breath, and tried to clear her head. The smell of clean earth and sweet grass enveloped her senses. She bolted upright, nearly blacking out from the blood leaving her brain. Wide-eyed, she slowly turned her head to scan her surroundings.

Two facts jolted her mind. First, she was definitely no longer in Zach's hospital room. Second, this was Yellowstone! Absolutely no doubt about it! After all, she backpacked in this park every summer. Her parents had instilled a love of camping and the outdoors in her since early childhood.

Fully alert now, she ran her hand over tufts of lush green buffalo grass. The rhythmic sounds of crickets, chirping birds, and the tranquil gurgle of a creek brought a sense of calm. The noisy humming of car engines, or the loud roar of a motorcycle speeding down the highway were sounds distinctly absent.

She inhaled deeply. Her lungs filled with crisp, clean mountain air infused with the scent of sage and pine. What a welcome contrast to the hot and pollution-laden air she breathed at home.

1

"This can't be possible. There's no way that crazy old man was telling the truth."

"I travel through time."

No. No way. She shook her head wildly. Time travel! Absolutely ridiculous!

But how the heck did I get here? Did she just land in an episode from *The Twilight Zone?* Any second now, Rod Serling would show up. Perhaps she'd find herself waking from a wonderful dream, one she wasn't sure she wanted to wake up from. Dreaming of Yellowstone was definitely good. Something she did a lot. Especially since her annual backpacking trip was only a few weeks away. She and Jana had been discussing possible itineraries for months already.

She shook her head again. This was too real. Her hand stroked the fine particles of soil where she sat. She ran her fingers up the long blades of sweet grass. It all felt real enough. She'd never had vivid dreams like this before. How could she have traveled over a thousand miles in the blink of an eye? Did that mean everything else was true as well, and she'd traveled back in time by 200 years? A sudden chill crept down her spine.

Do you have a better explanation? It's either real, or it's a dream. Pick one. Zach had told her the only way she'd finally be convinced he wasn't lying that he came from the nineteenth century would be to experience time travel for herself. A moment ago she'd been standing at his hospital bed, playing along with his claims that he could send her to the Yellowstone of the past, and now she was actually here! *Did you have to tell him you could survive a wilderness trip like this, Aimee?* Unbelievable! How could this be possible?

She rose tentatively to her feet, anticipating another round of the floating-through-the-air feelings she experienced moments ago. A slow sigh escaped her lips. Her world didn't tilt, and she stood firmly on the ground. In this endless sea of grass, she felt like an insignificant speck of dust, the only person in the world. The distant mountains stood like silent specters against the blue horizon, lending emphasis to the absolute solitude. She was on her own.

"Aimee Donovan, it would appear you're alone in the

2

wilderness," she stated the obvious, the reality of her situation starting to sink in.

A cold shiver ran down her spine, similar to what she'd felt five years ago when the police knocked on her door. The shocking news of her parents' deaths had left her all alone then, as well. Closing her eyes for a moment to pinch off the sudden burning sensation at the back of her eyes, she inhaled deeply, and pushed the memory from her mind.

She raised her hands in the air and looked skyward as she pivoted in a circle. "Okay, Zach," she called. "I'll play your game. You sent me into the past. It's 1810, not 2010." Her own voice sounded out of place amongst the sounds of birds and insects, but talking out loud was comforting. "I guess I finally get to put all those wilderness survival courses to good use."

Aimee lowered her hands. She spotted her backpack in the tall grass a few feet away and sighed in relief. Without it, she would be in some serious trouble. She turned her body in a circle and continued to scan the area, straining to identify familiar landscapes. Nothing but wide-open grassland in all directions. Forested mountains loomed in the distance to the north and south.

A wide smile spread across her face. The snow-capped peak to the north beckoned her like icing on a cake. The mountain welcomed her like a friend to guide her way. Mt. Holmes! Her knees weakened with relief. *You can do this, Aimee. You know this area. Even without a map, you've been here plenty of times.*

"This has to be the Gibbon Meadows area or somewhere nearby."

Think, Aimee, think.

She was completely alone in the wilderness two centuries before her time. The vast Yellowstone wilderness of 1810 was precisely that. She couldn't simply walk out of here. Heck, until she'd met Zach, she didn't even know there were any white men in the Rocky Mountains in 1810. The fur trapper era didn't get fully underway until the 1820's, if she remembered her history correctly. Only a few Native American tribes migrated through here.

"I need to find the Gibbon River. If it hasn't changed course much in 200 years, it's going to be around here somewhere."

Higher ground. She had to get to higher ground. Her survival depended on finding the Gibbon River and following it straight to the Madison River Valley. It's where Zach had told her to go. He'd said he'd come for her in three months and meet her there. So far, everything he'd told her had turned out to be true, and she had no intention to disregard his advice now. She could not survive three months without doing exactly what he'd suggested.

She gazed at the snowy mountain peak to the north one more time. "If I keep Mt. Holmes to my back, I should come up on the Gibbon River, and if I follow that, it will lead me right to the Madison."

A wide smile spread across her face. So far, so good. The distant high-pitched barking of coyotes reached her ears. Her face sobered, thinking about wild animals. Bears and wolves were abundant in the Rocky Mountains in the nineteenth century.

Aimee settled herself back on the ground and opened her backpack. The tall grasses swallowed her up on all sides. She had carelessly tossed a few things together at home to play along with Zach's wild claims that he could send her on the wilderness survival trip of a lifetime. She probably hadn't packed anything of real use to her now. She dug through her belongings to inventory what supplies she actually did have. She found nothing that she could use in her defense, should she encounter a wild animal.

"Damn! I didn't even think to pack my multi-tool." Her pulse rate increased. Did grizzlies in this time behave the same as the Yellowstone bears of the twenty-first century?

"Way to go, Aimee," she said aloud.

She counted three granola bars and a chocolate bar as her only sources of food. Her wool sweater, a couple of changes of clothing and underwear, her compass, flint, medical kit, a few toiletries, and her journal rounded out what she had thrown together in haste. She'd only gone back to visit Zach after her shift in the emergency room to indulge him in his mad fantasies.

Apparently, he hadn't turned out so crazy after all. Letting out a long sigh, she stared at her meager supplies splayed out before her. Hardly what she would ordinarily bring on a survival trip.

4

"How could you be so careless and unprepared," she mumbled, and shoved everything back into the pack.

Eager to be on her way, Aimee shouldered her backpack and held the compass in her right hand. She glanced at Mt. Holmes one more time. The mountain guided her way like a signal beacon, yet it was reassuring to have a compass. She squared her shoulders and adjusted the pack on her back, and started walking. The forested mountains ahead would be her first destination.

The bright sun shone directly overhead, casting almost no shadows. And if this was June, as it had been back home, she would have daylight for many hours yet. Right now, her main objective, aside from locating the Gibbon River, was finding a place to make shelter for the night. She was confident she could hike the distance to the Madison River in less than two days.

It didn't take long before she reached the banks of a shallow stream that meandered lazily through the grass. *Should I follow the stream, or keep going directly south?* A coin to toss would have made her decision easier. Following the stream might lead her to the river she sought. This was most likely a tributary. But if it wasn't, her hike might just get longer. The stream did flow more or less in a southerly direction.

Her mind made up, she followed along its banks for nearly an hour, but the forest appeared no closer than before. In the distance, the green grass disappeared beneath the largest bison herd she'd ever seen. The distinct smell of cow permeated the air.

"Okay, Aimee, decision time." She had no intention of a close encounter with those huge beasts. It could prove to be as deadly as meeting up with a grizzly. Two summers ago, she'd been one of many helpless people standing by to witness a woman gored by a bison. She shuddered at the memory. The woman had merely stepped on a stick while trying to photograph the beast. That was all it took to set the animal off. True, she'd been closer than she should have been, but the bison had charged without mercy, tossing her in the air like a rag doll. Aimee never found out what had happened to the woman after she'd been airlifted to the nearest hospital.

Her eyes roamed the vast herd. She'd never seen so many

bison before, and she stood in awe of their sheer numbers. If she had to venture a guess, this herd had to be at least two or three times larger than the entire modern day bison population put together. She couldn't even begin to count them all to get an estimate. The snorting and bellowing of the hulking beasts carried on the slight breeze. Most lumbered along lazily, plucking at the lush grasses in the meadow, while others laid in wallows, chewing their mid-day cud. Several orange-colored calves loped around their mothers, bucking and rearing in play.

After a few moments, Aimee set off again at a brisk pace along the stream. At least two hours passed before individual trees of the forest ahead finally took shape. The stream led her directly into the deeply wooded area. Tall lodgepole pines closed in around her, allowing only a few golden ribbons of light to penetrate the canopies and reach the forest floor. She rubbed at the goose bumps on her arms, trying to brush away her sudden apprehension. *It's just because it's colder here than out in the open, Aimee.*

The forest seemed to go on forever. Deadfall lay around everywhere. Her backpack grew heavier with each successive log she scrambled over. Time for a short break. Her thighs burned, and her pulse drummed loudly in her ears. She considered herself to be in excellent physical condition, but trudging over logs all day proved to be more exhausting than the longest Stairmasters workout she'd ever done.

A quick glance at her compass reassured her that she was still heading south. Reluctantly, she pushed off from the tree trunk she leaned up against, and forced her weary legs to move again.

An endless amount of time passed when the forest finally opened to a sunny clearing. "Oh thank goodness! I'm stopping here for the night." She held back a triumphant cheer. Shrugging the pack off her back, she rotated her shoulders and neck to ease her aching muscles. Without the burden of the pack, she suddenly felt light as air. She cupped her hands in the cool creek, splashing water on her face and neck.

The sun's rays shone on the rippling current, giving the illusion of thousands of shimmering diamonds, and Aimee shielded her eyes from the sparkling reflections. The icy liquid tasted better than anything she'd ever drank from a bottle, and it soothed her parched throat like ice cream on a hot summer day. Refreshed and hydrated, she set to work constructing a simple shelter. Dead trees and branches lay around in abundance. After dragging branches of various sizes to her selected campsite, she leaned them in a row against a large downed trunk, creating a v-shaped tunnel big enough for her to crawl into. She covered these with smaller branches to give extra protection in case of rain.

It was a simple shelter she'd learned to make in one of her outdoor survival courses. Finished, she rummaged through her pack for her flint, and set fire to a pile of kindling just outside her temporary home, adding larger sticks to feed the growing flames.

Her stomach growled and churned, a reminder that she hadn't eaten all day. "If I only had something to cook, that would be great."

There were no fish in the stream, and besides, she had nothing to catch them with. There weren't any berry bushes within sight, either. Too tired to explore the area further for something easily edible, she settled for a granola bar from her pack.

The last rays of the sun quickly disappeared behind the canopies of the tall lodgepole pines that stood sentinel at the edge of the clearing. Aimee briskly rubbed her hands up and down her arms to ward off the sudden chill in the air. She added more wood to her crackling fire, then pulled her sweater on over her head. Tired and alone, she curled up in her small shelter and hugged her backpack tightly to her chest as daylight fell behind the trees.

The events of the day had left her physically exhausted, but sleep eluded her. How was this possible? The warm glow of the fire gave little comfort as she lay there, staring into the absolute darkness, listening to the nighttime sounds of Yellowstone. Male crickets chirping their mating calls drowned out the chorus of frogs, the occasional hooting of an owl, and the rustling in the underbrush. The forest was about to come alive with a myriad of predators looking for an easy meal.

The sudden chill down her spine reminded her of nails scraping down a chalkboard. She'd never been scared before sleeping in the backcountry. The fun of backpacking was to get away from it all, experience nature and its solitude. However, she'd never gone out alone before. And right now, solitude and 'getting away from it all' took on a whole new meaning.

She reached for more wood to add to her fire. The dancing orange flames gave her little comfort. This was the real deal, not some simulated one-week survival trip into the wilderness where rescue was a phone call away. And she'd told Zach she was capable of just such a trip.

Heck! Who could blame her for not believing the man's stories that he was a mountain man from the past? He had been a patient in the emergency room where Aimee worked as a first year trauma nurse. She had liked the older man immediately. He'd been friendly and engaging, not rude like many of the other patients she had to deal with on a daily basis. His authentic-looking buckskins were similar to ones worn by actors in old west re-enactments she'd attended.

Zach's face had lit up with interest, and Aimee had soon found herself immersed in conversations with him about trappers, mountain men, and wilderness survival. When he told her he had traveled through time from 200 years in the past, she had contemplated calling for a psych consult. Nevertheless, his stories were fascinating. When he offered to send her to the past to experience "real" wilderness survival, she'd played along; even telling him it would be a dream come true.

* * *

After a sleepless night, Aimee struggled through dense forests and mountainous terrain. She must be somewhere close to the Gibbon Canyon. The stream she'd been following had to lead to the Gibbon River. Her thigh muscles felt like lead from climbing over logs all day, and her stomach was constantly protesting the lack of food.

She had found some edible plants along the way to add to her diet of granola bars, but none of it kept the hunger pangs away for very long. To keep herself entertained, she sang out loud. Hopefully, that would keep bears away as well.

Emerging from a particularly forested area, a wide canyon yawned before her. Her eyes scanned the scenery in wonderment.

8

As far as she could see, mountains blanketed in pine forests stretched toward the horizon beyond the deep scar in the earth. The flowing water at the bottom of the canyon looked like a tiny blue ribbon from her vantage point. This had to be the Gibbon River.

Relief washed over her like a warm ray of sunshine. She should reach the Madison River, and hopefully her destination, the following day.

A foul, sour odor filled the air, and she curled her nose in protest. Her heart rate increased. The smell could only mean one thing. Her eyes darted around frantically as her legs went rubbery from the jolt of adrenaline that flooded her system. She spotted the carcass of a partially eaten elk half-buried in dirt, confirming her worst fears.

"Oh, crap!" Her feet remained rooted to the ground in a paralyzing fear. When she finally willed her legs to move, a huge grizzly came charging at her from the woods. The beast let out a loud roar, baring huge yellow teeth as drool hung in long strands down its mouth. The breeze carried the stench of rotten flesh that emanated from the predator's jaws, and Aimee backed up quicker. Hopefully the bear was just bluffing, and it would realize she wasn't any threat to its food. Her heart pounded violently and her whole body shook.

Stay calm. Don't turn and run or you're dead. She had to force herself to heed her own words while every survival instinct in her body screamed at her to run away as fast as possible. She'd gladly give her right arm at the moment for a can of bear spray.

The bruin stopped its charge. It scratched at the ground with enormous paws, moving its head from side to side. Its large nose twitched back and forth, sniffing the air. The bear huffed several times, and then let out another earsplitting roar.

Realizing the grizzly geared up for another attack, her eyes widened. She stumbled backwards, nearly tripping on a rock. Just as she envisioned huge claws ripping her apart, the ground suddenly dropped out from under her feet. Her arms flailed wildly and she groped for any kind of hold on a rock or protruding tree root. Her throat tightened, and her jaw clenched. Her efforts prevented a complete free fall, but the downward

9

momentum proved too great to get a solid grip on any object. Her ribs jutted against unyielding rocks, knocking the air from her lungs. Roots and small trees cut into her arms and hands. When would she stop falling? It felt like an eternity, like she'd been sinking all her life. Her limbs became numb to the sensation of slamming against hard rocks. She stopped hearing the debris falling along with her. Her momentum increased, and her stomach rose to her throat. The sensation of floating through the air, then a sudden hard impact.

Coughing and spitting dirt, she gasped and sucked in several shallow breaths. Her lungs refused to expand for the air she so desperately needed. She lay still for a moment, listening, trying to calm her heart and trembling body.

Had she broken any bones? What if the bear followed her down the canyon? Cautiously, she raised her head, and gazed up the cliff. The predator was nowhere in sight. Her lungs finally allowed for a deep breath of relief. She turned her head slowly to the side, facing away from the rock wall. The bottom of the canyon still gaped hundreds of feet below her. A narrow ledge had stopped her full descent.

She lay still for a moment longer while her breathing and heart rate normalized. She tried to rise to her feet, but searing hot pain shot through her right ankle. She couldn't suppress a cry of pain. Tears stung her eyes, and she bit down on her lower lip, then sank back to the ground. Any hope that she would wake up to reality vanished instantly. No one could be in this much pain in a dream.

Aimee scooted back from the edge of the narrow outcropping, and pulled her backpack free of a pine branch. There was no way she would have survived a fall all the way down the canyon. Her arms trembled, and she slumped against the canyon wall. Staring at the little pine, she reached out and touched the sparse branches, silently thanking the tree for stopping her fall.

Stay calm. Don't panic. Her mantra replayed itself over and over in her mind. She mentally took stock of her options. Down was definitely out of the question. She would never make it. It was simply too steep. Getting back to the top might be an impossible task with her injury. And if she did manage it, the bear was still a problem.

The odds of anyone finding her here were less than zero. Perhaps in a hundred years or so, someone would discover her skeletal remains, creating all kinds of speculation regarding her twenty-first century effects.

The urge to scream in frustration, and at the same time give in to her growing fear and cry, raced through her. Taking a deep breath instead, she leaned forward to unlace her hiking boot, and pried it from her injured foot. Her hands ached and trembled, and were covered in bleeding cuts and gashes.

"I must look great," she scoffed, trying in vain to lighten the mood.

Her foot throbbed as she gingerly prodded and examined it. Being able to move it at the ankle was a good sign that it wasn't broken. Her medical training compelled her to stabilize and wrap the joint. From a survivalist point of view, she needed to keep her boot on if she hoped to get out of this canyon.

During her backcountry first aid training, she'd learned that a boot gave a sprained ankle adequate stability in an emergency. She slipped it back on, gritting her teeth as she tightened the laces. Later, and there would be a later, after getting safely off this cliff, she would wrap her foot with the ace bandage that was in her medical kit.

Aimee struggled to stand, hugging the wall of rocks, using them for support as she pulled herself up. If she lost her balance . . . She'd never get this lucky a second time if she fell off this ledge. Standing on her injured foot proved impossible. Without the ability to bear full weight, climbing out of the canyon would be nearly impossible. Emitting a loud growl in frustration, she eased herself back to the ground, and rummaged through her medical kit for a bottle of ibuprofen.

"Maybe if I take a large enough dose, I can get up this damn mountain!" she shouted into the wind, her voice echoing off the canyon walls.

Her calls sent several startled ravens that were perched on some outcroppings soaring into the sky. They squawked loudly in protest. Aimee grabbed for some rocks within her reach, and forcefully threw them deeper into the canyon in anger. *Whatever*

11

possessed you to tell Zach you could do something like this on your own? Were you out of your mind! Damn it, I'm not going to panic!

The hours dragged on with excruciating slowness. Aimee licked her dry and cracking lips. Dehydration happened very quickly at this altitude. Her empty stomach growled loudly in protest, but water was more important at the moment.

The ibuprofen proved to be useless. It eased the throbbing ache in her ankle, but not enough to bear weight. It was a futile exercise, but she called out for help several times, which only caused more pain to her already raw larynx. No one would hear her cries. Why even bother?

She huddled against the rocks late in the afternoon. The wind picked up strong and cold, whistling mercilessly through the canyon. Curling up around her pack didn't stop the shivers that vibrated her body through another sleepless night. The bright early morning sun refused to warm her. Maybe going over the ledge was the thing to do. The river below beckoned. She could quench her torturous thirst. *Sleep . . . I just want to sleep. I'll try climbing out later . . .after I get some sleep.*

12

Chapter Two

Daniel Osborne stood outside his small cabin, sharpening a large hunting knife on a whetstone, oblivious to the chill in the early morning air. His hands moved the shiny blade in rhythmic, circular motions against the smooth stone. Movement across the river drew his attention, and his hands stilled. Almost imperceptibly, he raised his head and scanned the tree line along the opposite bank. A lazy smile spread across his face. His focus returned to his work while he waited on the arrival of the man who emerged from the forest.

"Your senses are not as sharp as they once were, White Wolf." Daniel's adoptive brother, Elk Runner called in his native tongue. He loped up the grassy incline and stopped in front of the cabin. Straightening to his full height, Daniel's face brightened in a wide grin.

"I already saw you beyond the river." Daniel waved off the other man's words, then reached out and clasped Elk Runner's hand in greeting. "It is good to see you, brother. What brings you this way? I thought you were out hunting the bighorn with your family this month?"

"Three hunters and I were on our way to the canyon of the *E-chee-dick-karsh-ah-shay* to hunt the bighorn, when we came across a strange sighting."

"What did you see this time? A two-headed bison?"

Elk Runner ignored Daniel's mocking. "I left my hunting party and came here to tell you there is a crazy white woman wandering in the woods."

Daniel glared at his friend for a moment, then burst out laughing. "Yeah, and I'm *Tam Apo* himself."

"We followed her for half a day," Elk Runner continued, seemingly unaffected by Daniel's outburst. "She is alone, and appears lost. I did not see signs that anyone is with her. She wears strange white man's clothing, and chants loud words in the language of your father. I'm surprised you have not heard her, White Wolf, she makes so much noise."

Daniel's eyes narrowed. Elk Runner had certainly come up with a good prank this time!

"Do you remember the time when we were in our eighth summer, and you told me to stick my hand in a hollow log because you had seen a fox hide inside? You told me I would make our mother proud if I brought her a fox fur."

A slow smile spread across Elk Runner's face. "I remember."

"And I believed you," Daniel continued. "When I reached in to grab the fox, it was a skunk I pulled from the log. Do you remember how I was banished from entering the village for nearly a week? And how my father made me sit in the cold creek for an entire day?"

"We were children then, White Wolf," Elk Runner defended himself, a wide grin on his face nonetheless. "I would not mock you about this. There is a white woman wandering in the forest. Where she comes from, I could not tell, but I do know there is no man with her."

"I have a lot of work to do." Daniel poured some water on the whetstone to prove his point, and resumed sliding his blade across the stone's slick, flat surface. "You have really outdone yourself this time with your tales. You came all this way to tell me this so I would go on a needless search for this make-believe woman. Why did you not go to her and take her with you?"

"She is a white woman," Elk Runner argued. "I could not make my presence known to her. I cannot speak her language."

"You speak a little French." Daniel glanced up from his work.

"It was not French she was chanting. Besides, it is bad luck to talk to a person who is crazy in the head." Elk Runner made a circular motion with his index finger against his temple.

"Then why am I talking to you?" Daniel threw his arms skyward for dramatic effect.

14

"Why would I abandon my hunting party to come this far to tell you this if it was not true?" Elk Runner adamantly raised his voice. Daniel searched his brother's face. He did make a good point. Only something urgent would have him abandon a hunting trip. "I will take you to where I last saw her. Then you will see I do not lie," the Indian persisted.

"How far?" Daniel asked reluctantly.

He set the knife on the stone and ran his hand through his hair, pushing back the unruly strands that fell into his eyes. He shot Elk Runner a hard stare. If there was even a remote chance that something like this could be true, even though it was utterly impossible, he had to find out.

How would a white woman come to be here? It was ridiculous. Aside from himself and his father, only a few white trappers came through these mountains in any given year, and they were mostly Frenchmen who had wandered too far south from trapping up along the headwaters of the Missouri River. He hadn't heard anything this absurd in a long time.

"It is less than a day's walk from here, if we travel fast," Elk Runner answered. "Just beyond the falls of the Little Buffalo River."

"All right. I'll go with you." Daniel's chest heaved a sigh. What would he get himself into this time?

After sheathing the now razor-sharp knife in the belt at his waist, he entered his cabin to collect his powder horn, bullet pouch, a water bag, and a rolled-up blanket, all of which he slung over his shoulder. He picked up his tomahawk, long rifle, and gathered a handful of dried meat strips to put in his traveling pouch, and declared himself ready to go.

The two began their journey in silence. They kept a fast pace heading east away from the cabin. They made their way easily through a gently sloping, open meadow after leaving the small valley Daniel considered home, keeping to the left of what they called the Little Buffalo River. When the area became more wooded, they followed a deer trail single file along the river's banks.

By mid-afternoon, they veered away from the meandering river. The landscape changed from rolling meadowlands and

15

forest to steeper, mountainous terrain, and both men knew to avoid the canyon the water had carved, for it made travel a lot more difficult below the waterfall. Above the falls and beyond, the landscape flattened out again. When they came to yet another meadow, Elk Runner stopped and scanned the area along a shallow creek.

"This is where I last saw her." It didn't take him long to pick up a trail. An almost imperceptible narrow line of trampled grass followed close along the creek banks.

"I've never seen prints like these before." Daniel's eyebrows furrowed as he knelt down to examine the tracks more closely, his fingers tracing the odd grooves and circular patterns in the soft earth. His hand nearly covered one print. Whoever made these tracks must be of a small stature. Without exchanging further words with his companion, he followed the trail of peculiar footprints.

Finally, Daniel broke the silence. "How would a white woman appear in these mountains? There are no whites within a thousand miles."

"It is an omen that you should find this woman." Elk Runner shot him a serious look "The spirits are telling you that it is past time you took a wife, White Wolf. They have sent this woman to you, since you cannot seem to find one on your own."

"That must be it." Daniel's face hardened, and he clenched his jaw.

Elk Runner knew his thoughts about marriage. A wife would require that he give up his life as a trapper, which he was not inclined to do. Even Morning Fawn had wanted him to live with her family as was customary of a husband among her tribe had they married. A white wife was even more unthinkable. His father had always warned him about the frail and delicate nature of white women. Wasn't his mother proof of that?

His father hadn't told him about the malicious nature of white females, however. His eyes narrowed and his mouth contorted into a sneer as he recalled his one moment of weakness concerning a white woman. He quickly pushed the unpleasant memory out of his mind.

The tracks continued through the forest. "Whoever made

these prints is mad." His face darkened while he leapt over more deadfall. What fool would travel this way rather than seek out a deer trail?

"She will not be able to continue this course much longer. The canyon and falls are not far," Elk Runner commented.

The footprints finally led to a clearing overlooking the canyon. He stopped suddenly and held up his hand in silent warning before they were completely out of the forest. Several ravens perched on downed logs and in trees, making loud "kaah-kaah-ing" noises. Daniel scanned the area, and quickly found what he already suspected had drawn the ravens to congregate here. He pointed to the bony remains of an elk that lay strewn about. A coyote eagerly tore at some leftover tendons.

"This kill is several days old." Daniel exchanged a meaningful look with Elk Runner.

The two surveyed their surroundings and recognized the telltale signs of a bear charging at something. They didn't have to find more tracks to know what had happened. The person they'd been following had carelessly walked up on the kill. The bear had charged, sending the person over the cliff. The coyote's presence and unconcerned demeanor assured them that the grizzly had left the area. Hurrying to the edge of the canyon, they peered down.

Daniel's eyes widened. His gaze fixed on the female form that filled almost the entire area of a narrow outcropping along the canyon walls. Recovered from his initial surprise, he cleared his throat and shouted, "Hello down there."

When he received no response, he called again in French. "Etes vous bien." This time there was a slight movement.

"Find some twine and make rope. I'm going down there." Daniel shot a quick glance at his brother.

Elk Runner nodded and hurried off to do as he was asked.

Leaving his long rifle behind, Daniel climbed down the canyon wall, using jutting rocks and tree roots for support. Numerous thoughts entered his mind as he tried to come up with an explanation as to how a white woman appeared in this wilderness. As he reached her, she let out a soft moan. Her voice was barely audible, but she spoke in English, "Please . . . help me." Her eyes fluttered open briefly, and she tried to raise her head, but it seemed to cause her too much effort. She lowered it back to the rocky ground with a quiet moan, and lay still.

Daniel's eyes roamed over her. Dust and debris covered her strange-looking clothing, and cuts and bruises marred her face and hands. Her hair was matted with dirt and twigs. She had no outward injuries that would indicate a bear attack.

He pondered her unfamiliar clothing. Whites back east dressed in fine clothes, but he had never seen this type of material before. Her body curled around some sort of traveling pack, but this, too, looked unlike anything he had ever laid eyes on.

He removed his water bag from around his neck, uncorked the opening, and put one hand under her head to raise it slightly. "Can you hear me?"

The woman moaned faintly, but made no other sound.

"You need to drink." He touched the tip of the water bag to her cracked lips, letting small amounts of water trickle out. She swallowed weakly, and gave no resistance when Daniel took the water bag away. "Just a little for now. I'll get you out of here."

"Leg . . . hurt," she whispered weakly.

He stared at her legs. She flinched and let out a faint cry when he touched her right ankle.

Elk Runner finally appeared at the top of the canyon. He threw one end of a freshly braided twine rope down to him. "I'm going to tie this around her, and you'll have to pull her up," Daniel shouted up to his friend. "It's too steep for me to carry her."

Elk Runner nodded. Daniel tied the stiff makeshift rope around the woman's mid-section, and called to Elk Runner to start pulling.

The woman half awoke and grabbed hold of the twine in an effort to help get up the canyon. He was about to put a hand on a rock above him to begin the ascent, when she motioned feebly to her pack. He picked it up off the ground and turned it in several directions, then slung it over one shoulder.

Supporting her the best he could without falling himself, he proceeded back up the canyon wall. When they finally reached the top, she slumped to the ground again.

Daniel hoisted himself up over the edge of the canyon. "She

needs warmth or she will die," he said, his tone impassive. "Let's find a more sheltered place to make camp."

"She will need nourishment as well. I will go make meat," Elk Runner offered.

Daniel eyed the woman. What the hell was he going to do with her? A white woman, of all things! With a shake of his head, he bent down and scooped her up in his arms as if she weighed nothing. Scanning the surrounding woods once more for any sign of the bear, he strode off in the direction from which they had come.

Daniel carried the woman to a sheltered area about a mile from the canyon. He placed her on a bed of leaves and covered her with his blanket. Gathering kindling and wood, he quickly built a fire. He observed the woman's body shivering violently. She would not have lasted much longer on that ledge. It was remarkable that she had survived an entire night.

Every few minutes, he knelt beside her with his water bag, carefully dribbling the liquid into her mouth. Several attempts to speak produced no coherent words. Daniel had plenty of time to openly study her while he sat waiting for Elk Runner to arrive with some fresh meat.

Who are you? How is it even possible for you to be here?

His eyes drank in her angelic face as she slept. The color of her long wavy hair reminded him of autumn buffalo grass, and his hands curled into fists to keep from reaching out to touch it. The memory of her soft small body in his arms, and the curve of her breasts brushing against his chest, sent an unexplained heat through his veins.

The intoxicating scent of flowers on her clothing and hair, even through the layer of dust, lingered in his mind. Despite the numerous cuts and streaks of dried blood on her face, Daniel wondered if her skin would feel as soft as it looked if he ran a finger down her cheek.

Most curious about her appearance was her clothing. Daniel had never seen a woman in britches before, and it intrigued him. None of the Tukudeka women wore leggings, even in winter. Certainly no white woman in the eastern cities, or even in St. Louis, would wear britches. The many layers of material they

19

covered themselves with kept a man guessing as to the woman's shape underneath it all. Those pants, along with the shirt this woman wore, hid none of her feminine curves.

He couldn't even begin to explain where she might have come from. With the exception of his birth mother, he had never heard of a white woman in this region. She must be the wife of some French trapper. Was she a willing wife, or had she met a fate he'd heard about. River pirates were abundant along the Missouri, and women were often bought and sold. Perhaps she had been one of the unfortunate ones, and had been traded or sold to some Frenchman.

Was she alone because she had escaped him? Daniel scowled. Men got lonely in these mountains, but to take a woman against her will was despicable. He swore that if he found this woman's man, and she had been an unwilling wife, he might have to kill him.

He stood abruptly and ran a hand through his hair, clenching and unclenching his jaw as he paced by the fire. Why this sudden strong emotion to hurt someone over a woman, a white woman, he didn't even know?

Elk Runner found Daniel's camp sometime after dark. He brought two rabbits and a grouse. Silently they skinned, plucked, and gutted the meat, then skewered it on sticks to roast over the fire.

"What will you do with her?" Elk Runner finally spoke.

"You are the one who found her."

"I already have a wife." Elk Runner shrugged. "I give her to you. Besides, she is too small for my taste. She hardly has any meat on her bones."

"Take her to your village and have Little Bird tend to her until she is recovered." Daniel didn't relish the thought of spending any time with this woman. He had learned his lesson well years ago. Thankfully, he only encountered white women in St. Louis when he traveled that far to trade his furs. That amounted to once every couple of years.

"We do not speak the white man's tongue," Elk Runner reminded him again. "She would be better off with you at your cabin. You know the white man's ways."

20

"Perhaps we should find her man," Daniel suggested.

"I did not see any tracks that indicated she had a companion," Elk Runner said. "But I will go in the morning and retrace her trail. Perhaps I can find out where she comes from. Someone is probably looking for her. No one leaves a woman behind in these mountains. Unless," he added thoughtfully, "she is crazy like I said, and her man was trying to get rid of her."

Daniel's eyes perused the feminine creature lying there. She appeared small, frail, and helpless. Was she crazy? No man would deliberately get rid of her. In this wilderness, she would be a most sought-after prize.

"You can help me build a travois in the morning before you go. I can't carry her all the way back."

Elk Runner was right. He didn't have a choice but to take her back to his cabin with him. As he studied her some more, a peculiar sense of protectiveness took hold in him. The sensation was puzzling. Hadn't past experience taught him that a white woman was nothing but trouble? Even so, he would make damn sure no more harm came to her while she remained in his care. He would do no less for anyone else in need of help.

* * *

Aimee stirred awake. Faraway voices echoed in her head. There wasn't a spot on her body that didn't scream out in pain. Her pulse throbbed painfully in her injured foot. Lifting her heavy eyelids slightly, reality set in. Someone had rescued her. Her skin tingled as life-giving heat seeped into her body, although she still shivered under the blanket. Her mouth and throat didn't feel as if she'd swallowed a wad of cotton anymore, but she knew she had to be dehydrated. When she opened her eyes a bit more, the silhouettes of two men sitting by a campfire several yards away came into view. They were talking in a strange language. They had to be Indians.

Oh God, I hope they're friendly. Her mind conjured up a vague memory of strong yet gentle arms carrying her. Or had that been a dream? If these two meant to hurt her, wouldn't they have done it by now?

The vulnerability of her situation hit her full force. Dammit!

21

Zach should have known better than to send her off like this on her own, or at the very least, prepared her better. What had he been thinking? He must have known how dangerous this would be for her. Then again, what had she been thinking? She'd been thinking he was lying, that's what. And she had convinced him she was up to the challenge of a wilderness survival trip.

Snippets of her conversations with Zach echoed in her mind as she lay there, wondering how she was going to deal with this new predicament.

"If you had the chance to go back in time to the era of the trapper, live in the wilderness, just for a while, and experience it for yourself, would you do it?" . . . "Can't tell anyone" . . . . "I'll come for you in three months to send you home . . ."

She shouldn't be angry with Zach. He had warned her, and she just hadn't taken him seriously. But who in their right mind would believe stories about time travel? The last few days had certainly made a believer out of her. And wasn't this exactly what she had wanted for so long – to escape her reality - if only for a while?

One of her rescuers rose from his spot near the fire and moved toward her, jolting her mind back to the present. Her heart pounded in her chest. She tried to take deep calming breaths.

Okay, Aimee. You deal with all sorts of people on a daily basis in the ER. You can handle this.

The man knelt in front of her and wordlessly held out a water bag.

"Thank you." She reached for the offering while straining her eyes to see his face. She could barely make it out in the darkness, and the only light coming from the campfire's dancing flames cast moving shadows on his features.

"Are you hungry?" His deep voice and perfect English startled her. She hadn't expected him to speak her language.

"A . . . a little, but I need water more than anything else right now. I'm really dehydrated." She eyed the man, what she could see of him, warily.

"Let me know if you need more." He gestured to the water bag.

"Thanks." Aimee smiled weakly. He hadn't moved, and she

could feel his eyes on her. It was quite unnerving. If only he'd leave. As if he heard her thoughts, he abruptly stood and turned away to return to his place by the fire. He said something unrecognizable to his companion.

As soon as he turned his back, she managed to raise herself to a sitting position. She waited for the pounding in her head and the dizziness to subside, then put the tip of the water bag to her mouth, and moaned in pleasure at the wonderful sensation of the water soothing her parched throat.

She warily eyed the men several yards away from her. The one who had brought the water sat with his broad back to her again. The other man sat across from him, staring at her boldly while picking pieces of meat off one of the skewers over the fire.

If you think you're going to intimidate me, you're going to be disappointed. I've stared down much worse. Dr. Ashwell immediately came to mind. The man had the uncanny ability to make nurses cry.

The Indian's relentless stare annoyed her, along with the fact that she couldn't understand a word of what they were saying. Most likely they were discussing her.

* * *

Daniel called himself a fool for gawking at the woman after handing her the water bag. The light of the flames from the fire had illuminated different parts of her face, but soft eyes looked back at him, and her smile made his heart beat faster. He mentally shook his head, pondering his reaction to her. The woman's soft voice and manner of speech, which sounded different than anything he'd ever heard, even in the big eastern cities, held his attention.

"Maybe if you paid more notice to the meat, it wouldn't be burnt now," Daniel said gruffly, and sat in his place by the fire again.

Elk Runner grinned. He reached for a skewer of rabbit while looking in the direction of the woman in the shadows. "The woman has spirit," he remarked. "She is not afraid."

"Why would she be afraid of you?"

"All white women are afraid of my people."

23

"And how many white women have you known?" Daniel snorted.

"I've heard it to be so." Elk Runner shrugged.

"Maybe I will have a bite of food," she called out from behind him. Elk Runner was right. This little woman sure didn't seem to fear them, which was foolish. She should be afraid. A woman alone anywhere, much less in this wilderness, was a prime target for a lonely man.

Daniel reached for another skewer and brought it to her, once more kneeling in front of her. As she reached for the meat, her hand brushed his lightly. His own hand lingered, her satiny touch sending a tingling sensation up his arm. He held on to the skewer longer than necessary. The bewildered look on her face finally prompted him to let go. The memory of her cold hand on his remained, however, and burned into his skin. He wanted to touch her again.

"I'm sorry for being an inconvenience," she said. "I don't want you to have to wait on me. I injured my foot when I went over that cliff. I don't think it's fractured, but I'll have to take another look in the daylight to be sure." Her soft melodious voice kept him rooted to the spot in front of her.

"I'm Aimee Donovan, by the way, and it goes without saying that I am very grateful for the rescue. One more night on that ledge, and I would have been done for." She extended her hand in offer of a handshake.

His gaze moved from her face to the delicate hand she offered. No woman had ever wanted to shake his hand before. Here was his chance to touch her again, to feel her soft skin on his once more, but he held back. A moment later, she frowned slightly, and her hand moved away to rest in her lap.

Ask her where she comes from.

Her confident and self-assured manner had him question his original assumption that she might be on the run from a captor. This was not the behavior of a woman who had been abused by a man.

"We will travel in the morning. You should eat and rest." He turned and headed for his place by the fire.

* * *

Aimee chewed the meat slowly. She waited several minutes between bites to make sure she could keep the food down, and drank small sips of water in between. When she felt sure her stomach would not reject the nourishment, she pulled her backpack toward her and unzipped it.

She cringed. The sound of the zipper seemed to be amplified a hundred fold. She threw sheepish glances at the men by the fire. The Indian who faced her shot her a curious glance, but his companion didn't react to the sound. Once she found her ibuprofen, she discreetly opened the bottle and popped a couple of pills into her mouth.

She curled up in the soft bed of leaves, and shoved her backpack under her head for a pillow. She shivered under the blanket, and pulled it up to her neck. The subtle hint of rawhide and pine, and something else she could only describe as clean and pleasant, woodsy male scent saturated the blanket. It was an oddly comforting scent.

After spending two nights alone in the wilderness, the presence of these men was a reassuring welcome. The occasional cracking sounds coming from the underbrush in the darkness no longer haunted her into thinking she was some predator's next meal.

Her common sense told her that she should be afraid of them, but they hadn't given any indication that they meant to hurt her. She was determined to show no fear. Wasn't that what they did in the movies? Didn't Indians supposedly hold bravery in high esteem?

Sometime in the middle of the night, warmth radiated into her body from behind, and instinctively, even in her sleep, she moved closer to its source.

Chapter Three

Daniel lay awake, more uncomfortable than he'd been in a long time. He had noticed the woman's body tremble under the blanket. He settled down next to her after he was sure she'd fallen asleep, so she could absorb some of his body heat. She must have become aware of his warmth, for she had moved closer to him until her entire body pressed up against him. He stayed motionless. He didn't need a hysterical female waking up in the middle of the night.

As the hours dragged on with excruciating slowness, the feel of her softness next to him stirred a fire in him unlike anything he had ever felt. The pleasant scent on her clothing and hair enveloped his senses, reminding him of spring flowers.

To pass the long hours, he trained his mind and ears on the sounds coming from the forest. A pack of wolves roamed nearby. They had found the hiding place of a newborn elk calf, and announced their victorious hunt with gleeful barks and several howls. He'd heard the mother elk's bleating calls after the wolves made their kill. These sounds were familiar to him, comforting. They told him everything was as it should be in his world. What wasn't familiar was the steady breathing and soft moans coming from the woman pressed up next to him.

Before the first light of dawn, Daniel finally forced himself away. He stared down at her in the dawning light, wondering again, as he had all night, where she could have come from.

The sun had barely risen, and he and Elk Runner busied themselves cutting trees and saplings, making a travois for Aimee to ride on that he would drag behind him. It was the most practical way to get her to his cabin if she couldn't walk. He remained sullen and quiet as he worked, his movements more forceful than necessary. Why did this woman evoke such strong emotions in him? His dark mood did not escape Elk Runner.

"This woman has taken root in your mind," Elk Runner taunted. "And you liked sharing her blanket."

Daniel grunted, unwilling to be baited by his brother, who clearly enjoyed his discomfort.

"This travois is done." Elk Runner tied the last bit of twine to secure some branches together. "I will go now and find out if she is being followed. I will return to your cabin when I know more." After a moment's pause, he added, "You found her, White Wolf. You should keep her as your wife."

"It is not the white man's way," Daniel said between clenched teeth. "And you know I do not want a wife."

Elk Runner grinned. Daniel flung a tree branch at him, which he dodged skillfully. Laughing loudly, he turned and disappeared into the forest.

Alone with the sleeping woman by the fire, Daniel packed the leftover meat, and checked his rifle out of habit. With nothing else to do, he sat on a log and studied her yet again. He couldn't get his fill of watching her. She looked beautiful, even with her disheveled hair and dirty face. Was her hair an even lighter shade of yellow if she washed the dirt out of it?

Without a doubt, she could use a bath. He should take her to one of the many hot water pools in the area. It would soothe her bruised body as well as get her clean. He knew which pools were safe to bathe in, and which ones would boil a man in an instant if he fell in.

Why are you so concerned for this woman's comfort?

His reaction was merely due to the fact that he hadn't been with a woman in months, and he certainly hadn't set eyes on a white woman in over a year.

    * * *

Aimee stirred and slowly opened her eyes. One of her rescuers sat a short distance away, staring at her intently. She pulled herself to a sitting position, wincing at the throbbing pain in her ankle.

"Good morning." She yawned, and rubbed her fingers

27

against the temples of her pounding head. She glanced up as he walked toward her. Aimee drew in a sharp breath. With her first clear look at his face, it became obvious that this man was not an Indian. It had been easy to make that mistake in the dark of night. Although white, he could almost pass for an Indian.

Her eyes poured over his clothing and appearance. He wore a dark-colored breechcloth and leather leggings with fringes on the sides. His faded red flannel shirt had been poorly patched in a few places. Several leather pouches were draped around his neck, and over one broad shoulder dangled a powder horn made from the horn of a mountain sheep.

A tomahawk and large hunting knife hung from the wide leather belt around his waist. He wore un-decorated leather moccasins. His raven black hair fell to his shoulders, with some unruly strands tumbling over his forehead.

Aimee's eyes moved to his deeply tanned face, his square jaw line shadowed by a day's growth of stubble, and dark brown eyes that betrayed none of his thoughts as he moved ever closer.

Her pulse quickened as she met and held his hard gaze. She couldn't help but stare. Those penetrating dark eyes drew her in. She blinked, but couldn't look away. Dear God, she couldn't recall ever seeing a painting or drawing of a mountain man that looked like this guy. Images of rough looking, bearded wild men came to mind.

The man in front of her was quite simply . . . stunning. The feral, masculine virility he projected took her breath away, leaving her head spinning dizzily, and not from dehydration this time.

"Drink." He handed her a full water bag. "I wish to be on our way soon."

"Where are we going?" She felt tiny sitting on the ground while he loomed over her.

"I have a cabin less than a day's walk from here."

Aimee stared as a fledgling thought took root in her brain. It couldn't be *him*, could it?

"I still don't know your name," she called out quickly when he moved to walk away. He regarded her for a moment with those penetrating dark eyes.

"I am called Daniel."

"Nice to meet you, Daniel. Thank you again for saving my life."

The smile froze on her face when his expression hardened abruptly. His jaw visibly clenched, and his features took on a predatory look. His dark eyes turned even darker. Without another word, he turned and headed into the trees.

Puzzled by his abrupt departure and the savage, almost hateful look on his otherwise much too handsome face, Aimee watched him stride away. Shrugging, she couldn't help but smile. She couldn't believe her turn of good luck.

"Daniel will look out for ya."

"Does he know you're a time traveler?"

"No, and I don't want him to find out, neither. You gotta promise not to tell him how you got there."

Zach Osborne's son, the man she had been advised to find in the Madison Valley, had found her instead!

While her rescuer disappeared into the forest, Aimee unlaced her boot and pried it off her foot.

"Ouch." She sucked in a deep breath, then peeled off her sock and gently started poking at her ankle joint.

Now that it wasn't confined in the tight boot, she could actually see her throbbing foot start to swell. She poked a finger in the skin, and watched the indentation it created from accumulated fluid slowly fill again. There was no way now she could get her foot back into that boot.

As much as it hurt, she moved the joint, palpating with her fingers for fractures. She chewed her lower lip to keep from crying out as she performed her examination. The last thing she wanted was for Daniel to think she was a wuss.

With a sigh of relief, she concurred with her initial assessment that she hadn't broken anything, and that it was just a sprain. For all her lack of preparation for this "trip", she gave silent thanks that she had at least packed her medical kit.

However, her kit didn't contain an icepack. She glanced around for the stream that gurgled nearby. Even as she thought about a way to get there – crawling on hands and knees seemed to be her only option – Daniel appeared with a thick sapling that was forked at one end. He approached wordlessly, and held it out to her.

"You made me a crutch?" She beamed. "Thank you." She took the offered stick and pulled herself up to stand. Blood rushed from her head and she fought the dizziness that threatened to overcome her.

"Use the bushes if you need to." Daniel motioned curtly with his head to a stand of bushes. "How much longer until you will be ready to go?"

"I would like to soak my foot in the stream for a few minutes before I bandage it. It's only a sprain, but I'm afraid I won't be able to move very fast. I'll try my best to keep up."

Daniel's eyebrows shot up. The quizzical look on his face left her feeling weak and inadequate.

Just like with Brad.

Was he making fun of her? All the old insecurities came rushing back like an avalanche. Aimee squared her shoulders and held her chin up. She'd prove that she wouldn't be a burden. She wasn't going to fall into the same pattern all over again of kowtowing to a man.

Standing in front of him, she wondered how he cut a crutch that fit her height so perfectly. She felt completely tiny in his presence. He was more than a head taller than she, and seemed to be at least twice as wide. At five foot one, she was used to being small around most of her friends. And while Daniel wasn't overly tall, the proud and confident way he carried himself gave him an imposing appearance.

Grabbing her backpack, she hobbled to the stream and sank down in the dew-covered grass along the bank. She removed her other boot and sock, and rolled her pant legs up to her knees. Lowering her feet into the icy water, she couldn't suppress a gasp.

Aimee rummaged through her pack, and took out an ace bandage, her mirror, and a brush. She laughed at her reflection. Caked-on dirt mixed with dried blood, and several nicks and cuts crisscrossing her nose and cheeks. Her wildly disheveled hair gave her the look of an Amazon woman.

"If Brad could see me now." *No, I'm not going to think about him. For once, I'm where he can't hound me.*

She cupped her hands in the water and splashed it on her

face, rubbing gingerly to get the grime off. The crystal clear water beckoned, but it was too cold for her to contemplate a full bath. Instead, she found her small bottle of shampoo, bent forward as far as she could, and let her hair hang into the slow-moving stream.

"Sorry if there are any fish in here," she mumbled.

She made short work of lathering and rinsing her hair. The cold water gave new meaning to the term "brain freeze". She wrung her hair dry as best as she could, and ran her brush through the long tresses, using the bristles to rake some feeling back into her scalp. She gathered everything into a ponytail with the spare scrunchy she kept wrapped around her brush handle. Her other scrunchy was long lost. Some bangs and shorter side wisps of hair fell loose and framed her face. She hastily pulled her one sock and boot back on, then wrapped her ankle expertly with an ace bandage.

Aimee slung her backpack over her shoulders, and pulled herself up with the aid of her crutch. Turning around, she spotted Daniel leaning casually against a tree a short distance away. His arms were folded across his chest, and he watched her with those intense dark eyes. He frowned.

What am I doing wrong now?

Some sort of contraption she had not seen before lay on the ground at his feet.

"Okay, I'm ready to go now," she called out. "I feel a bit more human again. Thanks for being so patient."

"You will ride on this travois," he said curtly. His eyes roamed over her body, as if he was assessing her for something. His gaze lingered on her exposed legs, and she cursed silently that she'd forgotten to roll the pant legs back down to her ankles. *Too late now.*

"You want me to sit on that?" she asked skeptically, trying to draw his attention away from what he was staring at. "And then what? You're going to pull me?"

"You can't walk on your own."

"I really don't want to inconvenience you like this."

"We need to be on our way. I want to reach my cabin before nightfall." There was a definite note of impatience in his voice,

31

and it was probably best not to argue with him further. She grudgingly obliged and positioned herself in the middle of the travois. Daniel picked up the two poles at the end of the contraption, and headed out without another word, setting a brisk pace.

The ride jarred every bone and aching muscle in her body as the poles dragged over the hard and rocky ground, but she was determined not to complain. If her teeth would all be intact after this, she'd consider herself lucky. This guy had saved her life, and no doubt had to be hugely inconvenienced by her presence. She firmly closed her mouth and clenched her jaw to brace the jostling of her brain.

An hour later, Daniel had detoured around the edge of the canyon, and they reached the banks of the Gibbon River below the falls. Aimee was aware that he kept mostly to the meandering riverbank with its softer loamy earth. He had picked out the smoothest path possible, no doubt for her comfort. Guilt enveloped her. He showed no sign of slowing his pace the entire morning. He definitely had endurance.

Daniel seemed unconcerned when they passed close by a group of bison, while she gripped the poles of the travois until her knuckles turned white. She eyed the massive creatures nervously. A few of the beasts raised their heads from cropping at the lush grasses and watched them pass. Their eyes seemed to stare directly at her, and the hair at the back of her neck stood on end.

Quit being ridiculous! They're not giving you the evil eye. They're just curious.

Only when they had moved a safe distance away did she breathe easier. She observed more bison, and a large number of elk in the distance as the day wore on. Hawks lazily circled the cloudless deep blue sky in search of an unsuspecting meal.

The scenery was magnificent. She savored the crisp, clean air, catching the occasional scent of sulfur carried on the breeze, a reminder of the geothermal wonders of this area. The only sounds came from insects in the tall grass, birds in the distance, the occasional warning call of a ground squirrel, and the scraping of the travois poles on the ground. There was just no better place on earth.

By mid-day, Daniel stopped suddenly. He gently set the poles down, and Aimee raised her head and glanced around.

"Drink some water," he ordered, and handed her his water bag. He removed some meat from his pouch and wordlessly offered it to her.

She reached for the food, gritting her teeth at the pain that rushed through her arm at the slight movement. There wasn't an inch of her body that didn't ache. If only she had taken some ibuprofen before they started on their journey. She opened her backpack, discreetly took out the medicine bottle, and swallowed a couple of pills.

Daniel didn't sit down to rest. He stood off to the side, constantly scanning their surroundings.

"I would like to stretch my legs for a minute," she called, and hoisted herself up with her walking stick.

Once the dizziness subsided, she hobbled around awkwardly. She arched her back, her hands on her hips. Then she bent forward to touch her toes in an effort to stretch the tight muscles in her legs and back. Hobbling around for a few minutes, she waited for Daniel to say something.

He cast odd looks her way, and Aimee wondered what he must be thinking. The prolonged silence was unnerving. Conversation had always come naturally to her, but Daniel was apparently the silent type.

"How much further is it to your cabin?" she finally asked.

He didn't answer immediately. She'd almost given up on a response, when he said, "we will be there before the sun sets."

"It's really nice of you to take me with you."

She wished she could engage him in a little more talk than the few curt words he spoke to her. Watching him pick up the travois and head toward the river, she asked, "don't you want me to get on that thing first?"

"We need to cross the river," he replied without looking at her, as if that explained everything. "Stay where you are," he commanded almost as an afterthought while he hoisted the travois over his head and waded into the water.

"Okay, I'll wait here," she mumbled and shrugged, feeling completely useless.

33

Daniel deposited the contraption on the opposite bank and made his way back. Wordlessly he strode up to her and, in one swift motion, bent and scooped her in his arms.

"Whoa!"

Purely by reflex, her arms flew around his neck to hold on. Oh man, his face was way too close. A sheen of perspiration clung to the growing shadow above his upper lip. Her eyes locked onto the penetrating stare that came from underneath his dark lashes, and the unruly hair that fell forward over his eyes. Her heart hammered against her ribs. Awareness of his arms of steel, rock solid chest, and pure rugged maleness seeped into her body. Daniel's face remained hard and unreadable as he waded through the river a third time.

"Please don't drop me," she teased, trying to ease the tension, and at the same time ignore her wildly galloping heart.

Daniel didn't seem to think her comment was funny. His eyebrows furrowed into a dark scowl. The slight twitch of his upper lip reminded her of a wolf, ready to bare its teeth and strike, and she wished she could take her words back. Twice today she'd observed this savage, almost hateful look, and she wondered why he held such animosity toward her.

Safely on the other side of the river, Daniel placed her on the travois, picked up the ends of the poles, and silently continued at his brisk pace.

Chapter Four

It was late afternoon or early evening when the area they were in took on a familiar feel. Aimee turned slightly on the travois to look in the direction they were headed. The valley that widened before her was all too familiar.

Straight-walled mountains framed a meadow on the south side, and sloping wooded hills rose to the north. The river they had been following made a sweeping bend before another river, which seemed to flow straight out of the mountains from the south, joined this one. Together, they merged into one wide body of water that continued to flow west.

"The Madison!" she blurted out loud. Daniel turned his head and shot her a puzzled look.

Idiot! Aimee kicked herself mentally. *I shouldn't know this.*

Lewis and Clark had named this river in 1805, but much further to the north of here, not at its origin in this little valley. Their expedition hadn't come through the Yellowstone area. But Zach had also called it the Madison, so the name must have been widely used early on.

"Oh, look. Is that your cabin over there?" She awkwardly tried to cover up her slip. A log structure came into view around the bend in the river, nestled amongst some sheltering pines. The landscape looked familiar, but in her time there were fewer trees on the hillside to the north, and the worn path along the river's edge, created by thousands of tourists each summer, was also absent. It appeared so much more beautiful now, in its wild and undamaged state.

Daniel lowered the travois poles in front of the cabin, and Aimee hoisted herself from the ground with her stick. She

35

stretched her stiff muscles. Would her body ever stop aching? Daniel quickly surveyed the area, then he checked inside the cabin before he waved his hand for her to enter. Whatever he'd been looking for must have satisfied him.

Aimee had no idea what to expect. What did the inside of a trapper's cabin look like? Curious, she hobbled through the door into the dark interior. It took a moment for her eyes to adjust to the dim light. She scanned the single room. There was a rough wooden table in the center. Two logs split down their middle on either side of the table made up two benches. There were two bunks along opposite walls, each piled high with various animal furs and wool blankets. The back wall held a massive stone fireplace and hearth, and some shelves had been hung that contained tin plates, cups, wooden bowls, and various other containers. Two pairs of snowshoes, a hunting bow and quiver full of arrows, and several metal contraptions with chains, that she guessed were steel traps, hung on the walls. The entire cabin projected the man who lived in it - wild and rustic, without any frills.

"You can sleep here," Daniel said, and pointed to the bunk on the left. She hobbled over to the bed and deposited her backpack on it.

"I hope this isn't too much trouble for you, having me here," she apologized.

Daniel knelt in front of the hearth, gathered kindling from the wood box into a small pile, and struck his knife against a flint he produced from the pouch around his neck. Sparks erupted almost immediately, and Daniel blew air on the small flame, then added larger pieces of wood to feed the growing fire. Aimee had never seen anyone produce a campfire with such speed and efficiency. Of course he didn't reply to her comment.

"I won't be a bother to you, I promise," she tried again. "My foot should be better in a couple of days, and . . . I'll leave then." If he sent her away, she'd have to manage somehow on her own until Zach came for her. The thought sent chills of dread down her spine.

Daniel turned to look at her as if considering her statement. "You lost your way in the woods already."

"Not all who wander are lost." She couldn't help herself from quoting one of her favorite authors.

Daniel's eyebrows drew together. "Where do you plan to go? There are no people other than the Tukudeka and some Siksiska in this area."

"Some who and what?"

"The Tukudeka - the Sheep Eaters - and the Siksiska - the Blackfoot," Daniel explained. He stared at her again with those intense brown eyes. "Where did you come from?" His non-wavering stare seemed to burn a hole right through her.

There it was! Aimee expected the question. Unfortunately, she hadn't come up with any kind of believable story yet. Zach had been adamant that no one, including his son, could find out where she really came from.

"I sort of dropped into the area." She shrugged, knowing how crazy she sounded. "I'm actually from Ca...New York."

Daniel's eyebrows shot up. "That's a city in the east. How does a white woman travel this far, alone in the wilderness?"

Wow, he's actually talking. Wrong topic, though.

Struggling to remember any of her early American history, she answered, "Well, I always wanted to see things beyond New York. I . . . I hooked up with some settlers down the Ohio River to St. Louis. One thing led to another and somehow I ended up here." She shrugged again, and averted her eyes. The lie sounded stupid even as she said it.

"There are no white people within a thousand miles from here. Who are you running from?"

"I'm not . . ." She stopped herself and inhaled deeply. "Okay. I left a fiancé back home. I just needed to get away."

Oh man, these half-truths were really hard. Aimee knew how utterly impossible it was for a white woman to be in these mountains in this day and age, especially alone, but she couldn't think of one good scenario that was believable. She hoped her vague answer would satisfy him. It wasn't a complete lie. She had been looking for a way to get away from Brad. Just days before meeting Zach, she had broken her engagement. He hadn't taken it well. Brad never took "no" for an answer well. That was the problem.

37

"I don't know this word . . . fiancé." Daniel's resonating voice pulled her thoughts back to the here and now.

"Um . . . my intended, betrothed, the man I was gonna marry," Aimee explained.

Daniel's face darkened, and his body tensed. "Surely he is looking for you."

"I don't think so," Aimee said confidently. "He has no idea where I am."

"Who brought you this far from St. Louis?"

"N . . . no one," Aimee stammered. Damn! This wasn't going well. "I mean, I got separated from some people I was traveling with a few weeks ago." Okay. Lie number two. The vulnerability of her position occurred to her again.

Why did I agree to do this? Because you thought it was just some silly joke!

Daniel's accusing stare sent chills up her spine. She let out the breath she'd been holding after he turned his back to her to finish building the fire. When a sizeable blaze crackled in the hearth, he stood and headed for the door.

"Perhaps you'll tell me the truth later." He shot one final look of contempt her way, then abruptly left the cabin.

* * *

Daniel sat by his campfire, staring across the river. The sun cast a golden glow around the mountains that framed the valley. He needed to clear his head. He had expected Aimee to have a husband, but hearing her confirm it left him with an unsettled feeling in his gut. Someone promised in marriage, in his mind, was the same as being married. It gave him an odd feeling he couldn't explain. Why should it matter to him? The sooner he was rid of her, the better. This woman evoked a jumble of mixed reactions in him, leaving him agitated and confused. He was always in control of his emotions, whether he confronted an enemy, faced a predatory animal, or in the presence of a woman.

His mind recalled the events of the day, and this woman's odd behavior. He'd observed in perplexed fascination when she'd stretched her sore body. Those postures had only brought more awareness to her womanly curves. The entire morning, his thoughts had been on nothing but her shapely exposed legs, and

38

the fragrant scent of the soap she had used on her face and hair had played havoc with his senses. She seemed completely unaware of what she was doing to him. Her actions irritated and bewildered him. No decent woman behaved in such a manner, and definitely not alone in front of a man.

Her radiant smiles had left him mesmerized, while her sparkling blue eyes reminded him of some of the azure hot water pools he frequently encountered. He'd stood and watched, consumed by her loveliness. Visions danced before his eyes of a beaver lured by the enticing scent on one of his traps. The beaver struggled to break free as the trap snapped shut. Except in these visions, he was the beaver, and this little slip of a woman was the trap. In his mind's eye, the face of the enticing female he'd found morphed into another fair skinned woman's face, one he hadn't thought about in years. One he had never wanted to think about again.

Daniel threw more wood on his campfire. He had expected this little woman to demand more time to rest. Riding on the travois couldn't have been comfortable, yet she had uttered no words of complaint. He'd concealed his surprise earlier in the day when she told him she'd try to keep up, as if he expected her to walk on her injured foot. She sure had grit, he had to give her that, especially for such a little thing. *Especially for a white woman!*

Admittedly, she fascinated him. She had shown amazing strength and resilience so far. The way his body reacted to her when he touched her evoked foreign feelings in him. The memory of her arms wrapped around his neck, and the way she clung to him when he carried her through the river sent a fresh wave of desire through him. Good thing she hadn't been able to see the evidence of his body's reaction to her at the time.

Images of another white woman crept into his mind. Outwardly, the only thing Aimee and Emma shared in common was their fair skin - enough of a reminder of the hurt and betrayal he had suffered so many years ago. Daniel learned from his mistakes. He never made the same ones twice. His survival here in this harsh and unforgiving land depended on it.

Why did she lie to him? *She is a white woman. They all lie!*

What a ridiculous story! A woman did not travel alone from

New York to this wild land. Impossible. It was a difficult enough journey to travel from St. Louis up the Missouri, then south along the *E-chee-dick-karsh-ah-shay* - the Elk River to the Sheep Eater band of Shoshoni, and he'd also heard it called the River of Yellow Rocks by other tribes and French trappers. Not many men were hardy enough to make such a journey. She had to have run away from her man somewhere nearby.

Elk Runner would have some answers for him in a few days. If not, he might have to go in search of her man. But could he return Aimee to a man from whom she felt the need to run away? She was not his to keep if her man showed up, regardless of whether she wanted to go back to him or not.

Stop thinking about this! This woman is nothing to you.

Clenching his jaw, he strode back into his cabin. Aimee sat on the bed, unwrapping the bandage from her foot. Her head popped up, and her eyes met his with an expectant look. Daniel lit a lantern on the table to give her more light to see. He removed his traveling pouch and hung it on a peg on the wall next to the door. He removed the leftover meat from his pouch, and placed some on a tin plate, which he set on the table along with his water bag. Grabbing a buffalo robe off the other bunk, he left the cabin again with the rest of the meat.

* * *

Aimee's gaze lingered on the closed door. She didn't know what to think of Daniel. He wasn't anything like what she had expected. Then again, she really hadn't given it much thought before - maybe a younger version of friendly Zach Osborne, but certainly not this dark and intimidating, yet absolutely gorgeous woodsman. One moment, he did things that were kind and thoughtful, the next he gave her looks of complete contempt and even hatred.

She bit off a piece of meat, and chewed it like gum to soften it. She took up her crutch and hobbled outside. The last of the sunlight disappeared into the western horizon, and the clear twilight sky produced millions of twinkling stars. She rubbed at the goose bumps on her arms while she absorbed the tranquil scene. The rippling sounds of flowing water from the Madison mixed with mournful calls of loons seeking out their mates. The eerie howl of a lone wolf resonated off the mountains. Moments later, the high-pitched barking of several coyotes in the distance advertised they had made a kill.

She barely made out Daniel's silhouette sitting on the ground some distance away from the cabin. He had built a fire, over which hung a kettle on a metal tripod. *Just like camping.* A wistful sigh escaped her lips. If he noticed her, he didn't acknowledge it. She hobbled a short distance into the trees behind the cabin to relieve herself.

"Good night," she called when she returned, and waited by the door for a response. None came, and she reluctantly entered the dark cabin and shut the door. She would have much rather sat outside by the fire for a while, but something told her Daniel would not appreciate her company. She had to remind herself that he wasn't used to being around people, and especially not women. What a challenge the solitude would be for her.

Zach had told her to stay at the cabin, that Daniel would help her. What if Zach had misjudged his son, and Daniel would send her away once her foot healed? His demeanor toward her made it quite obvious he didn't want her here. How would she get back to her own time if he sent her packing, and Zach couldn't find her when he returned? And how much would Daniel press her for the truth on how she got here? Not that he would believe the truth any more than the stupid lies she had told him so far.

Yeah, you see, your father never told you this, but he travels through time and I met him in the twenty-first century. There's a lot you don't know, but it's not my place to tell you.

Aimee sank down onto her bunk. For the first time in almost a week, a complete sense of security enveloped her. She sighed and snuggled into the pile of soft furs, pulling several over her head. At least tonight she would sleep warm and comfortably.

* * *

Aimee woke the next morning, more rested than she had been since the beginning of this "trip." Her head didn't spin as it had the last couple of days, and black spots didn't swirl in front of her eyes when she sat up. Her ankle was definitely not throbbing anymore unless she moved it suddenly. The bandage had loosened up as well, a good indication that the swelling was going

41

down.

Sunlight filtered in through some burlap nailed to the wall, which covered the cabin's only window opening. What time was it? She stood. A tin plate filled with fresh wild strawberries, some pine nuts, and pieces of dried meat, sat on the table. Her stomach grumbled loudly. All she'd eaten the day before was dried jerky. Next to the plate was a tin cup with coffee, although it was cold.

Daniel's thoughtfulness surprised her yet again. She pulled her hiking pants on, picked up her crutch, and opened the cabin door, squinting against the bright sunlight. She stepped outside and went behind the cabin into the trees. She scanned the valley and surrounding hills for any sign of Daniel. After a few minutes, she gave up. He was nowhere to be seen. She left the cabin door open to allow more light to enter the room, and picked up the tin cup to savor her first sip of coffee in a week.

"Yuck!" Her face contorted in a grimace. She forced the bitter brew down her throat with a shudder. "I wonder if he's got any sugar around here."

Aimee ran her brush through her hair, and dabbed some Neosporin on her cuts, then left the cabin and hobbled in the direction of the river. She had been here many times before, but the experience was so different now with no one else around. The early morning air stung her lungs with each breath she inhaled. Enthralled, she watched the steam rise from the waters of the Firehole River as it came rushing out of the mountain and merged with the Gibbon to form the Madison. Across the river, several cow elk grazed the succulent grasses just in front of the tree line. The geothermal heat that radiated from the ground met the cold air above, which gave the scene an eerily primordial feel as the entire meadow was covered in a layer of thick fog.

Several hours passed, and Daniel still hadn't appeared. Where had he gone? It was really none of her business. She was here uninvited, after all. Well, at least not invited by him.

With nothing to do after her walk by the river, she perused the objects in the cabin more closely. Several burlap sacks were stashed in a corner. Upon closer inspection, and to her delight, they contained flour, cornmeal, sugar, salt, and even several types of root vegetables. Another sack was filled with what she guessed to be gunpowder. On one of the shelves she found a crock full of some sort of animal fat or lard, and some dried strips of meat hung from a crude wooden rack.

An idea took hold in her mind. She scooped a small amount of flour into a wooden bowl, then added water and several leftover berries from her breakfast. She covered the bowl with a piece of burlap, and set it on the hearth by the fireplace.

"Hopefully, we'll have some nice sourdough starter in a couple of days, and I can bake some bread," she said with a satisfied smile.

Figuring she could put the backcountry cooking course she had taken a year ago to some good use now, Aimee wondered if Daniel would appreciate a warm meal when he returned. She cut some meat and placed it in a bowl of water to soften. She peeled and diced some of the vegetables, and made a fry bread batter with flour and cornmeal. Talking to herself was more comforting than the complete silence, and soon she was singing out loud.

* * *

Daniel had almost reached his cabin, several rabbits slung over his shoulder, when an unfamiliar odor lingered in the air. It was definitely food, and it made his mouth water.

"What the hell?" The smell came from the direction of his cabin. Despite being worn out from lack of sleep, he increased his pace.

Last night he had sat by the fire, unable to sleep for the second night in a row. He had been acutely aware when Aimee came out of the cabin. What was he going to do with her? He had no choice but to protect her from the harshness of this land and its countless dangers. Somehow he had to figure out how to get her back to civilization.

For the better part of the day, he'd wandered the valley to check his traps, and scouted along creeks and tributaries of the Madison for beaver habitat that would make good trapping sites for later this fall. When his father returned from St. Louis in a few months, they could start setting traps for winter beavers. No matter how hard he tried to concentrate on his task, his thoughts kept drifting to the woman he had left behind at his cabin.

He had gone inside quietly at dawn with some food and

coffee, and stared longingly at her sleeping form on his bed. He remembered all too well the previous night, how her soft woman's body had molded itself to his side. Would she be as welcoming now if he slipped into bed next to her? Aroused and frustrated, Daniel had left the cabin quickly.

The most bothersome thing was that, regardless of her lies and fair skin, he wanted her. Had some French trapper found her, she would have most likely been violated many times over by now. Daniel cursed out loud at the thought. No one would lay a hand on her while she lived in his cabin. The only problem was that he didn't know how long he would be able to keep his own hands off her.

He loped easily up the rise that led to the small valley, and his cabin came into view. Smoke rose from the chimney, and the door stood wide open. From inside, a woman's voice was . . . singing. He'd never heard this kind of singing before.

"She is mad," Daniel sneered, and shook his head. Who in their right mind made this much noise? *She's going to attract the entire Blackfoot nation.*

Chapter Five

Daniel stood in the doorframe of his cabin. His eyes narrowed as he watched Aimee lean into the hearth and stir the contents of the iron kettle. Whatever she had cooking in that pot made his mouth water anew. The air outside and within the cabin was infused with delicious smells. Something inexplicable stirred within him as he stood there, silently observing her. His insides warmed. He'd never experienced coming home from a day in the woods to a prepared meal, much less a feminine presence.

Aimee removed the spoon from the pot. In a dramatic voice she announced, "Well, dinner's ready!"

She turned, and let out a startled shriek. Her hand that held the long wooden spoon shot up in front of her in an apparent act of self-defense. The quick move splattered liquid onto her clothes. Daniel was suddenly glad it was a spoon, not a knife, she clutched in her hand.

"Ohmigod! You almost gave me a heart attack!" She expelled a loud breath of air, and her hand grasped at her chest before she lowered her spoon.

"If I had been a Blackfoot warrior, that" – Daniel gestured at the spoon – "wouldn't be much of a weapon." He tried hard to suppress a grin.

"What, you're actually joking with me? I didn't think you had it in you."

"It wasn't meant in jest," Daniel said dryly. The hint of a smile left his face. "You make so much noise, I heard you a mile away. Anyone could walk up on you undetected."

"Oh." Aimee lowered her eyes. "Well, um . . . I made dinner." She seemed to stumble over her words. "I wasn't sure

45

when you'd be back, and I found food supplies in these sacks. I hope it was okay to use some of it."

"I already smelled your cooking from outside."

Her downcast eyes, and her subtle shift of weight from one foot to the other showed her sudden insecurity. Her quick action and recovery when she saw him in the doorway impressed him, even if her choice of weapon posed no real threat. He placed the rabbits he brought on the ground outside, propped his rifle next to the door, and removed his powder horn and traveling pouch.

Aimee turned, and reached for some wooden bowls and spoons from the shelf. "Are you gone all day a lot?" she asked.

"Most days," he answered absently. He still stood in the doorway. His eyes devoured her, and his gaze roamed over her backside. He contemplated her odd clothing. His pulse quickened at the sight of her form fitting shirt and britches that hugged every inch of her womanly curves.

Daniel clenched his jaw as he envisioned running his hands up and down the contours of her body, and burying his fingers in the long waves of her yellow hair that swayed seductively down her back with each of her movements. He had never seen a respectable white woman with loose hair before. He remembered the women in the east kept their hair tied up and covered at all times. Emma's hair had always been hidden beneath one of those silly caps women preferred to wear.

Is she aware at all of how beautiful she is?

"What do you do all day?" Aimee asked conversationally, which put a stop to his wandering mind.

"I run traps and scout for beaver," Daniel answered. She struggled with the heavy kettle that hung on the tripod over the fire. Moving quickly around the table, he reached for it, and pulled it off the hook.

Their eyes met, and he held her gaze for a moment. His stomach tightened. He moved the kettle away from the heat, and backed away to sit at the table. Aimee ladled out a portion of stew into a bowl, and set it in front of him.

"You must be pretty hungry after being gone all day," she said, and sat across from him.

Daniel forked a piece of meat from his bowl, and tasted it.

46

He followed it up with a tender piece of root. "This is good," he commented between mouthfuls. She'd prepared the meat and roots differently than what he was used to, but it had a pleasing taste. He ate in silence, and the woman sitting across from him thankfully didn't try to engage him in more talk. He was aware of her nervous glances in his direction, but he felt no need for discussion. He emptied his bowl, and refilled it again.

When he finished his meal, he thanked her for the food and left the cabin.

The early evening sun cast a golden glow around the mountain beyond the river. Daniel took the rabbits he caught earlier to the fire pit and began the task of skinning and eviscerating. Aimee emerged from the cabin. She'd stopped to watch him before continuing on to the banks of the Madison. In a hasty decision, he set the rabbits aside and caught up with her, his hands covered in blood. Wordlessly, he took the heavy wooden bucket she carried, and set it down at the water's edge.

"You don't have to do that," Aimee said. "I'm quite capable of pulling my own weight."

"I wasn't pulling you, I was carrying the bucket. Your foot will heal faster if you don't move around on it so much."

He reached for the bowls, and she hesitantly said, "Um . . . you should wash your hands first before you touch those bowls. I'd rather not catch salmonella or something next time I eat out of them."

"There are no salmon in this river." Daniel wondered what cleaning the bowls had to do with catching fish.

"Never mind." Aimee shook her head.

He washed his hands in the water, then dipped the bowls under the surface, and let the current rinse them out.

"You don't have to do that," Aimee repeated.

He shrugged. "I'm accustomed to doing for myself." Finished with the task, he dipped the bucket in the water to fill it, and then carried it back to the cabin.

He reached for the door, when movement between the trees beyond the cabin caught his eye. Daniel turned his head slowly, and stared into the forest. His hand inched toward the knife at his belt, and he stepped in front of the woman next to him. Seconds later, his hand relaxed on the knife handle. Elk Runner stepped from behind the trees. Daniel strode up to him, and the two clasped hands in a warm greeting. Ignoring the woman standing at his cabin door, he led his brother to the fire pit and offered him one of the rabbits.

Daniel wasted no time, and asked, "What have you learned?"

Elk Runner skewered the meat and turned it over the fire, taking his time with a response. "Her trail begins in the meadow near the bubbling mud," he finally said. "It is as if she fell out of the sky."

Daniel recalled Aimee's words from the day before. *I sort of dropped into the area.* He shrugged it off as ridiculous.

"Someone must have concealed their tracks," Daniel pondered.

"Does she say where she comes from?"

"She claims to be from a white man's city in the east, and she is running away from the man she is promised to marry," Daniel said. "But it is difficult enough for a woman to travel from the east to St. Louis, and impossible up the Missouri to this area."

"But yet she is here," Elk Runner remarked. "Your own mother must have made the same journey."

Daniel shook his head even though Elk Runner had a point. "My father accompanied her," he argued.

"There are ways to make someone tell the truth," Elk Runner suggested after a moment's pause.

"No," Daniel said quickly. "She has her reasons, and I will wait for her to tell me the truth when she is ready."

Elk Runner grinned. "If she is promised to another man, how long will you wait to see if he comes for her?"

"I have no intention of keeping her," Daniel said in exasperation.

Elk Runner gave a hearty laugh. "Your eyes betray you, White Wolf. As sure as the sun comes up every morning, you want this woman."

Daniel ignored his brother's remark. "If I have to, I'll wait until my father returns, then I will take her back to St. Louis myself before the first snow."

"You will not be able to stay out of her sleeping blankets that long," Elk Runner predicted with confidence. "This woman has you bewitched. It is like I said before. Perhaps the spirits brought her to you because they know a man should not live without a woman."

Daniel threw a stick in the fire, sending glowing embers into the air. Elk Runner tore a piece of meat from his skewer, and laughed.

* * *

Aimee stood by the cabin door. Daniel and his Indian friend seemed to be engaged in a heated discussion. They spoke in the Indian's language, which made it impossible for her to understand. The man seemed quite amused by some things, and whatever made him laugh visibly aggravated Daniel. She'd clearly been dismissed when the Indian showed up. Daniel hadn't given her a second look. Tearing her eyes away from the men, she headed into the cabin. She might as well call it a day. With a heavy sigh, she removed her pants, and crawled under the soft, warm furs.

Aimee's eyes focused on the dark ceiling above her as she lay on her back. Her thoughts strayed to the man outside who was such an enigma, and the intense feelings he evoked disturbed her. She had only known him for two days, but her attraction to him had been instant. His intense stare had sent her pulse racing, and the memory caused delicious tingling feelings in her gut. The entire room seemed to have shrunk earlier from his large and imposing frame. The purely masculine scent of him had enveloped her senses. He smelled of the forest - pine and clean earth, mixed with the scent of buckskin and wood smoke.

Her heart sped up at the memory, and butterflies fluttered in her stomach. Jeez! She'd never been affected like this in the presence of a man. She didn't recall ever having such exhilarating, electrifying feelings before. Brad had definitely never evoked such an intense reaction from her. That he'd been all wrong for her suddenly became crystal clear.

Brad Bigsby was a surgical resident, a city boy through and through, who wanted nothing to do with camping and the great outdoors. They had met shortly after she and her lifelong friend,

Jana Evans, moved from New York to California after graduating nursing school together. He had pursued her relentlessly until she finally agreed to go out with him. His controlling ways hadn't been immediately obvious.

After Brad's marriage proposal three months ago, his overbearing attitude had gotten so bad, it bordered on abuse. Recalling their last heated argument a little over a week ago, she didn't regret that she'd given back his ring and broken the engagement. He had told her in no uncertain terms that their relationship was not over. This unbelievable trip into the past seemed like her perfect temporary escape.

Now I just have to find the courage to truly stand up to him when I return home.

Her next relationship would definitely be with someone with whom she could share the splendors of nature. She would have to find someone who was more of an outdoorsman. Daniel's face flashed before her eyes. If only someone like him existed in her time.

Chapter Six

The next couple of days passed uneventfully. Daniel was gone most of the time. Aimee spent her days tidying up in the cabin, which she jokingly referred to as the nineteenth century version of a bachelor pad. She organized the dishes after washing an inch of dirt off the shelves. The table took nearly an hour to scrub clean. She didn't even want to know what all those little parts and pieces she scraped off the wood used to be. Most likely body parts of some animals that Zach and Daniel had butchered. The dirt floor would have to just stay the way it was. She could do nothing about that. She found a trunk under the bed Daniel had assigned to her that contained several homespun cotton shirts, a few buckskin shirts and pants, and various other articles of clothing Aimee couldn't name. As she folded some of the shirts, she couldn't resist holding one to her face, and inhaled the strong woodsy scent she'd begun to associate with Daniel.

She also took long walks along the river as best as her foot allowed, and prepared a hot meal each afternoon for when Daniel returned home from whatever it was that he did during the day. He never commented about her cooking, but the pleased look on his face when he returned from his outings, and the way he ate the food she prepared with gusto, told her he liked it. If he noticed the changes she'd made to the cabin's interior, he didn't mention it. Each morning when she woke, she found fresh berries, nuts and coffee on the table.

Aimee contemplated the appearance of her breakfast each morning. *How can a big guy like that move so quietly?* She considered herself a fairly light sleeper, and the hinges on that cabin door weren't exactly quiet. Daniel didn't come inside the cabin to sleep at night.

She stood in the doorway of the cabin, and sipped her coffee. It tasted much better, now that she had found some sugar. A couple of mule deer moved along the riverbank, dipping their heads to the water to drink. Aimee sighed as she stared at the beautiful scenery of the rivers across the meadow, and the purple-hued mountain in the backdrop. In stark contrast to her noisy condominium-lined neighborhood back home, this place was truly a slice of heaven.

She turned back into the cabin to check on her yeast starter, pleased with the many air bubbles that formed in the flour. It might be ready for some bread baking later on. She sat on her bed, and unwrapped the bandage on her ankle. The swelling was mostly gone, and it only hurt when she put full weight on her foot. She might even be able to walk without her crutch today.

"Ugh, I really stink." She tugged at the front of the shirt and sniffed. "I think I need to change clothes today and wash these."

She rummaged through her pack at the foot of the bed for a fresh pair of pants and shirt. *Better yet, I need a good bath and scrubbing.* The idea of bathing in the cold river wasn't too enticing, when another thought entered her mind.

The Firehole River flowed through several geyser basins south of here, and the hot water runoff from those geysers streamed into this river, which made the water actually somewhat warm. Due to the peculiar topography of this region, the Firehole, as well as the Yellowstone, were two of the few rivers that flowed in a northerly direction.

Wasting no time, she grabbed a blanket off her bed, and placed her fresh change of clothes on it along with her shampoo and soap. She wrapped this all up and headed out the door. A quick look around confirmed that Daniel had once again disappeared for the day.

She removed her clothes at the riverbank and stripped down to her bra and panties, ignoring the vulnerable feeling creeping up on her. The thought of feeling clean again eased her self-consciousness of bathing in the open. Nothing would deter her from her plans. It wasn't a whole lot different than wearing a bikini. With a quick intake of breath, she let herself drop off the riverbank, and gasped when she hit the frigid water. Grabbing for her bar of soap, she quickly lathered her arms and face.

Rather than leave the water after shampooing her hair, she swam to the inlet of the Firehole. The current was surprisingly stronger than she had expected, but she sighed in contentment when the water became noticeably warmer. The river was very loud where the water rushed out of a narrow gorge in the mountain, and tumbled over large boulders as it joined with the Gibbon.

Free and uninhibited, she splashed and laughed in the water, acting like a little kid at the water park. She'd had to grow up fast after a drunk driver claimed the lives of her parents not two months after her high school graduation. That was five years ago, and life had become way too serious too quickly. Right here, in this moment in time, she was free from responsibility, and it felt so good.

She tossed her inhibitions aside as she made a game of letting the current carry her downstream, then swam back upriver to do it again.

"Woohoo!" she shouted and laughed. Daniel had chastised her a few days ago for making too much noise, and she shrugged it off. Here, the deafening roar of the water would surely drown out anything she yelled.

* * *

Daniel had left before daylight to hunt fresh meat. He'd planned to stay close to the cabin today. Several hours later, he dragged a whitetail deer carcass back to camp. A piercing scream filled the air, much like the shriek of a bald eagle. Only, it was louder and more drawn out. A woman's scream?

Damn! Adrenaline flooded his body. What the hell kind of trouble had that woman gotten herself into now? He dropped the deer and ran over the rise leading to the valley. His eyes scanned the area, apprehensive about what he would find. Had a party of Blackfoot come to the valley? Everything appeared normal. His gaze swept across the valley a second time, and his eyes fixed on the unmoving body floating in the river. A jolt of adrenaline hit him. Was she dead?

"Dammit!" he shouted.

53

How the hell did she end up in the river this far upstream? Daniel dropped his rifle and sprinted down the slope. He dodged or leapt over the gaping holes left by countless ground squirrels that lived under the earth. Racing across the meadow toward the banks of the Madison, he yanked his pouches from around his neck. Without slowing, he unstrapped his belt, and pulled his shirt off over his head.

Visions of Morning Fawn drowning in a river entered his mind. Why was this happening again? Two years ago, he hadn't been there to save her. He wasn't going to let it happen this time. He pushed himself to an even faster pace. It felt like an eternity before he reached the riverbank. Without breaking stride, he dove into the water, and shook the hair out of his face when he broke through the surface. Pulling himself through the current with long and powerful strokes, he came up behind Aimee. He grabbed her by the waist in one swift motion and pulled her to him.

To his surprise, she immediately began to kick and thrash her arms and legs through the water.

"Get the hell away from me!" she shrieked. Daniel tightened his hold on her.

"Be still, dammit, so I can get you to shore," he growled in her ear. He treaded water in an effort to keep both of them afloat. Her fair skin slid against his in the water, and the stark contrast against his darker tone shimmered under the waves. Her lack of clothing suddenly jolted him like a lightning strike. His stomach tightened, and he ground his teeth. How much more could this woman torment him? Aimee swung her body around, and almost butted heads with him. She relaxed for a split second, as recognition filled her eyes.

"What are you doing? You scared me to death. Let go of me!" She squirmed in his arms, and tried to loosen his hold.

Daniel stared, utterly bewildered. Why was she fighting him? He pulled her more firmly against his body to control her thrashing. Her stomach was pressed tightly against his side, their legs entwined under the water in an attempt by both of them to stay afloat. His loins tightened.

"I heard you scream. I thought you were drowning," he

54

shouted over the roar of the water. Aimee continued to struggle. "Dammit, woman! Stop fighting me!"

"I didn't scream, and I'm definitely not drowning. But you're gonna be the death of me if you keep sneaking up and giving me a heart attack! I was taking a bath," she yelled back. "Let go of me. I can swim."

Dammit! She was going to drown both of them if she kept up with her wild struggles. He had no choice but to release her. She immediately swam upriver. He shook his head and followed. Relief washed over him that she was alive. The vision of her lifeless body floating in the current sent an icy chill down his spine. Her wild struggles had replaced his fear with anger. Recalling the feel of her unclothed body against his just moments ago sent renewed waves of desire through him. It took all of his restraint not to grab her again and pull her close to him once more.

What the hell was this woman doing to him? When he wasn't near her, all he did was think about her. The way she provoked him drove him nearly mad.

* * *

Aimee reached the riverbank and scrambled up the embankment. Her clothes and blanket lay in the grass where she left them. She could feel Daniel's eyes staring into her backside. She hastily wrapped the blanket around herself and turned to face him. The murderous look in his eyes gave new meaning to the saying "if looks could kill." His dark, angry scowl was more un-nerving than any ER doctor she had ever encountered. She took a few steps back as Daniel hoisted himself up the riverbank, and mentally prepared for the inevitable confrontation.

"What the hell were you doing in that river?" Daniel's voiced boomed. "That current is treacherous in some areas, and you can get towed under before you know what's happening."

She held her ground. Daniel stood mere feet from her, dripping wet and looking like an angry Greek god. He towered over her. Aimee swallowed hard at her awareness of his nude upper body. Her gaze roamed over the broad, well-muscled expanse of his shoulders and chorded arms, his lean torso, and his rock solid, well defined abs. *Does he go out in the woods and bench press 300 pound logs every day?*

"Answer me," he roared, taking hold of her arms in a strong grip, giving her a shake when she didn't respond.

She stood stiffly, unable to move. This wasn't happening again, was it? The memory of Brad grabbing her in much the same way seeped into her mind. But instead of his fingers biting cruelly into her skin, Daniel's grip, while firm, seemed almost gentle. In place of causing pain, the sensation of his warm hands sent surges of electricity through her veins.

Aimee's head cleared, and she matched his angry stare. Apparently, men were just as overbearing and controlling in this time as they were in hers.

"Take your hands off me, you . . . you big clod! I already told you, I was taking a bath." She glared up at him, and met his intense look with one of her own.

"Now you listen here." She raised a finger at him, even as he gripped her arms. "I don't need any more arrogant men barking orders at me. I get enough of that back home. You can say what you need to say in a nicer manner."

Daniel seemed to compose himself for a moment. But then, with pure contempt in his voice, said, "it's no wonder your man abandoned you. Could he not teach you proper respect?"

"My man," she said between clenched teeth, "did not abandon me. And as for respect, you men would do well to show some of that yourselves. Argh! I can't believe it's the same everywhere!" She squirmed to free herself from his grip.

"If he didn't abandon you, why has he not come looking for you?" Daniel demanded. He finally released his hold on her arms.

"I told you, he doesn't know where I am," Aimee said smugly as she stood and rubbed her arms. Her skin tingled from his touch. "Besides, he would never consider coming into the wilderness."

"But you would?"

"Obviously," she scoffed. "That's why I'm here."

"Then you have a lot to learn. This is not the city, *gediki.* Help is not around every tree to rush to the aid of a weak and foolish woman who gets herself in trouble."

56

She glared at him. "I am not weak, or foolish. I've done just fine in the wilderness, thank you very much. And . . . and if you think you know everything, then why don't you teach me."

Daniel stared at her in stunned silence. Aimee's heart did a little flip flop. Even angry, he was the most devastatingly handsome man she had ever seen.

"You want me to teach you to survive here . . . in these mountains?" Daniel repeated incredulously. "Impossible." He shook his head. "You're going back to wherever the hell it is you came from as soon as my father returns. You belong in the city. This is no place for a white woman."

Well, I finally know where I stand. Zach had said something similar to her at one point. She shifted uncomfortably and adjusted the blanket around her shoulder. Despite the blanket wrapped around her body, the cool breeze left goose bumps on her exposed skin, and she shivered involuntarily. Or was that due to Daniel's closeness?

"You've never mentioned your father," she said quietly, wanting to change the subject.

"He's in St. Louis, bartering our cache of pelts from this past winter." Daniel's voice had gone normal again.

'When will he be back?" Aimee asked, although she already knew the answer.

"Before autumn."

"So I can stay here until then, is that it? How can you stand having me around for that long since I'm so completely incompetent?" Her voice took on a shrill tone as she tried to control her feelings of rejection.

What the heck is coming over me? Good lord, I'm in the middle of the wilderness, turning into a sobbing female in front of the most gorgeous man I've ever met! I'm proving him right about the weakness of white women, and if I lose it now, I might as well jump back in that river and drown myself.

She swallowed back the lump in her throat and tried to control her cracking voice. "I might as well just leave now and try my luck on my own. I was doing pretty well, actually until I accidentally ran into that bear. That's not going to happen again."

Aimee bent to pick up her clothes, intent on heading back to the cabin. Daniel's hand reached out and took hold of her arm again, more gently this time. She glared at him, then at the contact his hand made with her arm.

"I told you to let go of me," she said in a tone she hoped sounded threatening.

Right now she just wanted to get back to the cabin and away from him. He was wreaking havoc on her nerves standing so close, and she hated feeling so uncomfortable and weak around a man. It was like being with Brad all over again. At times she almost thought Daniel might be attracted to her when he stared at her so intently, but those were fleeting moments, and she remembered the hate-filled looks from a few days ago. She kicked herself mentally for fantasizing like a love-struck teenager. In less than three months she would be back in her own world, and Daniel would no longer exist.

* * *

Daniel held her arm, and he studied her. Aimee's hair hung in wet strands down the side of her face and back. Water droplets dripped onto her exposed shoulders. His eyes followed the water's path as is ran down her smooth skin, and disappeared under the blanket between the valley of her breasts. He fought the urge to run his hands down her cheek and brush the moisture off her face. He stood close enough to inhale the flowery scent of her soap. For as long as he lived, he was sure he would never forget that scent, and it would always remind him of her.

"For your own protection, I could force you to stay," he said quietly. She opened her mouth in an expected protest, and he added quickly, "but I won't. If you want to die, that is your choice."

He paused briefly, and waited for a sharp retort. When she remained quiet, he couldn't help but taunt her some more. "According to the custom of some tribes, you belong to me."

"What are you talking about?" Aimee asked, the irritation back in her voice.

"Elk Runner gave you to me," he continued casually, knowing this would anger her again. For some reason, he enjoyed playing this game of taunting her. She was amazing when angry. Would she be as bold and responsive in his arms if he took her to his blankets?

"Elk Runner?" Aimee questioned. "Your Indian friend? I don't remember belonging to him, either," she added hotly.

"He found you," Daniel said, and shrugged. "Before he came to tell me of a crazy white woman in the woods, he followed you for a day."

Her eyes widened, and her lips parted slightly. What was she afraid of that Elk Runner might have seen?

"So he decided to give me to you?" Aimee questioned. "Isn't that just like a typical man," she spat. "Always thinking they can just own and control everything and everyone."

"If some Blackfoot warrior had discovered you first, you'd be dead which, for you, would be the preferable choice than coming upon another trapper." Daniel let his unspoken meaning sink in.

"I don't belong to you or anyone else, Daniel." She inhaled deeply. Obviously she was trying hard to stay composed.

"That is the way here in the mountains, just as it is in the cities in the east. You belong to your husband." No doubt, his comment would only provoke her some more. He was prepared, even hoped, that she would call him a filthy heathen, just as Emma had done. Perhaps then he could get this annoying attraction he felt for her out of his system.

She pressed her eyes shut, and inhaled another deep breath. Her mouth was set in a firm and stubborn line, and he waited for the angry words he was sure she couldn't wait to unleash on him.

"Well, I can see you're not an Indian, and you're definitely not my husband," she stated hotly. "I understand that a woman has no rights here according to a man's way of thinking, and I'm just someone's property. It's just my dumb luck that I came all this way only to be stuck with another control freak of a man. Let me tell you something right now." Her blue eyes shot icy daggers at him. "I'm not going to be owned or have my life managed by anyone." Aimee continued her rant. Her voice grew louder and faster with each word.

"I'm sick and tired of being told what I should and shouldn't do, like I'm a little kid and have no mind of my own. *'I don't want you to go on that backpacking trip, Aimee.' 'Why are you wasting your time taking these stupid wilderness first aid or backcountry*

59

cooking courses, Aimee?' 'You can't go out for pizza after work with friends because I'm taking you to the movies, Aimee.' Or this one; *'Aimee, why are you wearing these baggy rags to bed when you should be wearing a silk teddy.'* Oh, and here's my favorite, *'I prefer you to wear that black cocktail dress with high heels tonight and put your hair up in a French twist."*

She glared at him and continued, "Obviously, some things have always been, and always will be, the same!"

She forcefully pulled her arm free of his grip, and limped off as fast as her injured foot allowed. When she reached the cabin, she slammed the door shut with such force that it bounced open again.

Daniel stared after her, dumbstruck. The way she'd changed the tone of her voice, and her animated arm movements reminded him of a theater performance he'd once seen in Philadelphia. And what the hell was she talking about? He wasn't even sure most of her words were spoken in English.

"Damn all men for being so overbearing," she yelled from inside the cabin. His lips curved in a smile. She was right about the one thing he had understood from her tirade. No man would, or should, ever own her. She was strong willed, full of spirit, and irresistibly beautiful. Could he let her go back to a man who no doubt would try and break that spirit?

She's not yours to keep, damn it! Daniel ran a frustrated hand through his still damp hair. He desperately searched his mind for similarities between her and Emma, the woman he had professed his love to, and who had taken advantage of that fact and used him for her own means. To a young man of eighteen trying to learn about his heritage as a white man in Philadelphia after spending all his life in the wilderness, Emma had been the prettiest thing he'd ever laid eyes on. She had been a delicate flower, raised in a wealthy home, and lacked no comforts.

He couldn't recall ever seeing her with her hair uncovered, or her hands bare without gloves. Servants were at her beck and call. He now saw her from a man's eye, not the youth he had been seven years ago. She had been a spoiled young woman who would go to any lengths for her own gain, no matter who got hurt in the process.

Aimee, on the other hand, was not just a pretty face. She was radiant and breathtaking, spirited and exciting. She wasn't above working as she had shown when she took it upon herself to fix meals every day, clean the cabin, and insist on carrying the heavy water bucket to the river and back. Her delicate hands and satiny smooth skin spoke of wealth and privilege, not a life of labor. He was sure of it. How did a woman of obvious high social standing end up here, alone in the wilderness, a thousand miles from even the remotest white civilization? It only added to the mystery. She intrigued him as no one ever had; yet she was also secretive and full of lies. He would not fall for a woman's pretty face and deceptive ways again. Then why couldn't he seem to stop this insane attraction he felt for her?

With an annoyed shake of his head, he collected his discarded shirt and pulled it on over his head, then found the rest of his articles. He might as well go back and see if the deer he had killed was still where he dropped it, or if some predator had already scavenged it.

Chapter Seven

Aimee sprinkled flour on the table, dusted her hands with it, and pulled the lump of dough out of the bowl. She threw it onto her work surface, which sent a cloud of white dust into the air. Her clean t-shirt now sported white powder down the front. She pounded at the mass with her fists, and ground her teeth. She couldn't believe that she was stuck in the past with another overbearing, know-it-all-better man. The intense feelings Daniel evoked didn't help her foul mood. She'd known he was a strong man, but held against his hard body, and the vision of him without his shirt on sent her simmering hormones into overdrive.

No, Aimee. Knock it off. A good-looking man comes with a high testosterone level, which is synonymous with control freak, and you definitely don't need any more of that.

The cabin door creaked open slowly, and she tensed, then pounded the dough more forcefully than before. She glanced up briefly. Daniel appeared in the doorway. Her focus returned to her work.

"I'm making bread," she announced tersely. He hadn't moved further into the cabin, prompting her to look up again. His lips curved in a wide grin, and his eyes roamed over her. She shot him a questioning look, her eyebrows raised.

"I will teach you," he said quietly.

"Teach me what?" Her eyes narrowed suspiciously.

"You asked me to teach you to survive in the mountains. I will teach you."

She stared up at him, wide-eyed. The anger melted out of her, and a smile formed on her lips.

"Really?" she asked excitedly.

"Your first lesson will be how to skin and dress a deer. Come outside." He turned abruptly and walked out the door.

Aimee gaped at the closed door. She was genuinely surprised. He would teach her survival skills? She had thrown those words at him earlier for lack of something better to say. She never expected him to follow through. Her heart beat faster at the prospect of learning primitive survival techniques from this man. She formed her dough into a ball and dropped it back into the bowl. She'd have to punch it down again later. Quickly, she changed out of her clean clothes back into her soiled ones.

Dressing a deer. She could only imagine what all that would entail. She'd done plenty of dissections in nursing school, but an entire deer? She took a deep breath, squared her shoulders, and raised her chin. She was not about to back away from his challenge. It was obvious that he was testing her. Inhaling another deep breath for courage, she opened the door and left the cabin.

* * *

Daniel waited outside. A deer carcass lay on the ground next to him.

"Poor deer," Aimee mumbled.

Daniel glanced at her, his eyebrows drawn together. "Do you wish to eat?"

"What do I have to do?"

He handed her his hunting knife, and proceeded to instruct where to make the cuts to remove the hide in its entirety. He explained how to eviscerate the deer, and told her how important it was not to leave any entrails lying about, as it would attract predators.

From the look on her face, Aimee had never dressed fresh kill before. He meant to test her to see if she would back down from this unpleasant job, but the expert way she handled herself surprised him. Her knife cuts were made with peculiar fine precision as she sliced through muscle and tendons, but she didn't shrink away from the blood and gore. He almost stepped in and helped her when she wrestled with the carcass to strip the hide off the meat. She wouldn't ask for help, even as she struggled with the deer that probably weighed more than she did.

"You know," Aimee said teasingly, after succeeding in

peeling the skin off the carcass, "I'm going to have to take another swim in the river after this."

He scowled. The image of her nude, wearing only those pieces of fabric at her breasts and waist, was almost unbearable. "If you choose to swim in the river again, I might let the current sweep you away."

"Is that a promise?" she taunted.

Daniel remained silent. The things she said made no sense to him. Why would someone make light of possibly drowning?

An hour later, most of the deer meat, as well as the hide, hung up to dry in the sun. Daniel leaned against the cabin while Aimee headed for the river. She hadn't backed down from his challenge. She had performed the task without complaint, and she'd done it well. Was it possible that she could survive in these mountains? She obviously had managed to be on her own for a short time already. The thought nagged at him.

His father had always told him how frail and weak his mother had been. She had followed her husband into the mountains without question because she loved him, but she had neither the strength nor the spirit for this kind of life. Daniel could not picture Aimee as frail and weak. Everything she had done thus far spoke of strength and courage.

Aimee walked back from the river, a wide smile on her face. Something tightened in his gut.

"What else can I do?" she asked eagerly.

"That's enough for today," he replied. "I would look forward to some of that bread you plan to bake, though. It has been a long time since I've had bread like that."

"If you put some meat on a spit over the fire out here, I'll bake some bread to go with it." Daniel caught the satisfied look on her face before she turned and headed back to the cabin.

* * *

Aimee woke the following morning to a bare table. The usual cup of coffee and breakfast she'd become accustomed to wasn't there. She brushed her hair quickly and gathered it into a ponytail. After unwrapping and inspecting her foot, she decided that today she would try putting her boot back on. She stood and was about to pull her pants up over her hips, when the door swung open, and Daniel walked in. His expression hardened as his eyes traveled up and down the length of her body. She hastily zipped and buttoned her pants.

"I know this is your cabin, but how about you knock first next time before you just barge in." She shot him an exasperated look.

"I brought you these." Daniel held something out to her, apparently unperturbed by the heated look in her eyes.

She stepped toward him and reached for what he offered. Fingering the soft leather in her hands, she held a pair of moccasins, and her face brightened.

"You made these?" she asked with delight. "For me?"

"You need foot coverings. Your boots don't yield to the swelling in your foot."

Aimee was speechless. She wasn't used to a man's complete awareness of everything. His thoughtfulness surprised her beyond belief. She caressed the soft leather, and traced a finger along the even stitching on the sides. Her eyes stung, and she hastily tried to blink away the sensation. He was right. She hadn't been able to get her foot into her boot yet. She slipped the soft leather moccasins on. They were a perfect fit. Her feet felt wonderful surrounded by the downy rabbit fur that lined the insides of the shoes.

"They're so comfortable. How did you know my size?"

"Your footprints by the river."

"Oh, clever." Impulsively, she stepped up to him, put her hands on his shoulders to lean up and gave him a casual peck on the cheek. "Thank you, these are great," she said warmly, and stepped back. Her cheek grazed his for a mere second.

Daniel's hands reached out and spanned her waist. He held her for a moment before abruptly letting go. His Adam's apple bobbed up and down several times, and his eyes darkened considerably.

Oh God, I hope that wasn't a wrong message.

Aimee's heart beat faster when her eyes met his. The raw desire in Daniel's dark stare was unmistakable.

"Well, um, should I make some breakfast?" she asked, and moved away from him. Her skin still prickled from where his

65

hands had been moments ago.

"No," Daniel said, to her surprise. "This morning, you will find your own food."

"You're taking me with you today?" Her face lit up again.

"Only if your foot is well enough."

"I can walk fine on it," she said quickly. *I'll be sure to take some ibuprofen, though.* "When do we leave?"

"As soon as you are ready."

* * *

Daniel turned and left the cabin. Just outside the door, he ran a hand through his hair while his other hand clenched tightly in a fist. He had decided that he would start showing Aimee around his mountains, just to see what she was capable of, but mainly to keep her out of trouble. Now, recalling the sight of her half-undressed, he reconsidered his decision. How could he possibly spend an entire day in her presence after that vision? The brief glimpse of her exposed thighs combined with the innocent kiss she had given him had almost been his undoing.

"Damn." He couldn't remember any other time when he'd had to exercise such self-control. All he wanted to do was pull her into his arms, and lose himself in her sweet body.

He smiled, recalling her sharp reprimand when he'd walked into the cabin. Good thing there hadn't been a weapon handy. He wouldn't put it past her to throw a knife at him just then.

"Okay, I'm ready to go." Aimee emerged from the cabin. She carried her strange pack on her back. Daniel inhaled a deep breath and tried to erase the mental images in his head.

"You're still favoring that foot." Perhaps he could convince her to stay behind. Somehow he knew she wouldn't agree to that.

"I can keep up. I won't slow you down."

The corners of his mouth rose in a lazy grin, and his eyes boldly appraised her from head to toe. "I doubt you could keep up with me even if your foot was completely healed," he challenged.

"Oh yeah? Well I'll have you know I run at least 5 miles every day back home," Aimee countered, her hands on her hips.

His eyes narrowed. "Who do you run from?"

"No one, just to stay in shape." Aimee shrugged. "I bet I

could give you a good run for your money. I also work out, you know."

More words and phrases he didn't comprehend. This woman was such a mystery to him. He shook his head, gathered his rifle, and set off in the direction they had come from when he'd first brought her to the cabin. She fell in step beside him.

"Where are we going?"

"We will follow the Little Buffalo River for a while. There are places in the woods along the way where you can pick fresh berries." He avoided looking at her, and kept his eyes straight ahead.

"Is that what you call this river?"

"Why were you trying to follow this river when we found you?" He turned his head to look at her for the first time.

"What makes you think that?"

He scoffed. Her evasiveness was annoying the hell out of him. "The tracks you left made it quite obvious. You were following a tributary for days before your accident." He stopped and narrowed his eyes. "Why do you avoid answering my questions? What are you afraid of?"

"Look." Aimee let out a long sigh, stopping next to him. "There are things about me I can't talk to you about. Believe me, I would tell you, but I just can't. Can we please just not talk about my past?"

"I don't understand why you lie to me. If you are in danger, I can protect you."

"I don't need protecting. I just need a place to stay for a while." Aimee started walking again. She kept her eyes straight ahead to avoid his stare. "So, where are these berry bushes? I'm getting hungry."

Daniel clenched his jaw in frustration. Scowling, he picked up the pace again. After about a mile, he veered away from the river and entered the forest.

"Should we be worried about bears?" Aimee asked. "They hang out near berry patches, don't they?"

Hang out? "There is always danger from bears."

"Have you tangled with a lot of bears?"

"A few." He shrugged. "Why are you asking all the

67

questions, but you won't answer any of mine?"

"Because you're supposed to be teaching me about the mountains, remember? And a good student asks questions." Aimee grinned.

Daniel shook his head. He inhaled deeply to maintain calm. Why did she have to act so elusive?

"Well, then you need to begin to open your eyes. Look for tracks on the ground. Become aware of the things around you. Had you read the signs better, you would not have encountered that grizzly."

He pointed to a spot in the dirt. The grass all around was shorter and sparser than the surrounding area.

"Looks like bison tracks," Aimee said confidently after she bent down to look closely at the ground.

He raised his brows in surprise. Young boys among the Tukudeka learned early on to distinguish between elk and bison tracks. They looked very similar. That this white woman knew the difference impressed him. He nodded affirmation.

"How long ago?" he asked, crossing his arms over his chest. This question wouldn't be as easy to answer.

Aimee looked again and seemed to ponder his question. His lips raised in a smile when she didn't respond. Finally, she said, "not too recently, perhaps late yesterday."

His smile faded. "Why do you think that?"

"Because most of the grass is standing up again after it's been trampled on."

He studied her face. How did she know to read bison tracks so accurately, yet she couldn't see the signs of a bear kill? Stepping up to one of many lodgepole pines, he asked, "What about this mark on the tree?" He pointed to the trunk of the pine that had some of its bark stripped off.

Aimee walked up next to him, and ran her fingers across the yellowed scars. "A bison made those marks, rubbing his head against the tree. There's even a little fur hanging on. See?" She pulled a tuft of brown fur from the bark and held it up to him. Daniel's jaw clenched.

* * *

Aimee smiled sweetly. He could ask her all he wanted about

68

bison. This was basic junior ranger stuff to her. How many countless ranger-led hikes had she gone on in her life? And a favorite topic of discussion on those hikes had often been bison. She could practically lead one of these bison talks herself. She had to admit, though, that her guide this time was far more interesting than any ranger she'd met in modern times.

When Daniel didn't speak, she finally asked, "Well, how am I doing so far?"

He studied her for a moment with that intense look of his. "Where would you expect to find berries here?" he asked, rather than answer her question.

"I'd be looking around for sunny spots, I suppose, for berry bushes."

Daniel pointed out some strawberry patches on the ground, and huckleberry bushes among the thickets. She moved eagerly in their direction, when he took hold of her arm and pulled her back. She turned her head, and raised her eyebrows in a silent question.

"Bears, remember?" he warned. He scanned the area for a moment, and inhaled deeply. "Often, you can smell a bear before you see him," he explained.

"What do bears smell like?" She recalled the death and decay smell of the elk carcass, but she couldn't remember now if the bear smelled like rotten meat as well, or just the air around him.

"Most of the year, bears smell like the places they visit," Daniel explained. "In the early part of summer, they smell like the wet grasses."

"Sweet?" she asked. He nodded.

"The tundra smells like the earth and sage, and a bear has that smell as well. It is only much more distinct. You need to train your senses to pick up the differences. Bears like to roll in their food, or anything with a strong odor, so whatever they have eaten, they will smell like it."

"Ew. Okay. Kind of like dogs. They do that, too." She took a deep breath, but all she smelled was the pine scent of the forest. "What else?" she asked eagerly.

"Listen to the forest. What do you hear?"

69

She closed her eyes and inhaled. The tranquil sounds of the forest birds, the smell of fresh pine and musty earth, even the distinctive cow scent left behind by the bison, and the rushing sound of the breeze through the tops of the tall lodgepole pines, all had an intoxicating effect on her.

"I hear the wind and birds," she said softly.

"What kind of birds?" Daniel prodded.

She focused on the different sounds. "Oh! A woodpecker," she said in surprise. She had never paid attention to different birdcalls before. She turned her head to listen closer. "I hear ravens, and probably some kind of jay?"

"Any other animals?" Daniel pushed her further. "You must learn to separate all sound."

She sighed, but kept her eyes closed. Amazingly, she could, indeed, sift through the cacophony of chirps and make out individual animals. "Hey, that's not a bird . . . that was an angry-sounding squirrel."

She opened her eyes. In front of her, Daniel stared intently at her face. Her heart skipped a beat.

"Is it safe now?" she whispered.

Was he going to answer? She shifted her weight nervously. His intense eyes drove straight to her heart. She couldn't read his expression, but she wasn't about to back down and be the first to look away. Finally, he cleared his throat.

"There is no bear here," he answered, his voice sounding a bit raspy. He motioned with his chin to the berry patches.

Relieved for the excuse to move away from him, Aimee picked handfuls of berries, and between mouthfuls carefully placed some in her backpack. "There are so many. I would love to take some of these back and make a pie!"

Daniel stood off to the side while she ate her fill, and casually popped a few berries in his mouth from time to time. He was like a security guard – constantly trained on her to make sure she didn't make a wrong move. She tried to ignore him and concentrate on her task, but his eyes seemed to reach straight into her. Her skin tingled all over.

"Okay, I think I have enough," Aimee said after her pack was rather full. She wished he would catch her double meaning.

She'd definitely had enough of his continuous perusal, and was ready for a diversion. Daniel turned and led the way out of the forest.

"The last time I ate pie was in Philadelphia seven years ago," he said wistfully when the trail widened and they walked side by side. Aimee was surprised he volunteered this information.

"You're in for a treat, then. I make a mean berry pie."

* * *

For the better part of the morning, Daniel led her through the forest. He showed her how to read different tracks, signs to look out for that an animal had been in the area, where to look for edible roots and plants, and how to watch the skies for changes in the weather. Along with the berries, she filled her backpack with mint, wild onions, licorice, and various other roots and plants.

She listened attentively as she tried to absorb everything Daniel told her. Some things she already knew, others were completely new to her. The subtle animal signs he picked up on astounded her. Silently, he had pointed out a black bear sow and her twin cubs in the distance, a moose in the thickets that she would have completely overlooked, and countless other smaller animals. He knew which critter made every track they came upon. He read the forest for information as someone in her time would read a newspaper. It was most refreshing to get a glimpse of this wilderness that she loved so much in her time from this man who carved out a living here.

Aimee savored the beauty of her surroundings. Aspen trees grew in abundance. Beaver lodges lined the banks along streams, and countless otters played in the waters. With the coming of the fur trappers to these mountains within a decade of this time, the beaver would be trapped to near extinction. Wolves would be hunted until none remained, and without this predator, the elk would take over, and cause the destruction of the aspen from overgrazing. This was a Yellowstone unfamiliar to her, but it was as nature had intended before the encroachment of man.

Despite the differences, the landscape still held a certain familiarity, and she realized Daniel was leading them back in the direction of the cabin sometime in the early afternoon. Her foot throbbed with every step she took, but today was one of the best

71

days of her life. The raw, undisturbed landscape exhilarated her. No other hikers, no roads. *Just me and this gorgeous backwoodsman.*

Oh, geez, where were her thoughts taking her now? Daniel had proven to be an excellent teacher, and she enjoyed seeing her beloved Yellowstone through his eyes. Yet, as the day wore on, she found it harder and harder to concentrate on her surroundings, while she became more and more aware of him. He was as untamed as this land, and by far the most virile man she had ever met.

Chapter Eight

For the next hour or so, they walked single file along the banks of the fast-flowing Gibbon - Little Buffalo - River. Aimee couldn't help but watch the display of muscle movement on Daniel's back and broad shoulders that his shirt couldn't disguise. Visions of his nude upper body from the day before shamelessly entered her thoughts.

"Damn."

She'd been too busy staring at Daniel's backside to watch the ground beneath her, and carelessly tripped on a large rock, which caused her to lose her balance. Daniel's reflexes were lightning fast. He wheeled around, grabbed her, and pulled her close before she tumbled into the river. Aimee held on to his upper arms and balanced herself. His eyes burned into her. He held her so close, it felt like a lover's embrace.

"Easy," he whispered as he steadied her. She'd regained her balance, yet he didn't relax his hold around her waist. Aimee stared wide-eyed into his deep brown eyes. Her heart pounded in her chest, and it wasn't from the adrenaline of almost falling into the frigid water. She held her breath. No one had ever looked at her with such smoldering intensity before. It was as if he stared straight into her soul. *Get a grip on yourself.*

"I won't fall. You can release me now," she said softly. Daniel held her for a moment longer. His chest heaved, then he slowly loosened his hold around her waist.

"This has been too much for you today. I shouldn't have brought you this far." The frown was back.

"Are you kidding?" Aimee regained her composure. "I'm having a great time. I stepped on a rock is all."

73

"We will rest here for a while, and for once you will listen to me." The tone of his voice left no room for argument this time.

"All right, but will you take me out again tomorrow?" she asked eagerly.

"You need to give your foot proper time to heal." His jaw clenched. He seemed eager to say more, maybe even scold her again, but he didn't.

"My foot is fine," she argued. "Look, I want to experience these mountains while I have the chance. Today has been wonderful, and I don't want to just sit around that cabin all day. It's boring."

Daniel shook his head. "You are a stubborn woman."

"Damn right I am." She grinned. After a moment's silence, she asked hopefully, "will you take me to a geyser basin tomorrow?"

"What is a guy soor basin?" Daniel's perpetual frown deepened.

Oops, big slip up. Too late, Aimee realized that the term geyser had definitely not been in use in this time to describe the geothermal water features of this area.

"You know, the places where the water shoots out of the earth. And the hot pools and mud."

"How do you know of these things?" His eyes narrowed suspiciously.

"I've seen a few before my accident, and I would like to see some more," Aimee quickly said. *It's not really a lie. I have seen the geysers before now!* She wished she could tell Daniel the other truth. All of it. Then he would really think she was lying.

"It's a wonder you didn't fall into one and burn to death," he scoffed.

"Well, will you show me?" she prodded, ignoring his little dig.

Daniel met her eyes for a moment. "I will give you my answer tomorrow."

Well, that's better than a no. Besides, if she wanted to, she could find her own way to the lower geyser basins. All she had to do was follow the Firehole River.

Daniel reached into his traveling pouch, then held his hand

out to her.

"What's this?" she asked, examining what looked like a piece of black rubber.

"It's called pemmican. Eat."

She had heard of pemmican. It was a mountain man staple – ground up meat and lard mixed with berries, or something like that. Kind of like a power bar. It didn't look very appetizing. She sniffed it, then took a tentative nibble.

"Yuck! That is disgusting." She spit it out. Daniel took a large bite out of a piece he held.

"It's nourishment."

"Well, I'm not eating that." She handed her piece back to him.

"Another lesson about the wilderness." He shot her a hard look. "Never refuse food or water when it is offered, because you don't know when you will get another chance."

"I'll whip something up when we get back to the cabin." She stood. "Speaking of which, let's go. I know we've been heading in that direction for some time now."

* * *

Daniel grinned, and stared after her. She was not easily fooled. One more reason he wanted her. He'd been more than surprised today. He had assumed the little *gediki* would last a few hours on the trail with him. However, she had shown remarkable endurance. Her knowledge of some things and her ignorance in others added to the mysteries about her that he found intriguing. Whatever she was hiding, he was sure he'd find out in time.

By late morning, her limp had become more pronounced. Without telling her, he'd chosen a route that would lead back to the cabin. If he told her they were heading back so early, she would have tried to talk him out of it. Damn, she was stubborn. Her foot obviously still caused her pain, but why she wouldn't acknowledge that fact made no sense. Several times he had offered to stop and rest, and she had refused each time.

The feel of her soft curves pressed against him when he'd caught her around the waist to keep her from falling into the river had sent fire through his veins. He'd held her longer than was necessary. The urge to sweep some loose tendrils of hair out of

75

her face had been overpowering. Her soft skin, the slight flush of heat on her cheeks, and the healing cuts that crisscrossed her delicate features . . . he drank it all in. He hadn't been able to keep his eyes off her while he stood so close to her, his desire for this woman burning his insides. It took all his willpower to stay composed when all he'd wanted to do at that moment was wrap her in his arms and find out if her lips tasted as luscious as they looked.

His respect and admiration for her had grown all day, if that was even possible. He followed as Aimee walked on ahead after their short rest. She was determined not to show the pain she was in, making her body move stiffly in front of him. She would refuse any assistance he'd offer, so he simply walked behind her and enjoyed the view of her backside. He liked those britches she wore more and more.

* * *

Aimee sighed and deposited her backpack on the table. No way would she admit to Daniel that she had probably walked too far today. It didn't matter. It had been a wonderful day. She was confident her foot would be fine again tomorrow.

She poured the berries into a wooden bowl, sprinkled sugar over the top of them, and let them sit while she made a pastry crust using lard and flour. This would not be a true pie since she only had a Dutch oven to cook in. She would improvise the best she could, but her sweet tooth had to be satisfied. She definitely did miss her double fudge chocolate ice cream.

Low on firewood, she stepped outside the cabin to bring in more. Her eyes scanned the meadow, and her gaze fell toward the river. Daniel stood waist deep in the water with some sort of fishing line. Aimee stared. He wasn't wearing a shirt. Had he stripped off all of his clothes? Aimee couldn't remember ever feeling such undeniable physical attraction for a man. But it was more than that. She enjoyed his company, and spending time with him. She was convinced that somewhere under that serious, scowly exterior was a fun-loving, easy-going guy. She had seen that sexy grin of his more than once now.

She couldn't help but wonder what his thoughts were of her. He obviously had strong convictions that a white woman didn't belong in these mountains, but she was determined to prove to him that she wasn't incompetent. The looks of contempt she had seen on his face that first day were gone. Maybe she had just misinterpreted his dark and hateful expressions. What reason would he have to hate her? At times, he looked at her with that intense stare of his, making her wonder if it meant he was annoyed, or attracted to her.

She couldn't have misread the raw desire she had seen in his eyes after her innocent peck on the cheek this morning. How long had Daniel been without the company of a woman? Perhaps an extended abstinence had caused such a reaction in him. There was no way a man like him would lead a celibate life. Surely there were plenty of Indian women who would happily hop into bed with him.

Aimee walked toward the river. Reaching the bank, she sat down quietly and removed her moccasins, and wiggled her toes in the cool grass. Silently, she observed Daniel wade through the water, casting his line almost like a fly-fisherman. A swim would be really refreshing right now to wash some of the trail dust off, but she thought better of it. She was reasonably sure that Daniel wouldn't force himself on her, but she didn't want to test that theory, either. She should feel a lot more vulnerable. She was here all alone with this man, and no one would come to her rescue if he decided to have his way with her. He hadn't been threatening so far, and he made her feel safe and protected, even if he had acted surly most of the time.

Then again, what would it be like with a man like him? A little voice inside her head nagged at her. She smiled at the direction her thoughts were heading. Her sexual experience was limited to Brad. She had always planned to save herself for her wedding night, but Brad had shattered that aspiration rather quickly. He had wormed his way into her bed early in their relationship. To add to her disappointment, she couldn't help but find Brad's lovemaking rather unexciting. Sex with him was – as it always was with Brad – more about him, and less about satisfying her. Consequently, she had made more excuses than not to stay out of his bed.

And yet, here she found her thoughts straying to Daniel, and what it might be like with a man like him. Would he be gentle and considerate, or wild and fierce? Somehow she couldn't picture him as anything less than a perfect lover.

Oh, God, Aimee, get a grip! She mentally smacked herself. *This is absolutely crazy!*

Something wet and cold fell into her lap. Aimee jumped in surprise, jolted out of her sensual daydreams. She stared as a large trout flopped up and down on her legs. Her gaze shot toward the river. Daniel wore a wolfish grin on his face.

"You threw a fish at me?" she shouted in false anger. "I can't believe you threw a fish at me!" In truth, it was hard to believe. Mr. Tall, Dark, and Scowly had actually done something funny. Imagine that.

She bent down in pretense of picking up the wiggling fish, and gathered a handful of river mud from the bank, and squeezed it into a ball. As Daniel slowly waded toward her, still grinning from ear to ear, she aimed and threw the mud, hitting him in the shoulder.

"Hah! Take that!"

Daniel's grin faded quickly.

"Two can play at that game." Aimee kept taunting him, her hands on her hips.

Daniel emerged from the river, and she swallowed hard. Her eyes roamed over his glistening wet body as he advanced. His feral virility stunned her. Several large jagged scars on his chest stood out against his olive skin. Why hadn't she noticed them the day before? She swallowed nervously as her gaze traveled lower, and sighed in relief. He wasn't completely nude. He wore a breechcloth, but it didn't leave much to the imagination as to what it covered, and only served to accentuate his flat, rippled stomach and muscular thighs. The smoldering look in his eyes as he advanced sent her a few steps backwards, and the smile on her face froze.

Oh God! Is he really this angry because I threw some mud at him?

In one lightning fast, predatory move, Daniel grabbed her up and flung her over his shoulder like a sack of potatoes, and turned back to the water.

"What are you doing? Put me down!" Aimee shrieked. Her fists pounded his hard back while her feet kicked uselessly in the air. He waded into the water a few feet, and unceremoniously threw her into the river. Before she hit the water, her thought was one of disbelief that he carried the game this far. It seemed so uncharacteristic of him.

"You slimeball," she yelled as her head emerged from the water. She was actually pleasantly surprised at this new, playful side of him. At least it solved her dilemma of wanting to go for a swim earlier.

"How dare you!" she squealed in mock anger. Daniel dove into the river after her and came up inches from her face. She splashed water at him to ward him off. Daniel's hands shot up and encircled her wrists.

Flashing a devilish grin, he asked, "What is a slimeball?"

She couldn't keep up her false anger any more. "A slippery snake," she laughed. "Like you, who preys on helpless women."

Daniel's eyebrows shot up. "I thought you said you weren't helpless."

"You're right, I'm not helpless," she confirmed, and flapped like a fish to try and free herself from his iron grip. Daniel released her wrists, but snaked his arms around her waist and reeled her in close to him, while the slow current carried them downriver. She braced her palms against his chest, and a jolt of electricity seared up her arms at the contact with his warm skin.

"I thought you told me not to go in the river again." Her voice was slightly breathless.

Daniel's expression changed. His eyes darkened and any hint of a smile faded. Once again, intense desire registered in his dark eyes. Her heart rate accelerated, and she struggled to breathe. This game, she realized, was taking a turn in a very dangerous direction.

"Don't go in the river unless I'm here to fish you out."

Daniel's voice was low and husky. His hand came out of the water and wiped a strand of hair away from her face. His deep brown eyes fixed on hers. His fingers lingered, and caressed her cheek. Aimee's stomach tightened, and she groaned inwardly at the pure pleasure of that simple touch. His thumb traced along her cheek, and he cradled her face in his hand, his fingers raking through her hair.

Slowly, he lowered his face to hers. Aimee swallowed nervously. Her thoughts earlier might have strayed in this direction, but . . . *This is not right. I can't get involved with him. I'm not going to be here for long.*

It would do no good to give in to this temptation.

* * *

Aimee's body stiffened in his arms, and she whispered an almost inaudible "don't" as her hands pushed against his chest. Daniel pulled his head back and released his tight hold on her. Cursing silently for what he'd almost done, he moved them both closer to shore. What the hell had gotten into him? He wanted her like he had never wanted a woman. But he couldn't have her. Not only did she belong to another man, she shouldn't be here in the first place. He still had to figure out how to get her out of his mountains and back to civilization.

Daniel released her at the bank, and Aimee heaved herself out of the water, weighted down by her dripping wet clothes.

"Thanks for the swim," she mumbled hastily, then turned. Shivering from the cool late afternoon air, she walked briskly back to the cabin. Daniel watched her stride off, noticing how her wet clothing clung to every one of her feminine curves like a second skin.

"Damn." He punched the water with his fists. Why had he initiated this foolish game? He lost all reason when he was around her. He tore his eyes off her retreating form, and pulled himself out of the water to retrieve the fish he had caught earlier, including the one he had thrown at Aimee. He picked up her discarded moccasins in the grass and headed for the cabin.

* * *

The cabin door creaked open. Aimee turned and gasped in surprise. She quickly tucked the ends of a blanket under her arms. Her wet clothes lay in a pile on the floor beside her. She hadn't expected Daniel back so soon. After that little game in the river, and the fact that he had almost kissed her, she needed to draw some boundaries, or this – whatever it was – was going to get out of hand. She was terribly attracted to him, and could see herself in a relationship with him all too easily if circumstances were different. In her own time, this might have been a no-brainer. But nothing could come of this. She couldn't let herself get involved with someone, knowing it would have to end in a few short months. She didn't need that kind of complication in her life. And he probably didn't, either.

As she thought about this on her way back to the cabin, she realized that her casual, modern day behavior was probably sending him the wrong messages, perhaps even leading him on. She was a woman, all alone out here in this wilderness, and perhaps he thought she would be fair game to take to bed while she was here. Heck, he had already alluded to the fact that he considered her his property, based on Indian customs. She needed to work on her modesty and act more like a proper puritan. She wasn't sure she could pull it off, but here was her first opportunity as he stood in the doorway. He still wore nothing but that breechcloth, and his smoldering eyes boldly raked over her.

"Daniel," she gasped. "I . . .I . . . I'm not decent." Hopefully she sounded properly mortified.

"I brought your moccasins." Daniel stepped into the cabin and held out the shoes, rather than offer an apology. His eyes devoured her exposed shoulders and his gaze lingered on the swell of her breasts. She swallowed back the lump in her throat. For an instant, she felt like a prey animal, cornered by a predator.

"Daniel, could you please leave the cabin so I can get dressed." Her voice lowered demurely as she turned her back to him. With her eyes to the ground, she clutched the blanket to her chest. "Please give me some privacy. This is most improper." She glanced discreetly back over her shoulder at him, and the sober look on his face told her she had hit the mark. *Maybe I should have been an actress instead of a nurse.*

Daniel abruptly did an about-face and quickly left the cabin, pulling the door shut behind him.

* * *

Outside, Daniel raked his hands through his hair in frustration. For a moment he couldn't think straight. For a moment, all he'd seen was Emma standing there.

Daniel, what are you doing here? Those same words echoed

from the past. Emma with her clothes off, clutching her dress in front of her to cover up, the same horrified look on her face at having been caught in a compromising situation. Only Emma hadn't been alone.

She's not Emma!

He released a string of curses. This was not Aimee as he had come to know her. She would have told him to get the hell out of the cabin, maybe even thrown something at him in anger. Any proper lady would be appalled at getting caught in such a compromising state of undress, but he had never seen her act demure and proper before. Again, she confused the hell out of him.

"Damn." What the hell had gotten into him? He had never done anything as impulsive before as when he tossed her in the river. This woman was messing with his mind in ways that he couldn't comprehend.

Just now, for the first time, she seemed truly afraid of him, and it hit him like an arrow in the gut. He was becoming way too relaxed in her company, and her not-so-subtle reminder was like a dip in a frozen river.

Chapter Nine

Aimee dressed quickly after Daniel's abrupt departure, thankful that she had packed spare clothes and underwear. Three months in the same things would have been rather difficult. Hopefully her little puritan act had set up some boundaries. She would have to be more careful from now on how she behaved around him. What would be considered innocent behavior in her time could definitely be taken as forward and suggestive in this day and age. Thinking about it, kissing a man, even on the cheek, was probably not acceptable behavior. This whole situation was turning out to be far more difficult than she ever imagined.

She checked on her pie in the fire. It looked done. The aroma of cooked berries made her mouth water. "If only we had some ice cream," she said out loud.

She removed the Dutch oven carefully from the coals in the fireplace, and set it on the hearth to cool. Spying her wet clothes on the ground, she scooped them up and headed outside.

Daniel squatted by the fire pit, and skewered several fish on some sticks. He wore his leather leggings, but no shirt. Her heart beat faster. The memory of what had almost happened in the river played fresh in her mind. Forcing her eyes away, she quickly ducked her head and headed for some trees to hang up her clothes to dry. *Get your hormones under control, Aimee.* That had never been a problem with Brad.

Walking back to the cabin, she trained her eyes on the ground to avoid looking at him. She was eager to sample her pie, but stopped before she reached the door, and called out to him. "The berry pie is done if you would like some."

Daniel rose from his spot by the fire pit and moved toward

her. "I have work to do," he said, his voice tense. "What happened today will not happen again, you have my word. I have never forced a woman, and I don't intend to start now."

She looked up, and his jaw clenched and unclenched. The venom in his voice caused her to take a step back. He tore his eyes away, and strode past her to the woodpile. Aimee expelled the breath she'd been holding in. Even in the cool early evening air, her shirt stuck to her skin from the sudden perspiration on her neck and between her breasts.

Daniel picked up his ax and set a log of wood on the chopping block. He didn't bother to glance back at her. Aimee stared at the play of his taut back and arm muscles as he repeatedly split large pieces of wood with each blow of his ax. Yanking her eyes away from the sheer masculine display of strength, she turned and opened the cabin door. Maybe it was better that he be Mr. Scowly again.

She definitely liked the other Daniel from this afternoon better. It had been a pleasant surprise, but she had to put up boundaries for her own sake, as well as his. His proclamation that he wouldn't try anything like what he'd done earlier by the river again, put her mind at ease, even as it nagged at her. It would be all too easy to fall in love with him. She stopped cold at the thought. No, it couldn't be happening, could it? How could she even think that? Most of the time he acted as if he hated her. How could she be attracted to someone who despised her? Besides, it was crazy to even think this way. A relationship with him could never work. Her time here was limited. She turned and gave him one more quick glance before she disappeared into the dark cabin.

Aimee cut into the pie, placed a large piece on a tin plate, and headed back outside with it. Daniel still chopped wood, his arms and back glistening with sweat in the early evening sun. She set the food on the woodpile for him, and when he didn't turn to look at her, she silently returned to the cabin to eat by herself. Later, when she returned to clean the dishes, the plate she set out was empty, and Daniel was nowhere to be seen.

"Well, I guess an empty plate means he liked it." She shrugged, a little disappointed. What had happened to him in the course of a few hours? He had been pleasant all day, and the afternoon swim in the river was most unexpected. Did he think she would be willing to go to bed with him after that? He sure was a complicated man to figure out.

By the time she finished putting the food and dishes away, darkness had fallen. She sighed, and glanced around the cabin. The lantern's soft glow didn't give off enough light to see much, let alone do anything else. She would have sat and written in her journal, but it had been a long day. Cracking open the cabin door, Aimee strained her eyes to see. Daniel had let the fire burn down in the yard, and he was gone. She closed the door and crawled under the furs in her bed. With her hands behind her head, she stared up at the ceiling. Seconds later, she rolled over on her side, and punched her pillow. Visions of Daniel coming out of the river prevented sleep.

* * *

Daniel walked the familiar path along the riverbank, deep in thought. He was angry with himself for letting his feelings get out of control. He had been trying to fight his crazy attraction to this woman from the moment he first laid eyes on her. Sometimes the desire to just follow Elk Runner's advice, and take her to his bed became so strong, it caused him physical pain.

She was a mystery he couldn't figure out. One moment, she was sure and confident in herself, the next she acted like a complete novice. He only half-understood many of the things she said, but it intrigued him. Of all the women he had known, Indian or white, he had never been around a more beautiful or spirited woman. She had a zest for life and adventure, and didn't appear to be afraid of much. Daniel scoffed. She was probably afraid of him now, after what he had done this afternoon.

He frowned. He had been almost sure he saw desire in her eyes before he tossed her in the river. Had it been so long that he couldn't read the signs on a woman's face? What had come over him to do such a thing? She sure had enjoyed the game, though, or so it seemed. Until his foolish attempt to kiss her.

He stared at the waters of the Madison. Driftwood and debris bobbed lazily in the gentle current. He bent and picked up a large stick, and with a loud roar, threw it far out into the river.

85

Seeing the horrified look on Aimee's face in the cabin had conjured up painful memories from the past. Just because she was a white woman didn't mean she was like Emma. He had to keep reminding himself of that. Aimee had absolutely nothing in common with her.

Except that she lies! Why did she refuse to tell him the truth about how she came to these mountains?

He still didn't know what he should do with her. His biggest dilemma, of course, was how to get her out of the mountains. This was no place for a white woman. The logical thing was to take her to St. Louis, but it was a long journey, and he couldn't spare to be away that long. He had to prepare for winter. This was how his father and he survived. One would go to St. Louis in the summer with their fur cache to trade, while the other stayed behind and made preparations for the upcoming trapping season and the harsh winters in these mountains. If a man wasn't ready for winter here, he would die.

Aimee seemed to be oblivious to all the dangers of this harsh land. All the more reason to get her away from here. What if she got hurt, or worse? What had he been thinking when he took her up on her challenge to show her the mountains and teach her things? It was only encouraging her. But while she was here, she needed to know how to survive. Daniel's mind swung like a pendulum from one side of the argument to the other. In the end, he was as lost for what to do as when he started his walk.

* * *

Sunlight filtered into the cabin through the burlap covering the open window, casting a warm glow on her bed. Aimee pulled the covers back, and swung her legs over the sides of the mattress. She quickly dressed, and opened the cabin door. Daniel appeared to be gone again. She couldn't be sure if he'd been gone all night, or had left early in the morning. The buffalo robe he slept on near the fire pit outside looked undisturbed.

Where did he go this time?

She chewed her nails and scanned the river for any sign of him. The sun was already well above the mountains framing the valley. She'd been eager for him to take her out again today. As the early morning dragged on, Aimee grew more restless. She'd already tidied up the cabin. She sat outside, and wrote in her journal for a while, but couldn't concentrate as her irritation grew.

Why can't he tell me he's going to be gone? I'm not sitting around here all day. My foot feels fine.

She stared at the Firehole River in the distance, and an idea formed in her mind. She didn't need him to take her to a geyser basin. She could find her own way. It couldn't be more than a seven or eight mile hike to one of the geyser basins south of here. All she had to do was follow the river.

Her mind made up, Aimee packed her backpack. She grabbed her sweater off the foot of the bed, along with a blanket in case of cooler weather. She didn't want to deal with hypothermia again. She was confident she could make the trip in one day, but to be on the safe side, she wanted something to keep her warm if she had to set up camp somewhere.

She double-checked her pack for her flint so she could start a fire. *I'm going to be more prepared this time.*

Smiling in satisfaction, she wrapped some meat and leftover bread in cloth. Several water bags hung on the wall by the door. Without a second thought, she grabbed one and hung it around her neck. Daniel wouldn't miss it. He always carried one with him, so these were spares. A hunting knife hung next to the water bags, and purely on impulse she pulled it off the wall, too, and stuffed it in her pack. She was about to slip into her moccasins, but instead pulled her hiking boots out from under the bed. They would give her better ankle support.

"I bet he's going to be mighty ticked off when I'm not here," she said aloud, a smile on her face. She shrugged it off. *He doesn't have the right to tell me what I can and can't do, and besides, he always goes off without telling me.* She was almost out the door, when another thought struck. *I guess I could leave him a note. At least he'll know I'll be back. Zach said he went to school back east, so I'll assume he can read.*

She almost tore a piece of paper out of her journal, thought better of it, and found a strip of aspen bark instead. She rummaged through her pack for a pencil, scribbled a few lines explaining she had gone for a hike heading south, and would be back later in the day. She left the note on the table, and headed

87

out the door.

* * *

It was a beautiful warm summer day. The fresh mountain air, the slight breeze, and her beautiful surroundings put her in a good mood. If Daniel had accompanied her, it would have been a better trip, but she wasn't going to dwell on his constant mood swings. And just the few lessons she had received from him the day before gave her the confidence needed to handle this trip on her own.

She forded the Gibbon River at a shallow point, and kept the Firehole to her right. The river cut through the mountains for a few miles, and since she didn't want to end up hanging off a cliff again, she stayed in the valley to the east, and followed some animal trails heading south. Without the familiar two-lane highway that cut through this forest in her time, the going was slower than she expected, and she had to stop to get her bearings several times. It could be quite disorienting traveling through such dense forests, and she relied heavily on her compass.

You're not going to get lost. Just stay to the west, and you'll find the river. Would Daniel try to find her if she disappeared for days?

After several hours of walking over and around downed trees, a wide smile spread across her face. The sounds of rushing water close by meant that she'd met up with the Firehole River again, and the going got easier as she followed along its banks. Soon, the forest opened up to meadowlands, and the first plumes of steam made by countless geysers and hot springs from the lower geyser basins rose in the distance. She would love to go all the way to Old Faithful. What a sight that would be! No boardwalks, no thousands of people crowding around to see the famous geyser erupt. She would be the only one there. She'd save that hike for another day. Other than a short break for a snack, she continued along the banks of the river. It was now an easy flat walk to the geyser basin.

She made a large loop around a group of bison, and kept her eyes on the ground, ever watchful not to step in puddles. Even a harmless-looking water puddle could open the ground and scald her badly if she wasn't careful. The earth's crust in this area was very thin, and she didn't have modern-day boardwalks to keep her safe. If she stayed where there were a lot of bison tracks, she would be safe. If the ground could hold a one-ton bison, surely it would hold her.

* * *

"Damn that stubborn fool of a woman!"

Daniel pounded his fist on the table when he found her message. He had gone out early to scout the area, and thought about what he wanted to show Aimee today. He had finally come to the conclusion that she did need to know certain things, and if he kept her close by it would hopefully keep her safe as well. He returned to his cabin later than he had anticipated, after an unexpected detour around a large bison herd.

Taking several calming breaths, an uneasy feeling crept up his spine. What trouble would she get herself in now? Her message said she was heading south. Yesterday she had asked to see the boiling pools and mud. What had she called it? He couldn't remember the words she used. Was it too much of a coincidence that south of here were many such pools and shooting water? Daniel mentally shook his head. He had found her northeast of his cabin. It was impossible for her to know that heading south would lead her directly to these hot pools.

He hastily grabbed some supplies and headed out. It didn't take him long to pick up her trail. She'd crossed the Little Buffalo River at a shallow spot. Squatting, he touched one of her foot prints made by her odd boots. Why would she not wear her moccasins? Some rocks had scuffmarks on them, and the grasses were still bent. He guessed she must have a couple of hours' head start on him. God! The woman left a trail any blind man could follow! She sure made it easy for him, and he was confident he could make up her head start rather quickly.

He realized that she was once again following the river, this time the one the Shoshoni called the Burning River. Again, he had to shake off the coincidence that by following this river, she would find her hot water pools.

He bent down to examine her footprints along the banks of a small tributary that flowed into the Burning River. She must have stopped here to rest, perhaps eat something. Her boots had

89

scuffed some lichen off a large boulder. A squirrel ran past him, chatting loudly, and fled into a hole in the ground. Some grasses were bent a short distance away, and the squirrel hole looked as if someone had stepped on it recently. The squirrel hadn't yet repaired the damages. Examining the spot more closely, Daniel counted the tracks of several pairs of moccasins, perhaps five or six. They could have only been made by Blackfoot. The Shoshoni didn't frequent this particular area this time of year.

Daniel tensed. He scrutinized the tracks. The disturbed earth from Aimee's prints was still moist in some places, whereas these prints were dry. They had come across this area shortly before Aimee. She had to be behind them if everyone followed their present course, but for how long? An uneasy feeling crept up his spine, and his heart rate increased.

Out of habit, Daniel checked his rifle to make sure it was loaded and ready to fire. He tucked it securely under his arm, then hurried off at a fast jog, and followed Aimee's tracks, keeping a close eye on the set of Blackfoot prints.

* * *

Aimee reached her destination, an area that would be known in her time as Midway Geyser Basin. It contained the world's largest hot spring – Grand Prismatic Spring. Excitement built in her, and her pace increased. The thought that she would be one of the first white people to see this natural wonder sent a chill down her spine. All she had to do was find a place to ford the river. She stared at the wide expanse of the water, and realized she should have crossed further back. The water might be shallow enough that she wouldn't have to swim, but would definitely come up past her waist. At least it would be warm. She gazed across the river at the steep bank. Unlike this side of the river with its lush grasses, the other side was devoid of most vegetation, and appeared mostly gray and white in color, and was shrouded by gusts of steam – a telltale sign of the geothermal activity there.

She watched the steaming hot water runoff from Excelsior Geyser plunge loudly down the embankment into the Firehole. Brilliant colors of yellow and orange framed the runoffs, created by the heat-loving bacteria that lived in the geysers. She shielded her eyes with her hand, and watched this wondrous display of nature's awesome forces. Without sunglasses, the colors were almost blinding against the contrast of the bright gray earth.

There is so much more runoff here than what I remember.

An uneasy thought entered her mind. While Excelsior was an inactive crater in her time, in the 1800's, it was a very active geyser. Hadn't she read that it could shoot water over 300 feet into the air during eruptions? What if it erupted now, while she was here? As awesome as such a sight would be, she didn't relish the notion of being sprayed with scalding hot water.

She leaned her backpack against a tree, and contemplated what to do. Should she chance it and find a place to cross, or abandon her idea altogether? If she did cross, should she take off her clothing, or just let it get wet? She would dry quickly enough, but she also knew the risk of hypothermia in this mountain climate.

Movement in the trees further downriver caught her eye. Or had she imagined it? Her heart quickened with the thought that it might be a bear. She inched closer to a tree and steadied herself. Adrenaline flooded her system, and her legs turned to rubber. Peering out from behind her hiding spot, she scanned the trees where she thought she'd seen movement. She caught a flash of tan behind a group of sapling lodgepoles. Several figures moved like stealth commandos through the forest. Another wave of adrenaline shot through her, and her heart pounded in her chest. All this time, she was concerned about bears. She never considered the Indians who inhabited this area.

She didn't dare move out from behind the tree. It didn't appear as if those Indians had noticed her presence. They continued moving in the opposite direction. She clamped her hand over her mouth, sure that her breathing was so loud she'd be heard. She squeezed her eyes shut momentarily, and wondered how long she should hide. Daniel had told her that Blackfoot Indians were not friendly, but the Shoshoni were. But she had no idea how to tell one Indian from another.

Her pack sat a few feet away from her, and she reached for it tentatively, when a large hand clamped down over her mouth. She was pulled roughly against a solid figure behind her. For a split second, she thought she would faint from shock. Then she started to fight. She squirmed to break free of the iron grip her captor had on her. The more she struggled, the tighter his hold became around her waist. She bit down on the hand covering her mouth. Nothing deterred him. The man dragged her silently behind a thick stand of young lodgepole pines. She dug her boots into the ground. Her heart was going to pound right up and out of her throat. She was no match for him. *First a bear, and now this!*

The man stopped dragging her. Every inch of her backside was pressed against a solid wall of muscle. The pressure of his hand over her mouth increased, forcing her to lean her head back against his chest.

"Give me your word not to make a sound, and I'll release you." A familiar voice spoke quietly into her ear, and Aimee instantly relaxed.

"Not a sound," Daniel whispered again, and Aimee nodded. Slowly, he removed his hand from over her mouth. She gasped and inhaled deeply, then turned in his arm, which was still wrapped around her middle. His face was inches from hers, and he put his finger to his lips in a gesture for silence. Aimee gave him a questioning look. He gestured with his chin in the direction of where she'd seen the Indians. They were still there, but had moved further along some imperceptible trail.

How had Daniel found her so quickly? How was it that he could sneak up on her so easily!

Although grateful for his presence, she was slightly annoyed that she depended on him so much. What would have happened to her if those Indians had seen her? If Daniel hadn't come along? It seemed like all she did lately was get into predicaments, and Daniel came along for the rescue. *Dammit, I've never been this incompetent on a wilderness trip before.*

After a few tense moments of silence, she whispered, "Are they gone?"

He didn't look at her, nor did he answer. One glance at his face told her he was furious.

"Stay here, and don't move, do you understand?" he growled.

Oh boy, he's really pissed. "Where are you going?"

"Don't move from this spot, no matter what." Daniel gave

92

her a hard stare in place of an answer. He silently moved out from behind the small trees, and used every bush and tree he could for cover. Making his way through the forest, he followed the group of Indians.

"If he gets hurt, it'll be my fault," she whispered. Her stomach twisted in knots, and she chewed nervously on her fingernails. There were things here she couldn't possibly be prepared for, regardless of her training back home.

She sat on the ground, her knees drawn up to her chest, and shivered. Bile threatened to rise in her throat. She had gotten herself into this mess, and it wasn't fair that he be the one out there, putting his life on the line for her. Aimee rested her chin on her knees, and rocked quietly back and forth.

Daniel returned just as silently as before. He grabbed one of her arms and not too gently pulled her up from her sitting position, hauling her onto her feet.

"Get your pack," he ordered.

He turned and headed in the direction they had come from. Aimee sighed, and grabbed her backpack, then fell in line behind him.

So much for seeing Grand Prismatic Spring. It was best to keep quiet and not ask to stop. Right now was not a good time to cross the line with Daniel and demand to see the hot spring. He looked murderous.

Without so much as a word or backwards glance to see if she followed, Daniel kept a brisk pace across the open grassland. By mid-afternoon, there was a definite change in the sky. Dark clouds rolled in from the northwest, and moved in their direction. The wind had also started to pick up, and it got rather cold very fast.

The sky darkened and thunder rumbled. Wordlessly, Daniel changed direction away from the meadow and headed for the tree line. It was a bad idea to be out in the open during a mountain thunderstorm. The trees would offer some protection, but the possibility of lightning had Aimee worried. Thick raindrops pelted them. Daniel walked briskly until he found an area of dense young pine trees, and ushered her under the protective branches. Here, the rain was barely noticeable, although her t-shirt clung to her skin as if she'd jumped in the river with it on. Drops of water

93

ran down her face. She wrapped her arms around her middle and sat on a thick bed of pine needles, and shivered uncontrollably. She flipped open her backpack and checked for her cotton sweater and blanket, thankful that they had stayed dry.

"Okay, I can't take the silent treatment any longer," she finally blurted out. "How long are you not going to speak to me?"

"I don't think you will like what I have to say," Daniel growled. His eyes smoldered with anger. "You are a foolish woman, and you'll get yourself killed because you don't listen."

Oh my God, he's gorgeous! The thought jolted her as she met and held his dark eyes rather than cower from his gaze. She'd seen his stare often enough now, and it no longer intimidated her. Aimee studied his face. His wet hair glistened in the dimming light, and every now and then a water drop ran down the side of his handsome face. She tightened her hold around her middle to ward off the urge to wipe the water from his cheek. That would definitely not be appropriate. Clenching his jaw, Daniel broke eye contact with her and retreated out from under their protective canopy.

"Where are you going?" she asked, slightly alarmed.

"To find some dry wood for a fire." He hurried out into the rain. She inhaled deeply. *Again, he's out there in this weather because of me.* She ran a hand over her own wet face, and let out a loud breath. *Damn! What a mess I've gotten us into now!*

He returned minutes later with an arm full of twigs and tree branches. He laid a small pile of kindling on the ground. Before he had the chance to reach for his flint, Aimee grabbed hers. She efficiently struck it against the hunting knife she had brought. Small sparks fell on the kindling, and ignited the dry twigs. Aimee blew air on the kindling with long breaths, and a fire crackled within minutes.

Daniel's expression seemed to soften a bit, but the fire did little to warm her. She knew she had to get out of her wet shirt. At least her hiking pants were somewhat water repelling. She glanced at Daniel. His cotton shirt looked soaked as well.

"We're both going to get hypothermic if we stay in these wet clothes," she said, her teeth chattering. "And I bet you already know that," she added. "Survival one-o-one."

Daniel's forehead wrinkled.

"I have a dry sweater in my pack, and I brought a blanket," Aimee continued. "We can share the blanket and warm up."

This time his eyebrows shot up. He still didn't move or speak.

"Oh, for God's sakes!" Aimee sucked in an impatient breath. "What is your problem? I don't want to freeze to death just because you're mad at me for leaving the cabin today without your permission." All thought of acting like the frightened virgin went out the window at the moment.

"Close your eyes," she said, and turned around as best she could in the small space, grabbed the bottom of her t-shirt and lifted it over her head. She had to turn to pull her sweater from her pack. Daniel hadn't closed his eyes. She pulled the warm sweater on, smiling softly while her face remained hidden for a moment. *Typical male. Give them the opportunity, and they will always look.* Her heart beat a little faster at the prospect of snuggling up with Daniel to keep warm. So much for the boundaries she tried to set up the day before. This was a necessity for survival right now. Nothing more. She wasn't going to let her emotions get the better of her.

Under different circumstances, in a different time, she would give anything to be with a man like Daniel. But she couldn't afford to let herself get involved. She would be gone from here soon. Nothing could come of this.

She pulled the blanket from her pack. "I'm not sharing my blanket with a wet fish, so you'd better take off your shirt."

Daniel wordlessly unbuckled his weapon belt to pull off his shirt.

"Don't get any ideas, though. This is out of necessity. We'll both be frozen popsicles in a few hours if we don't keep each other warm. But that's all this is, okay?"

Aimee unfolded the blanket and held it out to him. He frowned. He still hadn't spoken. He scooted up behind her and wrapped the blanket around both of them. Aimee suppressed a groan. He felt nothing like a wet fish. His upper body radiated heat, and she let herself relax against his rock solid form. The strong rhythmic beating of his heart pounded through her sweater.

95

"We're not going to make it back to the cabin today." Daniel finally spoke softly near her ear, which sent shivers down her back that had nothing to do with the temperature. "Even if this storm lets up. We'll head back at first light."

He eased her down to the ground, and she pulled her backpack under her head for a pillow. The sounds of the crackling fire, and the raindrops hitting the soft undergrowth outside their little canopy, along with the heat coming off Daniel's body, soon lulled her into a contented sleep. Her last thoughts as she drifted off to sleep was how completely safe she felt, nestled against this big woodsman's side.

Chapter Ten

Sleep did not come for Daniel. He wasn't afraid of much, but this little slip of a woman scared the hell out of him. These insane feelings disturbed him. No one had ever affected him as she did. The worst of it was in knowing that nothing could ever come of this attraction. She was spoken for by another man, and besides, she did not belong in the wilderness.

Yes, he was angry with her for wandering off. He had never met a more stubborn and headstrong woman. How could he protect her and keep her safe if she didn't listen to him?

He had told himself he was not going to do anything as foolish as what he had done the day before, and make Aimee feel like he wanted to have his way with her. Of course, that's exactly what he wanted, but he would not let his emotions get out of control again. Suggesting that they needed to remove their clothing might frighten her again, and he had been thinking of a tactful way to suggest this without causing her to be alarmed. So he'd been quite surprised when she was the one to bring it up.

A hot wave of desire had swept over him at the sight of her nearly nude body. Her breasts were covered by one of those odd white undergarments that left absolutely nothing to the imagination. He'd cursed silently. Somehow the cold seemed the preferable choice. Being near her like this would surely be the death of him.

Aimee stirred and moaned softly in her sleep. Daniel gently wrapped one arm around her, and pulled her close to him. He drew in a breath, and savored the sweet, flowery scent on her hair and skin. He was a coward and no better than a thief in the night, but at least while she slept he could enjoy just holding her in his arms.

She had been completely trusting of him tonight. He was determined not to lose that trust. And that meant he had to keep his hands off of her. He also had to figure out how to take her back to civilization, and from there, how to get her out of his mind. He sighed deeply. It was probably too late for that.

* * *

Aimee woke to the delicious smell of meat roasting over a fire. She opened her eyes and raised herself to a sitting position. The cold morning air sent a chill through her, and she drew the blanket up around her shoulders. She buried her face in the fabric, inhaling Daniel's woodsy scent.

"Mornin'," Daniel smiled at her. He knelt by the fire, and turned a rabbit on a spit.

"Good morning." She yawned. Glancing around, she squinted at the sun's rays that streamed through the canopy of the trees. Countless birds chirped loudly, announcing that the storm had passed. The sky was blue and cloudless. Thick drops of moisture still clung to the tree branches all around.

She watched Daniel by the fire, and sighed. A warm, fuzzy feeling spread from her center outward. Her heart began to ache. He had kept her warm and comfortable all night, and not once made an inappropriate move. This morning, he provided food. Yesterday, he had surely saved her life . . . again. When he wasn't acting all dark and moody, he was by far the most wonderful man she had ever met. And, she was falling fast and hard.

She swallowed repeatedly. How could this happen? The unfairness of it all. She could not get involved in a relationship that would only last a few months. She was going back to her time. Aside from that, Daniel was adamant about getting her out of the mountains. He held fast to the belief that this was no place for a white woman. She buried her nose in the blanket and inhaled his scent one more time, then reluctantly pushed it aside and left her warm spot to head into the forest for some privacy.

When she returned, she ducked back under the branches to their camp, and Daniel handed her a piece of meat.

"Thank you," she said. "I'm famished."

"I wish I had brought that pie you made." Daniel grinned.

"You liked that, huh?" Aimee said between mouthfuls.

"I did," Daniel confessed. He already finished his meal, and put out the fire. "Are you ready to go?"

Aimee rolled up her blanket, and picked her shirt up off the ground. Thankfully it had dried in the night. Turning away from Daniel, she removed her sweater and pulled her t-shirt on and her sweater over it.

She found her brush in the backpack, and vigorously ran it through her hair. Daniel gathered his rifle, and ducked out from under the trees, and walked ahead. Aimee shouldered her pack, and ran to catch up to him. To stay even with his long strides, she had to walk fast.

"I want to apologize for yesterday," she said slowly. "I promise I won't leave again on my own. It was stupid of me, and I put you in danger." She looked sideways up at him when he didn't reply. She expelled a loud breath and leaned forward as she walked, trying to make eye contact. "You can be mad at me, but please stop with the silent treatment."

"I'm not angry anymore," Daniel finally replied. "But I will not come looking for you again if you foolishly choose to wander off by yourself," he added sternly, and met her eyes.

She nodded. "Fair enough."

They crossed a meadow and reached the banks of the Firehole before Daniel spoke again. "When will you tell me how you came to be here? You claim to have been on your own, but if that were true, you would have been dead a long time ago." He looked at her with raised brows.

Aimee groaned. "I already told you all you need to know," she said firmly. *I want to tell you everything,* her mind screamed.

"You are either running away from your man, or else he has abandoned you. Perhaps you are ashamed for being abandoned?" Daniel prodded. "Is that why you won't tell me the truth?"

Aimee shook her head. What could she say? If he wanted to believe she had been abandoned, maybe that was a convenient enough story to keep him from asking questions that she couldn't possibly answer. Her eyes roamed the landscape further ahead, and she enjoyed listening to the rushing sound of water from the river. Steam rising from heat vents near the water's edge created a surreal atmosphere when the hot vapors mixed with the crisp ambient air.

"Your man is a fool," Daniel said harshly.

Aimee simply wished he would change the subject. But her heart skipped faster at Daniel's words.

"Where did you learn to write?" Daniel prodded further. "Only wealthy men have the means to educate their daughters."

"So now you think I'm wealthy?" Aimee asked, grateful for a new topic.

"It would seem so," Daniel affirmed. "You've obviously had tutoring. And your hands are those of a gentle woman. They have not had to do much work."

Aimee stared at her hands, rotating them to view her palms and fingers. She'd done plenty of work. What was he talking about?

"I went to college in New York," she blurted before thinking. She cringed. *Damn me and my big mouth.*

"College?" Daniel laughed. "Women don't go to college."

"What I meant was I was educated at a college level by my tutor," she backpedaled.

"There is no need for a woman to have such an education."

She shot him an annoyed look. "Are you serious? And why not? Why can't a woman have an education, same as a man?" The little voice inside her head tried to remind her what century she was in.

* * *

Daniel chuckled. The idea of an educated woman was rather intriguing, although during the time he spent in Philadelphia, he'd heard of only a few seminaries that offered the means to higher learning for women. Emma certainly hadn't been interested in anything that didn't have to do with the latest fashion or the next big social event.

Remembering Aimee's angry reaction from a few days ago, he couldn't help himself but fuel the fire some more. "What would a woman need schooling for?" he asked. "White men in the east say that women don't have the intellect for advanced studies."

"Is that what you think?" Aimee raised her voice.

He smiled inwardly. Her reaction was just as he'd predicted.

"Well, let me tell you something, Daniel." She glared at him. "Not all women are stupid wall flowers who need a man to take care of them. Some women like to make their own decisions in life, and not be dictated to by a man."

"And you consider yourself among those women who do not need a man to take care of you." He couldn't hide the amusement in his voice. "This is why you ran away from your betrothed."

Aimee let out an audible sigh. "Ultimately, yes, that's why I ran away," she snapped. "He's nothing but a controlling jerk, and I had enough. I can't see myself in a marriage where I'm not an equal partner, and where my husband makes all the decisions for me."

Daniel didn't know what a jerk was, but it didn't sound like a compliment.

"Don't you want to find a rich husband? Isn't that what all women want?" he finally asked. Emma's face flashed before his eyes.

"Money doesn't buy happiness," Aimee retorted. "Brad comes from a well-off family, and he's going to make tons of money as a surgeon, but he's not the man I want to marry. There are things more important to me than wealth."

He kept silent for some time. Hearing her say she didn't want to marry the man she was promised to lightened his heart. Ultimately, though, she might not have a choice in the matter.

"Where is your family?" he finally asked. He couldn't wrap his mind around a woman all alone in the wilderness. Her family wouldn't have let her go on her own, would they?

"I don't have a family. My parents were killed in a car...carriage accident. I have no brothers or sisters. The closest I have to a family is my roommate, Jana Evans."

"Room mate?"

"Another independent, free-thinking woman I live with," Aimee said. Her face lit up in a bright smile.

"Two unmarried women living together?" He raised his eyebrows. "Is she your appointed guardian?"

"No, we're the same age."

"So you are both spinsters."

"Why would you consider me a spinster? That sounds like I'm some gray-haired old woman in a rocking chair."

"You seem past the usual age when a woman marries."

"Excuse me? I'm only twenty-three!"

Daniel perused her out of the corner of his eye for a moment. He had guessed her to be no older than twenty years, well past the age a young woman would have been married off. Again, the flawless skin on her hands and face made her look much younger, and supported his notion that she was a woman from a high social class. *Just the type of woman to stay away from.*

"Any woman would consider herself a spinster at that age if she wasn't married. But then I forget." His lips curved in a smile. "You are a rare woman who doesn't need a man."

* * *

Aimee inhaled deeply. *This is not the twenty-first century, you idiot!* She needed to change the subject fast before she continued to stick her foot in her mouth. Her gaze drifted to several river otters at play. They darted onto the banks, then scurried back into the water, diving and rolling through the current with ease.

Finally, she asked, "and what about you? Why don't you have a wife?" Zach had told her plenty about Daniel, but nothing about his personal life.

Daniel's face sobered. It took him a while before he answered. "I've had no desire to be tied to a woman. I have not met one who would lead the kind of life I do."

"What about the Tuku . . ? How do you say the name of the tribe you're friends with?"

"Tukudeka," Daniel supplied.

"Tukudeka. Isn't there anyone you're interested in?" Did she really want to know the answer?

"Morning Fawn was to be my wife," Daniel said without emotion. "She drowned two summers ago, before we were married."

Aimee studied his face for a moment. *That's why he was so mad at me the other day. He thought I was drowning.*

"I'm so sorry," Aimee said sincerely. The urge to touch him made her fingers tingle. She hooked her thumbs through the shoulder straps in her backpack instead. "I'm sure you loved her a lot."

Daniel shrugged. "I knew her all my life," he said indifferently. "My foster mother wanted me to marry her. I would have honored the match out of obligation to her, not because of my feelings for Morning Fawn."

Was that relief she felt? Would she have been jealous of Daniel's feelings for a dead girl?

"Come on, there has to be someone you care about? You can't tell me you've never been in love."

Daniel's hard stare told her she wasn't going to get anywhere with her question. It was probably best to change the subject. "For a mountain man, the way you talk is quite . . . refined. You don't sound like an uneducated dimwit."

"Dimwit?" Daniel's eyebrows pulled together.

It was her turn to grin. "Someone who's not too bright in the head," she offered, and tapped her index finger against her temple.

"My father's upbringing. He is always honoring my dead mother in some way, and he knew she would not want me to be without an education. She certainly wouldn't stand for it if I spoke like a . . . dimwit. He taught me to read, write, and cipher numbers during the winters when we were snowed in. Then I spent two years in Philadelphia with my father's sister and her family. I attended Philadelphia University."

"Wow! I think you've just set a record," she said incredulously, surprised that Daniel divulged so much information about himself.

"Set a record?" Daniel looked confused.

She giggled. "I've never heard you talk so much all at once."

Daniel stared at her blankly.

"From your tone, I gather you didn't like living in Philadelphia much." Aimee was eager to keep the conversation going; glad he was finally talking to her.

"My father thought it would be good for me to live among civilized people and learn some culture." His voice suddenly filled with contempt.

"I can't picture you anywhere but here." She looked him up

103

and down, admiring his profile. He walked gracefully, as if on air, with light, fluid movements. He carried himself tall and erect, always alert to his surroundings. His rifle was cradled casually in the crook of his arm, but she didn't doubt for a second that it was ready to fire at a moment's notice. "You must have been like a fish out of water back east."

"This has always been my home. I was born in these mountains, and I don't wish to live anywhere else." Daniel's face was impassive as he scanned for any danger in the distance.

If you only knew the truth.

They walked along in silence for a while, each absorbed in their own thoughts. Aimee kept going over some of the things he had – and hadn't - said, and the way in which he had said them. Finally, she ventured, "So, who was she?"

Daniel visibly stiffened next to her.

"The girl who broke your heart," she prodded. Things about him were starting to add up now. At least she had a theory. His dark looks of contempt that first day. The penetrating stares. Even the near-kiss in the river. She'd bet a month's pay that she reminded him of someone, and his body language at the moment, and the expression on his face when she glanced up at him, told her she had hit the mark.

"No one I wish to speak of," he finally said.

"I take it she's someone you met in Philadelphia?" She couldn't imagine any woman who wouldn't be absolutely beside herself to have the attention of a man like Daniel. What a stupid twit for rejecting him.

"This is not something I wish to talk about," Daniel said firmly. "It is in the past, and long forgotten."

"But now that I'm here, the memories are coming back. I remind you of her, don't I?" she asked softly.

"You share nothing in common with . . . her," he finally said.

"I'm sorry she hurt you," Aimee said sincerely. "Whatever she did, I know you didn't deserve it."

Daniel's jaw clenched and unclenched. "You have nothing to be sorry for." He frowned. "No more talk of the past," he said with finality.

Aimee's curiosity was bursting at the seams, but she wouldn't press the issue. Maybe another time she could bring it up again. What would cause a man like him to have his heart broken by a woman? She wanted to reach out to him, take away the hurt look in his eyes. Right at this moment, this dark, intimidating man looked more like a big puppy that had been kicked around. Under his hard, tough as nails façade was a deeply caring guy with a tender heart.

"How did you find me so easily?" she wondered, wisely changing the subject.

"Your boots leave heavy tracks," Daniel answered. His body relaxed again. "But even in your moccasins, it would have been easy," he said through a grin.

She couldn't help but stare at him. The easy smile on his face made him all the more stunning. What stupid woman would let him go?

"Do you think those Indians are still in the area?" she asked in order to conceal her true thoughts.

"They were heading further south, following elk tracks," Daniel said. "They were not on the hunt for white women yesterday."

"Oh, very funny." She rolled her eyes at him.

"Why do you wear clothes like a man?" Daniel questioned after minutes of walking in silence.

"How would you like to walk around in a dress?" she countered, and Daniel flashed her another bright smile.

Oh, God, you're melting my heart.

"I don't recall women in the east wearing britches or letting their hair down and uncovered. Is this a new acceptable fashion?"

"I never took much stock in what's fashionable." She shrugged. "I wear what I like and what feels comfortable, not what other people say I should wear."

Her last conversation with Brad popped into her mind. She glared at Daniel through narrowed eyes. "Do you disapprove of my choice of clothing, too, like you disapprove of me having an education or being a . . . a spinster? And don't you even dare tell me to put my hair up!" She wagged a finger at him.

Daniel's grin widened. "I don't mind your clothes. They are much more practical here than if you wore a dress. And I never

105

said I disapprove of you being educated or unwed. As for your hair," Daniel paused and she noticed his eyes darkening. "It would be a shame to hide it away under some cap."

His arm moved, ever so slightly, away from his side. He hesitated for a moment, then dropped it back down again, his hand clenched in a fist. Had he wanted to reach up and touch her hair? Aimee's face grew hot. She never blushed! Why now, with him? Just the question of why made her blush all the more. It was time to take off the sweater.

Chapter Eleven

By noon, the Gibbon River came into view. They were about to emerge from the woods, when Daniel suddenly stopped and held up his hand, and he stepped in front of her.

"What is it?" Aimee asked apprehensively, and peered around his wide shoulders. Wordlessly, he took hold of her elbow and maneuvered her toward some trees to their left.

"Stay here," he said firmly.

"Daniel, what is it?" she asked impatiently.

He pointed in the direction of his cabin, but she couldn't see anything out of the ordinary.

"I didn't leave a fire burning in the fire pit yesterday. And even so, the rain would have doused it. "

Now that he'd pointed it out, Aimee noticed a tiny wisp of smoke rising in the air where the cabin was located. Daniel's sharp senses continued to amaze her.

"Don't move from here until I come for you." He shot her a warning stare, and disappeared into the dense foliage.

Who could be at the cabin? Had Zach returned already? Perhaps he had changed his mind about letting her stay for three months, and decided to come for her early. She wasn't sure she wanted to leave yet. There were so many things she hadn't seen or experienced yet. *You want to spend more time with Daniel, too.* Aimee brushed the thought aside.

What if it was Blackfoot, and they had taken over the cabin? Would Daniel be able to fight them off by himself? What help could she be? All she had was the hunting knife, and she wasn't entirely sure she could use it against another human being.

The minutes dragged on, and seemed like an eternity to

Aimee. *Dammit. I want to know what's happening.*

Daniel suddenly appeared out of nowhere and beckoned her to follow.

"What's going on?" She jogged to keep up with him.

"Some Tukudeka hunters are at the cabin. They are in need of help. One of them is injured." Daniel's voice sounded grave. He stopped abruptly and gave her a hard stare. "After we cross the river, you will go to the cabin and wait there."

Oh, this was just great. More orders. "Why do I need to go to the cabin? Maybe I can help. How badly is he hurt?"

Daniel didn't reply. His jaw set firm, and anguish filled his eyes. When they reached the banks of the Gibbon, Aimee had a clear view of the cabin. Two men stood by the fire pit, a third lay on the ground. She squinted to see better. The man squirmed but didn't get up.

"He's hurt bad." Perhaps she could be of some help. Without waiting for Daniel, she ran to ford the Gibbon at the shallow spot. After wading through the knee-high water, she sprinted quickly up the meadow toward the yard. Daniel caught up to her, and headed her off, a dark scowl on his face.

"I told you to go to the cabin! Dammit, woman. Don't you ever listen?"

"What's wrong with that man on the ground?" Aimee asked, undeterred by Daniel's glare. She took a closer look, and recognized the Indian as Elk Runner.

"My God, Daniel, is that an arrow sticking out of his abdomen? What happened to him?"

"They were surprised by a party of Blackfoot while on a hunting trip. Their village is too far, so they came here," Daniel hissed.

She headed toward the injured man, and Daniel pulled her back.

"This is no sight for you," he said firmly.

"Like hell it's not!" She shot him a defiant look, and pulled her arm free, then pushed past him. She was back in the ER; a new trauma patient had just been brought in. This was her territory.

She rushed over to the injured man on the ground. His

breathing was fast and shallow. A grimace contorted his face. He was in obvious pain. Aimee was completely undeterred by the other two Indians staring at her as she dropped to her knees beside Elk Runner. She assessed him quickly and expertly, lifting his lids to check for pupillary reflex, his pulse, his breathing. She took note of the arrow protruding from the man's lower left abdomen. His leather shirt was soaked in blood.

"He's in shock," she announced, and peered up at the Indians and at Daniel, who now knelt next to her. "We need to stabilize him and get that arrow out, or he'll bleed to death internally." Aimee wriggled her backpack off her shoulders and found her medicine kit. She stuffed her rolled-up blanket under Elk Runner's knees to elevate his legs.

"Daniel, I need boiling hot water, now, and a few more blankets!" she ordered. When he didn't move, she shot him her fiercest look, then said, "If you want this man to live, you need to do what I say, and do it now! I need boiling water, and if you have any alcohol around here, I could use that as well." *I'm starting to sound like Ashwell.*

Daniel spoke quickly to the two Indians before he disappeared behind his cabin. One of the Indians set a kettle of water over the fire.

When Daniel returned, Aimee sliced open the man's leather shirt with the hunting knife. She expertly palpated around the wound to try and figure out where the arrow's trajectory was, and which organs might be affected.

"An ultrasound would be really nice right about now," she mumbled.

Daniel wordlessly handed her a cup.

She looked up at him. "I can get that arrow out."

"A wound like that is fatal," he stated solemnly, his voice filled with anguish.

"No, it doesn't have to be." She shook her head. "If the arrow didn't puncture his stomach or intestines, there's less chance of sepsis to set in. From the looks of it, it might be closer to the kidney."

"I don't understand your words."

The worry and pain in Daniel's eyes tore at Aimee's heart. "I can help your friend," she said encouragingly. "You have to trust me."

"Have you seen a wound like this before? It is an agonizing death."

"I have treated many wounds like this," Aimee said firmly. "And this will only kill him if infection sets in. If it stays clean, he can heal."

"You speak words I don't understand. How is it you know all this?" Daniel ran a hand through his hair in frustration.

"Look, I'll explain later, but right now I'd like to get this arrowhead out of his gut and get him sewn up, okay?"

Daniel gave a bewildered nod of his head.

"But you have to do what I say, when I say it, understand?" she continued. "No questions asked. And first, I need more of . . . what is this?" She smelled the contents of the cup Daniel had brought her. "Rum?" she answered her own question. "I guess it'll have to do. I need more of this. We both need to soak our hands in it. Please tell your friends to either step back or support Elk Runner's head, and keep him still. This is going to hurt."

She didn't dwell on the barbaric way she would have to perform surgery on this man. She had assisted in countless emergency knife stabbing and gunshot surgeries, so she had complete confidence in her ability. But those procedures were always done under anesthesia, not while the patient was awake. And unfortunately, she had nothing to give this man to knock him out. She did have lidocaine, however. Technically, she shouldn't be in possession of this drug, but a veterinarian friend she'd gone backpacking with on several occasions had given it to her. They had both agreed that it was a useful drug to carry in the backcountry. Now it would hopefully numb this wound enough to let her remove the arrow and stitch him back up without too much pain.

Supplies for minor surgeries were always with her. The trauma nurse in her wouldn't have it any other way. She glanced down at her medical kit, knowing she had a limited supply of needles and syringes, betadine, sterile gauze, and suture material.

Aimee unzipped her kit. She rummaged for her bottle of lidocaine, and ripped open the plastic cover to a small syringe.

She stuck the needle in the bottle's rubber stopper, and pulled back on the plunger to withdraw some of the drug.

Elk Runner's companions murmured to each other when they saw her with the syringe, and one of them shouted and tried to grab her when she started inserting the needle under the skin around the entry wound. Daniel said something quickly to the Indians, and they backed off.

"This is to make it numb," she explained. "It will make the pain less when I pull this arrow out of him." Her eyes met and held Daniel's for a long moment.

"Is that water boiling yet?" she finally asked. Daniel nodded in affirmation, and she thought for a moment. "I need you to pour that cup of rum over my hands," she finally ordered. Daniel did so without question. "Please bring me another cupful, and I need you to put two spoons into the boiling water."

If he thought her requests were strange, he didn't say so. He wordlessly and quickly did her bidding.

"I'm going to hold this shaft steady, and I need you to break it off," she said to Daniel when he returned. She held the protruding arrow to minimize the movement internally when Daniel broke it off with one quick effortless snap.

Once the spoons had been in the boiling water long enough to be considered sterile, she said, "remove those spoons from the water, but be careful to only touch the very top of the handles, Daniel."

He carefully did what she instructed. When he gave her a questioning look, she said, "The boiling water kills bacteria, which would kill Elk Runner if it got in his wound. That's why I had you boil the spoons. They should now be sterile and safe, but if you touch them, you will get bacteria on them again."

"I don't know what bacteria is," Daniel said with a confused look on his face.

"Well, baby, this is where I know more about survival than you do." She smiled. "Just as I trust you to know more about surviving these mountains, you'll just have to trust me to know how to doctor up a wound like this, okay?"

Daniel merely nodded.

She selected a scalpel from her medicine cache, and made a

111

quick incision in the skin on either side of the hole where the arrow disappeared into Elk Runner. He barely flinched, which meant the lidocaine had taken effect, at least on the surface. She sighed in relief. She wasn't sure she could go through with her operation if this man felt the entire procedure. The lidocaine would only minimize the pain as it was. She suddenly gained a deeper appreciation for the origin of the phrase *bite the bullet*. Elk Runner might have to do just that to get through this.

She took the spoons Daniel held, and used them to gently pry the tissue apart. "Hold these again, and . . . and don't move them," she ordered. Daniel obeyed. Taking a deep breath to steady her nerves, she stuck her finger inside the hole. The two Indians standing close by kept murmuring.

When Elk Runner let out a loud moan and began to squirm, she retracted her finger quickly and drew up some more lidocaine, squirting it directly into the wound. A minute later, she inserted her finger again, and felt around. She could feel the arrow clearly penetrate the abdominal wall, but luckily it had missed the stomach and intestines, and had stopped just short of the kidney.

"Oh, phew, that was lucky," she mumbled. She swiped her arm across her forehead. There was nothing she could have done if it had penetrated a vital organ. Under these primitive conditions, he would die of septicemia. Daniel was right when he'd said this was an agonizing death. She had no antibiotics to give him. All she could hope for was to keep the wound as clean and sterile as possible, and that his body's own immunity would fight off any organisms.

She wrapped her finger around the arrowhead and pulled it out. Blood flowed immediately out of the wound, spilling over and seeping down Elk Runner's torso like thick red paint. Quickly, she pressed her free palm over the wound to slow the bleeding. She tossed the arrow aside and grabbed a handful of gauze squares she had laid out in preparation. She stuck a few inside the wound to buy a few seconds time while she tore open a pack of suture material.

Pausing for a moment, she opened a new syringe and drew up some of the hot water, into which she mixed some of her betadine solution. Her eyes darted to Elk Runner's face. He was drenched in sweat, his eyes focused at the sky. She couldn't imagine a modern-day patient remaining so calm under these circumstances.

Aimee squirted her betadine mixture into the wound and wiped it out with sterile gauze. She did this several more times, and by feel, sutured the tear in the abdominal wall. When she was satisfied it was closed, she told Daniel to release his hold on the spoons. She dabbed at the wound again to wipe off the blood, then quickly and efficiently sewed the skin together. She poured a little betadine wash over the now-closed wound, applied some Neosporin ointment, taped a large gauze square over the incision, and wrapped her spare ace bandage around Elk Runner's torso.

Finished, she straightened her back and sighed in relief. She'd done all she could. She knew Daniel cared deeply for his friend. It would devastate him if he died.

When she looked up, three pairs of eyes were staring at her in utter disbelief. Elk Runner's companions murmured excitedly, and pointed at her supplies that were now littered all over the ground. She heard them repeat the word *puhagant*, while motioning to her.

"I'm sort of a healer back home," she offered tentatively as an explanation. She shot Daniel a sheepish look. She figured in this time, she could run circles around any doctor, so the fact that she was only a nurse was an irrelevant little detail. She hastily gathered the trash, and threw it in the fire. Glancing around, she made sure nothing remained. She was not going to be able to explain all of this. Her only focus had been to save Elk Runner's life, so discreetness with her modern supplies was forgotten.

"Tell them," she motioned with her head toward the two Indians, "to keep an eye on him, and he needs to lie still and be kept warm."

Aimee's eyes swept the area a second time to make sure she hadn't missed anything that should be thrown away. She repacked her medical kit and shoved it in her pack. With a final glance at Elk Runner on the ground, she stood to her feet.

"I've never seen anything like what you just did." Daniel loomed in front of her, and looked down at her intently. "Who are you?"

"You know who I am." She avoided his stare. "Just a city girl lost in the wilderness."

"This is what white healers do in the east?"

"Where I come from, we do," Aimee replied vaguely.

"You speak with strange words sometimes, and you don't behave or think as any woman I have ever met. One day you will tell me the truth, but I won't ask again."

"Thank you." She gave him a grateful look. She was tired of the lying.

"Will he live?" Daniel nodded at Elk Runner.

"He's got a good chance. As long as infection or septicemia, um . . . blood poisoning doesn't set it, he should survive. I took all the precautions I can under the circumstance. The wound needs to stay clean now, and it should heal. Internally, there's no damage to the vital organs.

* * *

* * *

"They can't move him yet!" Aimee shouted and ran from the cabin several hours later. She had gone inside to put her things away and remove her hiking boots. Her moccasins were definitely more comfortable. She'd set some meat in water to soak to prepare a meal for the men. To her horror, Elk Runner was getting up from the ground with the aid of his companions. He clutched his side, and his face contorted in a grimace. "It's crazy for him to try and travel. He has internal injuries that need to heal. Tell them, Daniel." Her eyes darted from the Indians to Daniel. She ran up to him, waving a hand toward Elk Runner.

"I can't make them stay here against their will, Aimee," Daniel tried to reason with her. "These people live in seclusion most of the time, and they want to return to their camp."

"Then at least tell them to leave Elk Runner here with us. In a week or so, he should be okay to go."

"He won't stay." Daniel shook his head.

"I can't believe you people," she ranted at the Indians, throwing her hands up in the air. "This is insane. First you think he's going to die, then I save his life, and now you're going to kill him after all!"

There was nothing she could do or say to keep her patient

114

from leaving. She had to concede that this was a different environment; these were hardened people, not like what she was used to. It was either survive or die in these elements, no matter what got thrown at them.

* * *

Daniel stood by silently as Aimee unleashed her temper on the Tukudeka hunters. They seemed to be too stunned by her behavior to react. Women rarely behaved disrespectfully around men. He chuckled quietly, and folded his arms across his chest. She reminded him of a mother grizzly protecting her young.

"Call off your woman, White Wolf," one of the men finally called to Daniel.

His grin widened. "I can no sooner call her off than I can call off a blizzard in the winter." He gently tugged on Aimee's arm. "Let them go, Aimee. They can't stay." Turning to Elk Runner, he said, "Perhaps it would be wise to stay."

"Have you followed my advice, brother?" Elk Runner asked weakly.

"No," Daniel said quickly. This was one conversation he wanted to avoid.

"She is a brave woman, White Wolf. She will make a good wife and give you strong sons. She also has powerful medicine," he said in awe. "Tell her I am forever grateful to her for my life. And if you do not take her as your wife soon, I may take her back as my second wife, no matter that she is too small."

Daniel laughed, and so did the other two men. "I will think about what you have said."

Aimee remained quiet as the hunters left the valley. Daniel thanked the heavens that she didn't direct her temper at him.

"What does *puhagant* mean?" Aimee asked when they were once more alone. "I heard them use that word over and over again."

He studied her for a moment before he answered. "A *puhagant* is a person who has been favored by the spirits. Such a person is one of the most powerful of the warriors among the Shoshoni. It is said that they possess powers no other man has. Many warriors go on vision quests to attain this status, but few succeed. What you did today was powerful medicine, and they

115

believe you are blessed by the spirits as a great healer."

"Oh . . . well, I don't know about being favored by any spirits."

"Perhaps Elk Runner was right, and you did fall out of the sky." A grin spread across his face. "You are most definitely a great mystery."

"What else did Elk Runner say?" Aimee's eyes narrowed.

"He said he is grateful for what you did for him, and he considers taking you back and making you his second wife." He could barely maintain a serious facial expression. "Even though you are too small for his taste," he added.

"Oh, you men are just infuriating." Aimee spun on her heels and disappeared into the cabin.

Chapter Twelve

Aimee had the time of her life in the days that followed. She soaked up all the knowledge Daniel threw at her about the mountains and forests. While he was gone on his trapping expeditions each morning, she prepared the meal that she would cook in the evening, and looked forward to their forays into the woods. He was a patient and able teacher. He seemed more talkative with her now and more relaxed, and she enjoyed every minute she spent with him. She was especially relieved that he no longer questioned her about her past. She sometimes caught him looking at her in a way that made her heart do flip flops, but not once did he make the slightest attempt to touch her, whether intentional or accidentally. He was truly a man of his word.

Her feelings for him grew with each passing day. Daniel was an amazing man. As gruff and surly as he had seemed a few weeks ago, he acted mostly kind and friendly now. She often lay awake at night, fantasizing about being held in his strong arms, being kissed by him, or what kind of lover he might be. It was for the best that nothing happened between them. Her heart would ache enough when she returned to her own time.

"Today you will learn how to load and shoot a rifle," Daniel announced one morning while they shared a breakfast of leftover venison and cornmeal mush.

"Why do I need to learn to shoot?" she asked, a little shocked. She had seen and treated enough gunshot victims at the hospital to know that she didn't want to have anything to do with guns.

"You've done well learning the deer trails, so now it's time you track one and make a kill," Daniel said enthusiastically. "You have earned this privilege."

"No way!" She shook her head. "I am not going to kill Bambi, no way."

"What's a bam bee?" Daniel asked, confusion in his stare.

"Bambi is a deer. I can't kill a deer, Daniel."

"You eat meat," Daniel stated, his incomprehension as to her logic clearly visible on his face.

"I know that. I should really be a vegetarian, but I do like a good steak. But that doesn't mean I have to be the one killing it."

"Vegetarian?" The skin between Daniel's eyes couldn't furrow any deeper.

"It's someone who doesn't eat meat," she explained hastily. "Please don't ask me to shoot and kill something. I just can't do it."

"I have given up some time ago to understand your ways." He shook his head with a smile. "I've seen you catch fish, but you won't kill game?"

"Fish are different," she argued. "Oh, don't give me that look, like you think I'm high," she added in exasperation. His "look" only intensified, with her unfamiliar phrases.

"Are all white women as difficult to understand as you?" he asked in an exasperated tone.

"That's what all men say."

"They say you are difficult?"

"No, I don't mean me personally, but women in general," she huffed. "Men always complain that the minute they think they've got a woman figured out, the woman does something to completely confuse the man again."

Daniel nodded. "I would agree with that."

"Well, that's because men are simple-minded and uncomplicated." Why was she having this conversation with him? "All a man needs is food and . . ." she stopped herself. Oh, she really didn't want to go there! Why did she have to open this can of worms?

"Food and what?" Daniel pressed.

She took a deep breath. "Give a man food and sex" - *there I said it* - "and they're as happy as clams."

Daniel coughed and almost choked on a piece of venison. A split second later, a thoroughly devilish smile spread across his face as he intently peered up at her from across the table. She held her breath. God, why did he have to be so damn good-looking, especially with that heart-stopping smile of his!

"Well, your cooking's been real good so far," he drawled. His eyes smoldered as he stared at her.

She waved her hands in front of her, palms out, and abruptly left the table. "Okay, this conversation has gone far enough. You are a typical man, Daniel, and it brings me to my final point,"

"Point?"

"Men are pigs."

She grabbed her plate off the table and quickly left the cabin. Things had been so nice the last couple of weeks. Talk of sex would ruin all that. Or would it? She groaned out loud as she put some distance between herself and the cabin.

* * *

Daniel chuckled, and shook his head. He couldn't believe where this conversation had led. He had to conceal his surprise at hearing her use such a word. He could picture a dozen eastern women, his aunt included, who would absolutely faint if they heard that word spoken out loud. Aimee seemed fairly at ease with the subject, just as she was at ease with the way she dressed, and even sometimes undressed to a point, around him. She hadn't acted shy or frightened since the day he had walked in on her in the cabin when she was wrapped in only that blanket.

The day he almost kissed her.

He inhaled deeply and followed Aimee outside. She cautiously knelt at the river's edge and rinsed out her bowls. His insides grew hot at the memory of that day. What would have happened had she not pulled away?

He had given his word that he would not repeat his actions, and he had kept it. With every passing day his admiration and desire for her grew, but he'd kept his emotions well hidden and he never touched her. She needed to return to her own people in the big city, and somewhere out there was the man who could legitimately lay claim to her.

Admittedly, he enjoyed every moment he spent with her. She

119

was adventuresome, determined to the point of being stubborn, and without fear of most tasks he put before her. His days had definitely not been dull with her around, and he was glad she was at ease in his presence again. The fearful way she had acted that day, which was not her normal way, had disturbed him greatly.

Movement between the trees to the west drew his attention, and he tensed. It was not the random movements of deer moving through the forest. He recognized the shapes of people walking along almost single file, some riding horses. Reflexively, he reached for his rifle.

A distraction was good right now. He didn't like where his thoughts led him. He knew that what he felt for Aimee was more than merely a man's need to bed a woman. He cared for her as he never thought possible. But he could not allow himself to show his feelings. Once he took her back to St. Louis, she would be forever out of his life, and he hoped he would forget about her in time. He was selfish for thinking she might be able to live in these unforgiving mountains. His father had taught him better than that. Zach had loved his wife dearly, but in the end, love hadn't been enough to save her life.

Before they emerged from the woods, Daniel recognized most of the group as Shoshoni. The women wore deerskin dresses that came past their knees, and the men all wore buckskin shirts and leggings. Their clothing and hair was unadorned with fur or feathers, yet the leatherwork was of the finest quality. Some women carried woven baskets on their backs, and a large number of dogs pulled travois behind them.

Daniel scanned the group. He hoped to see Elk Runner among them. It was past the number of days that Aimee had asked him to come back so she could look at his wound.

His gaze fell on Aimee by the river. She was looking at the group as well. She had become much more alert to her surroundings in the last few weeks. His heart swelled with pride.

As they emerged from the forest, several families of strangers accompanied the familiar members of Elk Runner's clan, but also several families of strangers. They were not Shoshoni. Several men rode horses, and most wore no shirts. Breechcloths, leggings, and moccasins made up their attire. The men's hair was braided in two long braids, most adorned with fur and feathers. Several of them carried rifles. The women also wore their hair in braids, and their dresses showed obvious wear.

"Where are all these people going?" Aimee asked as she joined him in front of the cabin and waited for their visitors' approach.

"They are on their way to higher country for the summer hunting grounds," he explained.

"Is Elk Runner among them?"

Aimee's eyes intently scanned the many approaching faces. There were about thirty adults, including old men and women, and at least a dozen children.

"Wow, they have a lot of dogs!" Aimee remarked. "There's got to be at least twice as many dogs as people."

"The Tukudeka don't have horses. They use dogs to carry their belongings, and for hunting the bighorn. Those men," he gestured with his chin, "on horseback call themselves the children of the large-beaked bird."

"Large-beaked bird? I've heard of Crow Indians, but never large-beaked bird Indians."

"I have not heard them call themselves that, but I suppose they could be referring to a crow. In their language, the word for their tribe is Absaroka."

Remembering Aimee's comparison of men to pigs from earlier, he couldn't help himself, and added, "Their women walk and carry their belongings."

"Typical," Aimee scoffed. He grinned.

"Why don't you have a horse?" Aimee asked suddenly, watching the progression.

"My father takes our horses to St. Louis. He needs one to carry the furs. I prefer to be on foot, because I can go places where horses can't."

"I see." Aimee nodded. "Oh, look, there's Elk Runner!" She pointed to a man who broke away from the group and reached them before the others. He and Daniel clasped elbows in friendly greeting.

"How are you, brother?" Daniel asked.

"I am well, thanks to your woman's healing," Elk Runner

grinned brightly, and nodded to Aimee. She held up a hand in greeting.

"We are on our way to the summer camp further north, and my wife wanted to bring your wife a gift." Elk Runner paused for a moment, his eyes searching Daniel's face. "She is your wife now?"

"Why are the Absaroka traveling with you?" Daniel asked evasively.

"Several of their men and women were killed by Blackfoot several days ago. They asked to travel with us for a while." Elk Runner smiled knowingly and shook his head. "She is not yet your wife. You have more endurance than any man I know, White Wolf. Her man is not coming for her."

Daniel refused to be baited by his brother. He greeted his foster mother, Gentle Sun, and the men from the group of Crow Indians.

"Tell Elk Runner I'd like to look at the wound and take the stitches out," Aimee called to Daniel, after he'd made his rounds. Daniel translated. Elk Runner held up his shirt to expose his abdomen. She touched and pushed gently against the incision, and seemed pleased with what she saw.

"I need to get scissors from my pack to remove the sutures." She hurried off and disappeared inside the cabin, and reappeared moments later. She moved slowly toward the group, and had an uncertain look on her face. Her lips formed a smile, and all eyes stared at her. How would she handle herself around these people? Would she be afraid of them?

Two small boys ran up to him excitedly, calling repeatedly, "*Dosa bia'isa.*"

"These are Elk Runner's sons." He laughed, and scooped the smaller boy up and hoisted him onto his shoulders. The little boy squealed with delight.

Talking ceased, except for a few whispers. Daniel understood their curiosity. The only whites most of them had seen, other than his father and himself, were the occasional Frenchmen who wandered through this region. None of them had ever seen a white woman, let alone one with yellow hair.

His insides warmed, and he smiled at her in encouragement. She inhaled deeply, raised her chin, and walked up to Elk

Runner. She gestured for him to lift his shirt again, which he did.

"Ask him if it hurts when I press here." Elk Runner shook his head when Daniel translated.

"She has a gentle hand." Elk Runner grinned at Daniel. "But you would not know this, would you, White Wolf?"

Daniel's eyes narrowed. Irrational jealousy swept over him, seeing her hands all over his brother's stomach. His own gut tightened. She worked the tips of the sharp scissors under each of the stitches, and pulled the cut strings through the skin.

"There. Done. It looks really good," Aimee said. Daniel clenched and unclenched his jaw when she favored his brother with a radiant smile.

"My wife would like to present a gift to *Dosa haiwi*," Elk Runner said formally after Aimee stepped away from him.

"Whatever you do, don't refuse anything," Daniel warned her. Her head tilted up, and she raised her eyebrows in a silent question.

Little Bird, Elk Runner's wife, stepped forward next to her husband. She was a short, plump woman. His brother's newest son rode in a sling at her hip, crying heartily. Unaffected by the screaming infant, Little Bird held out a large animal skin for Aimee. She smiled and gestured for her to take it.

Aimee's face lit up, and she returned the smile as she took the gift offered to her. She stroked the fine sheepskin coat, the workmanship of the finest quality. The Tukudeka were known for their excellent leatherwork, and their hides were highly valued.

"We are forever grateful to *Dosa haiwi* for saving my husband's life," the woman said.

Daniel translated, omitting the Indian name they had given her.

"It's beautiful!" Aimee exclaimed. "And so soft. Thank you," she smiled and nodded brightly at Elk Runner's wife. Then she turned to him. "How do you say thank you in their language?"

"*Aishen*," he answered.

"Aishen," Aimee said to the Indian woman.

"Eh shun," Daniel corrected her pronunciation. Aimee repeated the word again. The woman nodded and smiled.

Several of the children gathered around Aimee, staring at her in fascination. A few of the bolder kids touched the fabric of her pants, then shyly retreated.

"It's okay." Aimee smiled warmly at them. "You can touch." She kneeled down and held out her hand, and gestured to the little ones to come back to her. Instantly, half a dozen smaller children encircled her. All of them touched her hair in wonder. Aimee took it all in with a smile. Little Bird finally shooed the children off. Her infant was still squirming and crying in his sack on her hip, and she finally took him out to hold him.

"We should speak with the Absaroka warriors," Elk Runner said. "Hear what they say about the Blackfoot raid."

Daniel glanced at Aimee. Elk Runner slapped him on the back.

"Little Bird will look after her. Come, White Wolf. Your woman is not a child that needs to hang onto your shirt tails."

"If you were not my brother, I would slit your throat," Daniel growled. When had he turned into such a fool? Elk Runner laughed heartily, and headed toward the warriors. To save face, Daniel followed without a backward glance at Aimee.

* * *

Aimee's gaze followed Daniel as he walked off. She realized he needed some time to visit with his friends. Why did he act so annoyed with Elk Runner? She shrugged it off. They behaved like true siblings, constantly bantering back and forth.

"May I hold the baby?" Aimee turned to Little Bird, and made hand signals to indicate what she was asking. The young woman handed her the infant.

"I think he has a tummy ache," Aimee cooed. Instead of cradling him in her arms, she held him face down, and gently swung her arms back and forth, and up and down. The baby immediately stopped his crying in this new position

She handed the infant back to his mother, showing her that by holding the baby this way and putting a little pressure on the stomach, it might soothe him. The woman smiled brightly at her, and nodded. Aimee looked up across the yard. A group of men stood together away from the women and children. Her eyes were drawn like magnets to Daniel, who stood out as the tallest in the group. He appeared to be in a lively debate with one of them.

She inhaled sharply when Daniel suddenly turned to look her way. Her heart skipped a beat, and the smile froze on her face. She hadn't seen that look in his eyes since the day in the river.

* * *

After the children lost their fascination with her, Aimee seized the opportunity to retreat inside the cabin to attend to some bread dough she had completely forgotten about. After punching the dough down, and setting it back in the bowl, she returned the scissors to her backpack, taking care that all her supplies were packed away properly. It wouldn't do to have anything laying around, in case Daniel decided to enter the cabin. She'd taken great care to keep all her things hidden from view, to ward off unnecessary questions.

The cabin door creaked open and closed. Aimee straightened, then turned her head. She held back a gasp of surprise as she came face to face with an Indian. She recognized him as the same man she had seen talking to Daniel earlier. He wore no shirt, only a breechcloth and leather leggings, and his weapon belt hung at his hips. His ebony hair was long and the braids framing the sides of his face were wrapped in fur. She backed against her bunk and couldn't maneuver around. Her mouth went dry when the man continued his intense perusal of her. His gaze lingered on her hair.

Glancing quickly in all directions, she found nothing that was within reach that she might use in her defense. He moved to stand closely in front of her. His hand reached out and fingered her hair. He spoke words she didn't understand, his voice quiet but demanding. Aimee shook her head, and pointed to the door.

"I need to go back outside now," she said firmly. When she tried to move past him, he blocked her way and his words became more forceful.

"I don't know what you're saying, but you need to let me pass." Her gaze didn't waver from his eyes. She held her chin up, and hoped that she projected bravery even as her heart raced nervously. She tried to push past him, only to have his hand snake up and encircle one of her wrists. Just as she tried to pull away, the cabin door swung open forcefully, and she sighed in relief when Daniel's large frame filled the entry. The Indian released her, but after a quick glance at Daniel, his stare returned to her face.

Daniel's voice was calm and quiet when he spoke to the other man. Slowly, the Indian moved aside.

"Come over here," Daniel commanded, and she quickly complied. Daniel's face was hard and unreadable, but she knew him well enough by now to recognize the seething anger in his eyes. "Leave the cabin." He moved to stand between her and the other man. She took a step toward the door, then turned back.

"He didn't do anything, Daniel. It's okay." The last thing she wanted was a fight between these two.

Daniel ignored her comment and spoke again to the Indian, who hadn't moved. With hand gestures and firm words, the two men conversed. To Aimee's relief, no one made a move to reach for their weapons. Finally, the Indian pushed his way past Daniel and left the cabin.

Daniel turned to face her. "The next time I tell you to do something, I expect you to obey," he growled.

Taken aback for a moment by his harsh words, her temper flared. "Oh, do you now? Since when do you have the right to order me around?" Were they back to that again?

"Since you are my responsibility," Daniel said heatedly.

"What did he want, anyways?" She was in no mood to start this old argument again.

Daniel's eyes traveled up and down her body in a way that made her shift weight from one foot to the other.

"You." His eyes burned holes right through her.

"Oh." She had already guessed as much. "So, you explained that I'm not available?"

Daniel's face actually lightened, and his lips curved in a grin. "He made me an offer for you that I had a hard time refusing."

"He what?" She stared at him in stunned disbelief. "So, how much am I worth?" she asked angrily.

"He offered three ponies, two buffalo robes, and various other pelts," Daniel answered casually. "I told him I wouldn't take less than seven horses and six buffalo robes."

"I can't believe you think you can just barter me away like that. I don't belong to you. What if he meets your price?" She stated heatedly.

Daniel's grin widened. "He won't. No woman is worth that much, and this was the only way to peacefully settle this situation." He paused, and all humor left his face. His eyes turned even darker as he stared down at her. "Understand this: you will know when I consider you to belong to me." With those words, he left Aimee standing in stunned silence to ponder his meaning.

Chapter Thirteen

Aimee left the cabin a short while later. She observed the hustle and bustle as people moved around and set up camp. Apparently the Indians had decided to stay in the valley for the night. It felt strange, having so many people about after weeks of solitude. Instead of feeling lonely, she had embraced the peacefulness of no other people around. Odd, since she was considered quite the socialite back home.

Daniel stood among a group of men, all inspecting hunting bows and lances and various other weapons. The sight brought a smile to her face. Some things were just timeless, she mused. It didn't matter what century it was, but men apparently always wanted to compare their toys with one another, to see who had the biggest and best. The only thing that changed over the years was the type of toys in question.

Longing for some peace and quiet, she walked along the banks of the Madison. She stayed a safe distance from the water. Daniel had warned her days ago not to get too close to the edge. Recent thunderstorms in the higher mountains had caused the water levels in the rivers to rise. What had been a peaceful river a week ago now had areas of whitewater and spots where the undertow was dangerous.

She'd walked quite a distance from the cabin when excited shouts alerted her to a commotion further down river. Several boys no older than seven or eight years ran toward her, waving their hands frantically in the air. Instantly alert, she turned her head to see if anyone else was within earshot behind her. She had walked further than she thought. The cabin and Indian camp were well around the bend.

The boys gestured wildly at her and pointed down river. A small body tossed around in the turbulent water.

"Oh my God!" Aimee kicked off her moccasins and sprinted barefoot along the shore of the river. The water moved so fast, she wasn't sure if she'd catch up.

"Go! Get help!" She waved her arms in the direction of the camp, and hoped the boys understood what she wanted. Several boys took off in the direction she indicated. A couple followed her. When she finally caught up with the tumbling body in the river, she jumped into the fast-moving water without a second thought. Ignoring the bitter cold, her head broke through the surface of the water. She gasped for air, then pulled herself through the current while her body was churned and pelted by rough waves.

She continued to struggle through the current, her target bobbing out of the water then disappearing from sight time and again. She herself struggled to remain above the waves, swallowing and choking on mouthfuls of muddy river water. Her arms and legs became heavy like lead, but she finally caught up with the lifeless body of the child, and pulled him to her. Struggling to keep them both afloat, she backstroked toward what she hoped was the shoreline. She tried frantically to hold the child's chin up above water.

Exhaustion overtook her quickly as her arms and legs grew heavier by the second. How much longer could she keep going? Strong arms reached out to her and a man called her name.

"Here, take the boy!" Aimee shouted. She passed the child over to the arms reaching for her.

"Give me your hand, I've got you both." Daniel's voice sounded frantic.

"No, the current is too strong. Just take him." She thrust the boy at him and with a final burst of adrenaline, kicked her arms and legs into motion.

She fought against the strong force of the water, but it was no use. She wasn't going to make it. She had no more strength left as she struggled to keep her head above water. Invisible anchors tugged at her legs and pulled her under. The thought to give up entered her mind, but strong arms encircled her waist and pulled her through the current. Moments later someone lifted her onto dry land. She coughed and gagged, and forced herself onto her knees, where she coughed some more to expel the river water she had swallowed. Tentatively, she raised her head, and Daniel knelt in front of her. He was dripping wet. The look on his face was one she hadn't seen before. Did he look scared?

"The boy?" she finally managed to choke out.

Daniel shook his head. She found a renewed reserve of strength at his meaning.

"No! I know he was alive when I had him. He can't be dead!"

She lifted her head and spotted a group of people around a lifeless little body on the muddy ground. A woman's wailing spurred her to action. She stumbled to her feet, even as Daniel tried to pull her back.

"Let me go!" She pulled away from him and fell to her knees in front of the boy. With trembling hands, she felt for a pulse and put her ear to his chest.

"He's not dead! He's got a pulse!" She wasted no time. She started rescue breathing. One breath every five seconds. After several attempts, she started chest compressions. Thirty compressions, one breath, two breaths. Finally, the little boy gave a strangled cough. He coughed and sputtered some more, and expelled river water from his lungs. She turned his body onto his side, and slapped at his back. The group of people around her murmured, then shouted. The woman who had been wailing fell to her knees and hugged her child firmly to her. Then she looked at Aimee, her expression one of thanks and awe. Aimee nodded and smiled weakly in return, then slumped back on her rear. The full impact of her exhaustion finally overtook her.

"He needs to be kept upright, and warmed up," she whispered weakly. Hopefully Daniel was close by to understand. She was about to collapse completely to the ground, her body shaking violently from the cold, when strong arms pulled her against a wall of warmth. She was lifted and held against a steely chest. Craving the warmth, she wrapped her arms around Daniel's neck and laid her head against his shoulders as he carried her back to camp.

* * *

Daniel had never experienced fear such as this before. He recalled being frightened as a child plenty of times, but blinding fear for another person when he saw Aimee in the river was an emotion completely foreign to him. He wanted to throttle her in anger when she thrust the child into his arms and pushed away from him in the water. He'd been left with no choice but to get the boy to shore first, then return for the brave little woman who was losing her battle with the churning river.

He watched in wonder alongside the Tukudeka as she seemingly breathed her life force into the boy's body. He had no explanation for what he saw. Who was this woman? This was the second time he had witnessed her bring someone back from the brink of death. He had never bought into the superstitions of the people who had raised him, but in this moment, he found himself wondering if magic and supernatural forces did actually exist. Right now, those were the only explanations he had for what he had witnessed. Would that explain how she ended up in these mountains, and how she had survived on that ledge?

He carried Aimee inside his cabin. Magic or not, she was as real and soft as any other woman, one he had come to care for more than he wanted to admit. He didn't want to let her go when he gently laid her on his bunk. Exhaustion had overtaken her and she had drifted out of consciousness. Quickly, he started a fire in the hearth. He had to get her out of her wet clothing, even though she would probably be furious with him when she woke.

There were no buttons or strings to undo on her shirt. Awkwardly, he pulled it up and over her head. He shook his own head in the process, and contemplated her odd clothing again, even though he was used to them by now. Her pants were another dilemma. There were no ties that held them together at her waist, and he fumbled with the strange button. When he finally had that undone, he still had to pull and tug to get the britches past her hips. In frustration, he thought to just cut the cursed things off her, but thought better of it.

Aimee stirred at his none-too-gentle treatment, and he strained to hear her murmur, "just undo the damn zipper."

131

Baffled, he had no idea what she was talking about. Her hand reached where he'd undone the button at her waist, and tugged on the small metal charm that dangled there. Her britches widened, and she managed to wriggle out of them herself.

Daniel had no idea how to remove the contraption at her breasts, and he wasn't going to try. He quickly pulled some blankets and furs over her, and cursed himself for staring at her near-naked body. He gently brushed some strands of wet hair out of her face as he leaned over her. Slowly, he lowered his head and brushed his lips over hers for a feather-light kiss, while his fingers caressed her cheek. Molten heat coursed through his veins and he quickly pulled back.

"My brave little *gediki*," he whispered. His lips widened in a smile. He tore his eyes off her sleeping face to rummage through the trunk under his bed for a dry shirt for himself.

His cabin door slowly opened, and his foster mother, Gentle Sun, and Elk Runner's wife, Little Bird, entered quietly. Another woman, the mother of the drowned boy, was with them.

"We will tend to your woman." Gentle Sun strolled past Daniel, and pushed him aside, mindless that he was nearly twice as tall as she.

His woman. If only it were true.

"Go now. Elk Runner and some of the other hunters are going to bring back fresh meat. It has been decided there will be a hunt and celebration in honor of *Dosa haiwi* and her bravery. The spirits have sent her to you, and she has been a blessing to the people as well."

Daniel silently bowed his head to his mother in respect. He didn't want to leave Aimee's side, but he would not disobey the old woman. With one more glance at the sleeping woman in his bed, he grabbed his rifle and left the cabin.

* * *

The men returned from a successful hunt late in the afternoon. The elk would feed the entire group this night. Talk around the camp was only of Aimee and her bravery for jumping into the river to rescue the child, and the magic some had witnessed when she brought him back to life. Daniel played along good-naturedly with the men who teased him about the powerful woman he had chosen as his wife. He was thankful that Elk Runner kept his mouth shut and didn't reveal the truth of the matter to anyone. Aimee would no doubt have a dozen suitors by night's end if they knew he had no claim to her. As it was, that Absaroka warrior had already tried to barter for her.

He was anxious to see if Aimee was all right. He hadn't wanted to leave in the first place. If she was awake, she couldn't communicate with anyone. She might need him.

The sound of her voice and jovial laughter carried to his ears as he approached his cabin, and it set his heart racing with joy. The urge to see her overwhelmed him as he opened the door. Immediately, the women's chatter died as he entered.

"My son, I have taught you better manners than to enter a woman's lodge unannounced." Gentle Sun's firm voice assaulted him.

Woman's lodge? What the hell. This was still his cabin.

His gaze drifted from his foster mother to the bunk where he had left Aimee hours before. She sat between Little Bird and the other woman, while Gentle Sun stood at the hearth. The breath left his lungs at the sight before him. Aimee raised her eyes slowly to meet his, a soft smile on her face. The baby on her lap caught his attention. He cooed and gurgled as she held him in a sitting position. Daniel's eyes fell on the deerskin dress Aimee wore. The two women on either side of her braided and adorned her hair with shells and feathers.

He had never seen anything as beautiful as the fair-skinned, fair-haired woman on his bunk. He knew her curves all too well from her unusual white man's clothing. Seeing her in that dress, however, raised his awareness of her femininity to even greater heights than he cared to experience, especially since three glaring women confronted him at the moment.

"The mighty fearless hunter is left speechless by his woman's beauty," Little Bird remarked, laughter in her voice.

"His eyes will drop out of his head if he keeps looking at her like that," the other woman chimed in.

"Mother, you will no doubt be a grandmother again very soon." Little Bird motioned with her head to Gentle Sun. "If we leave them alone now, White Wolf might not let her join the

133

celebration tonight."

"It would be about time my other son gifted me with some grandchildren," Gentle Sun croaked.

The women all laughed in unison. Aimee's head turned from one to the other before meeting his eyes again.

Daniel cleared his throat, annoyed by the women's teasing. Irrationally, he was irritated by their presence. Aimee appeared to be getting along just fine without him. He wanted to be the one she sought, yet there she was, sitting with the other women, having an apparently good time. His sister-in-law had read him correctly, though. At the moment, he could think of nothing he wanted to do more than sweep Aimee into his arms and truly claim her as his.

"You are well?" he managed to ask.

"Yes, your family has been wonderful," Aimee replied softly. Her complete acceptance of these people made his heart swell, and overwhelming desire for her swept through him. He gave a quick nod, and then turned and left the cabin before his body betrayed his thoughts, which would only give the women more fuel for their jokes.

The women soon emerged from the cabin to help with preparations for the celebratory feast. Aimee stayed alongside Little Bird, and watched her grind nuts and berries. She helped make cakes, and sliced meat to hang over cooking fires and in pits that were dug into the ground.

Daniel observed her from afar, and tried in vain to conceal the hunger in his eyes. She showed none of the disdain against the Indians that he had encountered from whites back east. Aimee was genuinely warm and friendly with these people who were like family to him. She obviously loved children. She played games with the younger ones, and each time she held Elk Runner's infant in her arms, a new wave of desire spread through him.

He tried not to think about what it would be like to see her holding a child, their child, in her arms. That could never happen. His white mother had died in this wilderness, giving birth to him. No matter how she dressed, or her abilities on the trail, Aimee was still a white woman. Like a beautiful spring flower, she would wither and die in these mountains. Neither lasted long in this harsh environment.

* * *

The people broke camp early the next morning. Aimee and Daniel stood by as the group prepared to depart. Aimee gave Gentle Sun and Little Bird a warm hug in farewell.

"I wish I understood their language, and could speak with them," she said when they were alone again. "I think I did learn a few words, though, *Dosa bia'isa.*" She glanced up at him expectantly. Daniel's eyebrows raised in surprise.

"I know that's what they call you, and they call me *Dosa haiwi,* although I don't know what these words mean."

Daniel smiled. "To the Tukudeka, I am known as White Wolf, and Elk Runner gave you the name White Dove. But I prefer to call you *gediki.*"

"Meaning?" She faced him, her hands on her hips.

"It refers to a wild cat." Daniel's look dared her to have a sharp comeback. She had none. His little nickname gave her the warm fuzzies all over even as she wondered if being referred to as a wild cat was flattering or not.

"Well, I . . . ah, think I'd better change out of this dress and back into my practical clothes." Lost for words, she rushed to the cabin, leaving Daniel to stare after her.

135

Chapter Fourteen

Several days later, Aimee knelt at the banks of the river, a large pile of clothing next to her. She dipped her shirts and pants in the water, and sparingly dribbled some soap on them, then rubbed the fabric together vigorously to scrub everything clean. She'd grabbed several of Daniel's shirts as well. Inspecting the garments, she wished she had some thread and needles to patch up some of the holes in them.

"Aimee."

She glanced up at the sound of her name. Daniel had returned early from one of his forays. He looked as if he must have run for quite a while. He breathed hard, and his hair was a mess. He stopped in front of the cabin, and waved her to him. The urgent look on his face startled her, and she rushed to his side.

"What is it?" she asked anxiously.

"Bring your wash," he commanded.

Aimee headed back to the river to retrieve the pile of wet clothes while pondering his distressed behavior.

"Stay in the cabin, and don't make a sound to give away your presence," Daniel said when she returned. His voice had an edge to it, and his body looked tense. "Do not come out until I come for you."

"Why, what is it?" The insistence in his voice made her nervous.

"Do as I tell you for once. Give me your word that you won't leave this cabin for any reason until I get you," he repeated.

"Daniel, I don't understand why . . ."

"Your word!" he growled impatiently. "Or I will bind you to

your bed and gag you."

"Okay, fine. I'll stay put," she said in exasperation. He stared at her for a moment, then shoved her inside the cabin and pulled the door shut. Why didn't he just tell her what this was about?

She paced nervously, then sat on the bed and strained her ears to listen. Was it Blackfoot? If they were being attacked, shouldn't Daniel be in the cabin with her, rather than face them out there alone?

Outside, the rhythmic thudding sound of an ax repeatedly striking wood carried into the cabin. *He's chopping wood? What the heck is going on?* She left the bed. Her hand was on the door handle when she heard a strange voice with a French accent called out "hello the camp." Overcome with curiosity, she clenched her fists at her side, and sat on her bed to stay away from the window. She lay down, and stared at the ceiling, trying to listen. Why was Daniel hiding her away from visitors? He didn't hide her from the Indians.

* * *

Outside, Daniel stood by the woodpile. He swung his ax with more force than necessary to split the logs on the chopping block. His rifle lay within easy reach at his feet. A voice called out from behind, and he turned. Two white trappers rode their horses into the yard.

They arrived sooner than he'd expected. He had stumbled across their tracks earlier in the day, and followed them for half the morning. When it became obvious they were heading for his cabin, he had cut through the forest to head them off. Until he knew whom he was dealing with, he had to keep Aimee hidden away. He couldn't take the chance of them finding out about her. Perhaps he should have tied her up. She never listened to him. He didn't want to think about what might happen if these men saw her. He knew he wouldn't hesitate to spill their blood to keep her safe.

Daniel walked out to meet the men. He called a greeting to each one of them in turn.

"Daniel Osborne, it has been a long time," one of the men said with a thick French accent, and reached his arm out. Daniel shook his hand heartily. Without being invited, the trapper dismounted his horse. The other man did the same. "You are well?"

"I am well Francoise," Daniel replied. "How are you, my friend?"

"Very well, very well," the Frenchman smiled brightly, exposing stained teeth. "How is your father? We did not see him last month in St. Louis."

"Oh? You must have crossed paths. Presumably he is still there. He doesn't like to admit it to me, but I believe, as he is getting older he prefers city life to the mountains. Something he always swore would never happen." They all laughed.

The three men slipped into conversation that was a mixture of French and English.

"He is more likely enjoying the company of the ladies." Francoise stroked his goatee smugly. "That is something sorely lacking up here. The Shoshoni do not like to share their women. The Absaroka, on the other hand," he smiled, showing more of his rotten teeth, "they will accommodate any visitor with a woman for the night. The unfortunate thing is, they won't let you take one with you. A man gets pretty lonely up here, especially in the winter. A woman to keep the bed warm at night would be nice."

Daniel cursed inwardly.

"Word in the mountains is that you have taken a wife, Daniel." Françoise leered.

"Who told you that?" An overwhelming urge to hit something, or someone, washed over Daniel.

"We met a group of Absaroka two days ago, and heard the most curious story," Françoise said, rubbing his chin some more. "One of them said you had taken a wife. And not just any woman, but a white woman."

Daniel's hands itched to wrap around that damn Absaroka's neck and choke the life out of him for having such a loose tongue.

"It is about time that a young man such as yourself takes a wife. It is not good to live such a solitary life. I remember when I was your age, I sometimes serviced two or three women in one night." He and his companion slapped each other on the back, laughing. "I'm not sure I could do that anymore, eh, Pierre?"

"Sit and have some coffee," Daniel said, trying to hide his

138

growing annoyance. He gripped his ax handle until his knuckles turned white, and motioned to the coffee pot on the tripod over the fire pit.

"Thank you for your hospitality, Daniel," the man named Pierre said, and poured himself some coffee. The three sat down around the fire.

"So, is it true?" Pierre asked, his eyes darting around the yard.

"I have taken a wife, yes," Daniel conceded. He had to think fast. This was a complication he wasn't prepared for.

"Where did you find a white woman, Daniel?"

"I traded her from a river man up on the Missouri," he lied smoothly.

"It would have been wiser to marry a Shoshoni, Daniel. You are practically one of them."

"If you tire of her, we will take her off your hands," Pierre offered. "I'm sure we can make good use of her, eh, Françoise?" They laughed again. "Where is she? Let's have a look at her." Both Frenchmen turned their heads in all directions.

"My wife," Daniel said slowly in a cold, quiet voice, "is none of your concern. And if you speak of her again in an insulting manner, you won't walk out of this camp alive."

"We meant no disrespect." Françoise laughed nervously and waved a hand in defense. "A woman of beauty is rare to behold in these mountains, and we only wished to make your bride's acquaintance."

Daniel's eyes narrowed as he nodded. He tried not to let the tension show on his face. His muscles were coiled tight as a snake ready to strike. He would have loved nothing better than to beat these men into the ground.

After exchanging nervous glances, the two Frenchmen quickly changed the subject, and talked about good beaver trapping areas, the growing demand for fur in the east and across the ocean, and mutual acquaintances. Finally, they said their farewells.

"Give our regards to your father, Daniel, and perhaps we can meet your bride next time," Francoise said, waving as they mounted their horses and rode on. Daniel kept his eyes on them until they disappeared into the forest. Only then did he go to his cabin. When he opened the door, Aimee bolted upright from her prone position on the bed.

"That was quite a story you told those men," was the first thing out of her mouth. "Since when am I your wife?"

"If you understood that, surely you heard them talk about what they would like to do to you," Daniel said with disgust.

"You really think they were going to just jump me?" Aimee persisted.

"Believe me, you don't want to meet men like those two." Daniel scoffed. "And I didn't wish to kill two men because of you today." He ran his hands through his hair and paced the small cabin like a caged animal.

"What is that supposed to mean?"

"What will it take to convince you?" Daniel whirled around and snarled at her. "Animals like that have only one thing on their minds when they see a woman. And one look at you would make them behave like bull elk during the fall rut. Is that what you want? To have them leering at you with nothing on their minds but you on the ground on your back?" He turned abruptly and stormed out. He had to get his emotions under control. The thought of what those two frenchmen would do if they laid eyes on a beautiful woman like Aimee caused the blood to boil in his veins.

"Hey, no need to get so worked up. They're gone now," Aimee said from behind him a moment later. He turned to face her.

"I will follow their trail for a day and make sure they leave the area," he said gruffly. He inhaled deeply, trying to calm himself. He studied her face for a moment. "I will not let any harm come to you," he added as if to himself.

"I know that, Daniel." Aimee smiled softly. She placed her hand on his upper arm. It was an innocent gesture, but the sensation was like a jolt of lightning, even through the fabric of his shirt. His body reacted instantly. He swallowed hard and cleared his throat. Right now, his emotions spiraled out of control.

"Aw, hell!"

In one fluid movement he pulled her to him, one hand at the

back of her head, his other arm coiled around her waist. He tilted her head and claimed her mouth with the hunger born of weeks of pent-up desire for this woman. Kissing her like a starved man who'd finally been given a morsel of food, Daniel savored the feel of her soft body pressed to his. It's what he'd longed to do since he first laid eyes on her. She squirmed in his embrace, and the pleading noises that came from her throat finally brought him back to his senses.

Dear God! What was he doing? Had he completely lost his mind? Apparently so, where this woman was concerned. He was doing exactly what he wanted to protect her from. How long had she struggled to get him to stop? His blinding need overruled everything else. She was so small, she didn't stand a chance against him. How easy it would be to just take her. The thought scared the hell out of him. Abruptly, he broke away from her. Disgusted with himself, he released a string of curses and quickly headed into the trees behind the cabin.

* * *

Aimee gasped, struggling to control her breathing and racing heart. She wanted to call him back, to run after him, but her mouth and her legs wouldn't obey. She just stood there, stunned by what had happened. She definitely hadn't been prepared for Daniel's unexpected onslaught, and had just stood stiffly, crushed against his hard body. The primal assault on her mouth had ignited a fire in her veins and her body began to melt.

Aimee fervently wished this wasn't simply Daniel trying to make a point. He was trying to intimidate her, make her see that she was no match for a man's assault. But God help her, the desire that had built in her as he slashed his lips across hers was more powerful than an impending eruption of Old Faithful.

She'd wanted desperately to wrap her arms around him and respond to his kiss. Her arms had been trapped, however, against his chest, and the more she tried to squirm to free them, the tighter his hold on her had become. She had yearned for his touch for weeks. Her body was still liquid fire, but this was not how she had envisioned their first kiss.

She should be appalled at what he had done, her common sense told her. This was not a lover's kiss, yet it hadn't exactly been brutal, either. Her lips tingled from the assault. What would a true kiss of passion feel like? Her body was still a molten mass of goo at the sensations he evoked.

As her breathing returned to normal, she realized that he had successfully made his point. She was completely helpless if a man tried to have his way with her here. No, not any man, just this man.

* * *

Daniel followed the Frenchmen's tracks for part of the next day until he was satisfied that they were heading in the direction they had said. Disgusted with his own behavior, he had stayed away from his cabin the day before until he was sure Aimee had gone to bed. He had no words to tell her he was sorry for what he had done.

He must have scared the hell out of her this time. Heck, he had scared the hell out of himself. Truthfully, he didn't regret that he had kissed her, just the way in which he went about it. And that kiss only left him starving for more. The thought that he could lose control so easily around her renewed his conviction that he had to get her out of these mountains. He would kill any man who dared try to hurt her, and she was not safe from men like those French trappers. And apparently she wasn't safe from him, either.

He returned to the cabin in a foul mood late in the day. Aimee sat on a log in the yard in front of the cabin, writing in her journal. It was something she did almost daily. She looked up and gave him a hesitant smile as he approached. As always, seeing her smile at him set his heart on fire.

"Everything all right?" Aimee asked tentatively.

"Fine," he said without looking at her. He strode over to the woodpile, grabbed his ax, and gathered large chunks of wood onto the chopping block. He was about to take a swing, when Aimee walked up next to him.

"Did I do something wrong?"

Daniel lowered his hatchet, and braced his heart. "You can't stay here any longer," he said roughly. "It's not safe for you here."

"What happened now?" Aimee asked in exasperation. "Is it because of those two trappers from yesterday?" She paused, and glared at him. "Or the point you tried to make after they left? I

142

got the message, so don't worry. I'm a helpless woman at the mercy of every man in the wilderness."

He clenched his jaw and cursed silently. His hand gripped the axe handle.

"If you want to send me away, fine." Aimee threw her hands in the air. "But I don't have anywhere to go. I wish you'd stop telling me what's best for me. I can make my own decisions, damn it!"

"I will leave my father a message, and take you to St. Louis. I should have done this when I first found you." He ignored her tirade. "We can prepare to leave in a couple of days."

"I don't want to go to St. Louis," Aimee argued.

"You belong in the city," Daniel growled angrily. "I'm growing weary of having to look out for your safety. You have kept me from my work. I have to prepare for winter, and with you here, I can't get anything done." He stared at her coldly. The shocked look on her face, the pain in her eyes, almost crumbled his resolve.

"Well in that case, don't let me keep you from your work any longer," Aimee yelled.

She wheeled around and stormed into the cabin, and slammed the door. Daniel stared after her. It was best that she be angry with him. Tomorrow he would go hunting so they had meat for traveling. To hell with what she said. He had made up his mind. He was taking her back to the city, even if he had to tie her up and carry her all the way there.

* * *

Françoise had noticed Daniel's evasiveness and tension regarding his wife, and he wondered at the reason. The Crow warrior who had told him about Daniel's woman had mentioned her beauty and unusual light hair coloring. Just the description the warrior gave him set his loins afire. His sexual need had gotten so great he gave the warrior two beaver pelts to find him a woman to relieve his need. But it hadn't been enough. He wanted to see this white woman for himself, and perhaps he could steal her away from Daniel. The more he thought about it, the more he came to the conclusion that Daniel was keeping her hidden for good reason.

A slow smile spread across his lips. *Oui*, that was it. Daniel certainly knew that he needed to hide his woman away from leering eyes.

"Pierre." Françoise turned in the saddle to face his companion. "I think we should be more neighborly and introduce ourselves to Daniel's new bride."

"What are you saying?" the other man asked.

"If there is a white woman in these hills, I would wish to meet her." He shot his companion a meaningful look. "When is the last time you had a white woman, my friend?"

"Two months ago in St. Louis," Pierre frowned. "But if there is one available close by." He grinned malevolently at his partner, and spit out some tobacco juice.

"I grow tired of dark-haired, dark-skinned Indian girls. Even the whores in St. Louis were dark-haired."

"Let us ride east from here and circle back. We can be back to Daniel's cabin by nightfall. We will watch, and if he leaves in the morning, we can make our introductions." He sniggered.

"What if he doesn't leave her by herself?" Pierre asked.

"Then we may have to kill our young friend," Françoise sneered. "But I would much rather have the opportunity to steal his woman away. I have always liked Daniel and his father. It would be a shame to have to kill him."

"What are we going to do when we have her?" Pierre asked eagerly.

"We will ride hard for a day and put distance between us and the cabin. No doubt he will try and search for her, but we will cover our tracks." Françoise ground his groin against his saddle in anticipation. "My friend, in a few days' time, we won't need to seek out the Absaroka women anymore."

* * *

Tears of frustration flowed unabashed down Aimee's face as she sat on her bed. *Why did I have to fall in love with him? Why did everything have to be so complicated?* She had no doubt in her mind that, had she met someone like Daniel in her own time, she would have let him know how interested she was. Here in this time, she couldn't do it. It would be hard enough to leave when the time came.

144

Let go of your stupid fantasies, she chided. *He's proven over and over again that he doesn't want you here.* If he removed her from this valley, how would Zach find her? She had to stay right here or else she wouldn't be going home.

Daniel again didn't come in for their customary evening supper together, and she didn't bother looking for him. She went to bed still angry. The next morning, he was already gone when she woke, and the sun had barely come up yet. He had left her usual cup of coffee on the table.

Out of spite, she decided to go for a swim, even in the chill of early morning. She had followed Daniel's advice and not gone in the river again when she was alone. The water levels had receded just as quickly as they had risen the last few weeks, and the waters once again flowed calmly. Out of sheer rebellion, she grabbed a blanket, and her soap and shampoo, and headed across the meadow. To hell with him. *I dumped one guy because he's overbearing, I'm not about to let another one tell me what I can and can't do.*

She had just reached the banks of the river, when movement in the tree line to the east caught her attention. Two riders approached. They were white men, dressed in buckskins and fur hats. A jolt of adrenaline shot through her. She looked from the riders to the cabin, and tried to judge the distance. Would she make it? She dropped the blanket and the spare clothes she carried, and made a dash for the cabin. The men on horseback saw her move and urged their horses into a gallop. There was no way she was going to outrun them, but she was sure as hell going to try.

One of the riders pulled his horse to a stop in front of the cabin door, effectively blocking her way. In a split second's decision she ran to the left to try and head into the trees behind the cabin. She heard the two men laugh and whistle behind her.

"Son of a bitch," she muttered between gritted teeth. Her self-defense training back home hadn't prepared her for being chased on horseback. She hadn't even reached the trees when she sensed her pursuers right behind her. Heavy hooves clomped behind her and a horse's hot breath blew against her neck. A hand grabbed for her arm. She stumbled and fell face forward to the ground. The man was on top of her in an instant.

"Now, *Cherie*, don't run away from Françoise," the man whispered close to her ear, his foul breath making bile rise in her throat. "We didn't get a chance to meet the other day." He hauled her to her feet. Aimee kicked and thrashed, and she screamed Daniel's name.

"*Mon Dieu*, you are a wild one!" Françoise panted. He clamped his hand over her mouth. The other man jumped off his horse and helped Françoise wrestle Aimee into submission.

"Tie her hands and put something in her mouth," Françoise ordered. Then he leered at her, exposing rotting teeth. "I see now why Daniel hid you away from us, *Cherie*. You are more beautiful than I could have imagined." He stroked the side of her face with a dirty hand. Aimee jerked her head away.

In her mind, she called him every foul name she could think of. The other man tied a piece of leather over her mouth and around her face to keep her from screaming again.

"She is something to look at." Pierre's eyes raked boldly over Aimee's body. He reached out a hand and groped at her breasts. "So young and ripe," he said in French. "Are you sure we can't sample her here right now?" he asked his companion. "I am as hard as a rock just looking at her."

"No. Help me get her on my horse. We must be away from here quickly. There will be plenty of time to enjoy her soon." Françoise waved his hand impatiently. He swung into the saddle, and reached for her arm.

Aimee struggled again, and twisted and turned in Pierre's grip as he hoisted her onto the front of Françoise's saddle. Françoise's hand dug painfully into her skin as he held her wrist. Adrenaline flooded her system. She managed to twist away from the horse, and kicked out at Pierre. He backhanded her across the face, then grabbed her around the waist and threw her up into the saddle.

Aimee's heart hammered in her chest. This wasn't happening to her. Françoise tugged her in front of him, and roughly pulled her up against his chest. Her eyes filled with tears of frustration.

Her four years of high school French came in mighty handy

146

now. For the most part, she understood what they said. Daniel had been right again. She swore never to doubt him about anything ever again, if she got the chance. How could this be happening? She never imagined she would have to worry about the possibility of being gang-raped here in the wilds of Yellowstone!

The two men kicked their horses into a fast run, and headed north. The man, Françoise, held her tightly to him as they rode, smelling of tobacco, whiskey, and the foul, sour odor of someone in desperate need of a bath. She swallowed back the bile that rose to her throat. Her mind raced with possible ways of getting away from these men. She was helpless to do anything at the moment.

Where had Daniel gone off to? Irrationally, she directed her anger at him for leaving her this morning. How long would it be before he returned to the cabin and found her missing? He had told her he wouldn't look for her if she went off on her own again.

No. Surely he would realize she hadn't wandered off. There were too many tracks left behind. She inhaled slow and deep to calm her panicked nerves. Daniel would search for her, but would he find her in time before these men raped her?

Chapter Fifteen

Daniel followed a familiar deer trail in search of game since dawn. He needed to be alone to clear his head. He would take Aimee back to civilization. It was for the best. He obviously couldn't trust himself around her. In time, he was sure he could stop thinking about her, and his life would return to the way it had been before, the way he always liked it. He and his father would trap beaver in the fall and spring, and sit around their warm fire in winter and tell stories late into the night. In summer, he would go hunting for bighorn sheep with Elk Runner. It all sounded lonely to him now.

He had just come across some fresh deer tracks, when these mingled with prints that gave him cause for alarm; hoof prints. He knelt down to examine them more closely. Two horses had come through here very recently.

Francoise and Pierre. Could they have circled back around and were in the vicinity? He followed the tracks for several miles. An uneasy feeling crept up his spine. They were headed for his cabin.

Daniel broke into a run. He abandoned the deer trail, and cut through the forest. He dodged low-hanging branches, leapt over downed logs, and ran in a straight line for his cabin. A wave of cold dread washed over him, and he cursed his carelessness. He shouldn't have left Aimee alone. He should have known those bastards couldn't be trusted.

"Aimee!" he yelled at the top of his lungs, long before his cabin came into view through the trees. From a distance, a pile of clothing and a blanket lay strewn along the banks of the river. He kicked open the cabin door. One glance told him nothing had been disturbed. The interior was neat and tidy as always since Aimee's appearance. Her backpack sat at the foot of her bed where she always kept it. He ran back outside and called her name repeatedly.

Taking a deep breath to calm himself, he read the signs on the ground. Hoof prints were everywhere in the yard. He followed them to the tree line behind his cabin, where an obvious struggle had taken place. These men had been in a hurry, and they took Aimee with them. There was still a chance he could catch up to them, before . . .

"Dammit!"

He didn't even want to think about what they were doing to her, perhaps at this very moment, or what they might have done to her already. He knew exactly what he would do to them once he found them.

A deadly calm flowed through him. He rushed inside the cabin, removed his powder horn and bullet pouch from across his shoulder, and tossed his long rifle on his bed. He reached for his most prized possession hanging on the wall above his bunk - his hunting bow made from the horns of the bighorn sheep. He only carried this weapon to hunt large game such as bighorn sheep and buffalo, for it was more powerful than the rifle, and deadly accurate. He slung a quiver full of obsidian-tipped arrows over his shoulder, readjusted the tomahawk at his belt, unsheathed his knife, and checked it for sharpness. Leaving the cabin, he took off at a run, and followed the horse tracks into the forest.

* * *

Aimee's face burned hot and pulsed from when Pierre had slapped her earlier. The jolting wild ride on horseback didn't help matters. The Frenchmen kept up the grueling pace for what seemed like an eternity, but they slowed down as they headed up a mountain pass. She tried hard to concentrate on her surroundings. They traveled pretty much the same way she had come over a month ago. They skirted around a small geyser and hot spring area at one point, and Aimee vaguely recognized the area. If they stayed on their present course, eventually they would reach the Grand Canyon of the Yellowstone. Another sight she longed to see, but definitely under different circumstances.

149

The two Frenchmen kept up a lively chatter after several hours, sometimes arguing as to when it would be safe to stop. They rode their horses up several shallow streams, presumably to try and cover their tracks, and make it harder for Daniel to find where they had gone. After a while, Françoise removed her mouth gag.

"No need for this anymore, *Cherie*," he whispered in her ear. She shuddered involuntarily, and her skin crawled in disgust. "If you try to scream here, no one will hear you. Soon you will be screaming with passion."

"Over my dead body," she hissed through clenched teeth.

"Oh, what a shame that would be, for it is a beautiful body to behold," Françoise cooed. His hand around her waist moved up and fondled one of her breasts. "*Non*, I am sure we will be enjoying you for a long time, wild one. Where did Daniel find such an exquisite creature?"

Aimee didn't reply. She squeezed her eyes shut. She willed her mind to become numb, and tune out all feeling as the man continued to grope at her.

"When is it my turn?" Pierre asked. "She can ride with me as well. I want to have a feel, too."

"You will get your turn soon enough," Françoise said gruffly. "For now she stays with me. This was my idea, so I get her first."

Pierre made a disgusting noise, but didn't argue the point. It was apparent that Françoise was the leader here.

At some point they would have to stop, and perhaps she could try and make a run for it. If she could escape into the dense forest where the horses couldn't follow, she might have a chance.

"Where are you taking me?" Aimee asked when they veered in a more northerly direction.

"Ah, *Cherie*, we are headed for the *Roche Jaune*, not that it should matter to you where we go," Françoise answered.

So she had been correct. They may not be going to the Grand Canyon, but they were headed for the *Roche Jaune*, the French name for Yellowstone River, nonetheless. She had covered many hiking trails in that area, and she hoped to see some familiar landmarks that might help her in her escape.

Aimee was not used to sitting astride a horse, and her inner thigh muscles screamed in pain. Several times she wanted to ask if they could stop for a while, but then thought better of it. At least while they were on the move, she was safe from what they intended to do to her when they did stop. It was only a matter of time. The horses couldn't keep moving forever, and it was well into late afternoon. At this point, Daniel wouldn't find her in time. They had covered a lot of ground fairly fast, and Daniel was on foot.

Please, let me be strong to endure this.

She had dealt with her share of rape victims in the ER, and it was always a horrific experience. What would this do to her? There had to be a way out of this situation.

Thoughts of Daniel flooded her mind. *I love you, Daniel.* An overwhelming feeling of regret came over her. Why hadn't she told him how she felt about him, and seen where that might have led. Her mind drifted to the day he tossed her in the river when he almost kissed her, and the gentle way he held her the night of the storm under the canopy of pine trees. Would he look at her with desire in his eyes after these men were through with her? Would she even ever want to be with a man again after such an experience?

The horse underneath her stopped, jolting her out of her thoughts. The Frenchmen had stopped in a clearing surrounded on all sides by forest. A small creek gurgled as it meandered snakelike through the tall grass. Perfect! She had plenty of opportunities to make a run for it here.

Francoise and Pierre both dismounted their horses, and Francoise dragged her out of the saddle. Her feet touched the ground, and she couldn't hold back a cry of pain. Hot needles shot through her leg muscles, and she buckled to her knees.

"*Cherie,* you need to get up and walk. The cramps will go away." Francoise hoisted her back up. Aimee suppressed another cry as he hauled her off to the creek.

"Drink."

She fell to her knees and put her mouth to the water. At first, she wanted to tell the Frenchman to go to hell, but Daniel had told her to never refuse an offer of food or water.

How was she going to make a run for it if she could barely

walk? Struggling to stand on her feet, she suppressed another cry of pain. With her hands tied, she couldn't even rub her sore muscles.

"We will make camp here," Francoise announced. Pierre was already busy unsaddling the horses, which vigorously plucked at the tall grasses.

"We will rest for a while," he spoke to his companion in French. "The woman needs some time to relax her legs. She is obviously not used to riding. Even I am not that barbaric to take her when she is in such discomfort. She will not be able to spread her legs for us."

Pierre made a noise of objection. "What does it matter if her legs are cramped? I have an ache, too, between my legs, and it needs to be satisfied soon."

"It will be, my friend. But give her a little time to rest."

Aimee stood by silently, taking in all they said. She didn't understand everything word for word, but she got the general idea that they would wait a little while before having their way with her.

"Do you think we are being followed?" Pierre asked after he returned with a pile of wood.

"We rode hard and fast. Even if he followed us, he is on foot, and I believe we covered our tracks well. He will not be able to track us in the dark. We will be long gone from here in the morning if he finds this place," Francoise said. He turned to Aimee. "Cherie, we will have some supper first, and then the entertainment, no?"

"Go to hell," Aimee spat.

"Oh, but quite the contrary." Françoise smiled. "It will be pure heaven, I am sure."

After the men built their campfire, Pierre went off in search of meat. Aimee heard several shots. These two were very confident, she thought when she heard the noise. Maybe they were too confident, which could work to her advantage. The sound of gunshot could travel quite far, and maybe if she got lucky, someone would hear.

An hour later, as the sun started to set, a couple of birds roasted over the fire. Aimee sat and leaned against a tree, away from the trappers. They hadn't untied her. The soreness in her legs was only a dull ache now, but whenever she shifted, the muscles tightened painfully. Moving her legs at all was pure agony. Her head pounded. She wanted to close her eyes and drift off to sleep, but fear kept her awake. Francoise sat closest to her, his rifle next to him, and Pierre leered at her every now and then from across the fire.

Aimee scanned the ground nearby for something, anything she could possibly use as a weapon. One thing was for sure. She was not going to let them have their way with her without a fight. Come what may, she would try and hurt them as much as they planned to hurt her.

Her eyes darted to where Pierre roasted the meat over the fire. He looked up at her and smirked. "Very soon, ma petite."

Aimee turned her head in disgust. Her mind raced while her eyes continued to scan the ground for something that might help her defend herself. There just had to be a way out of this situation. She refused to believe that this would be her fate.

* * *

"Pierre! Françoise! Release the woman before I kill you both!" A loud voice broke through the sounds of crickets, and echoed through the forest. Startled, Françoise and Pierre both grabbed their rifles and darted around, pointing their weapons into the forest.

Aimee's head shot up and her heart pounded in elation. Daniel! He had found her! She scrambled to her feet, ignoring the shooting pain in her inner thighs. She scanned the trees in all directions, but couldn't see anything. Where was he?

"Show yourself, Daniel," Françoise called out. "We were trying to do you a favor by taking the woman off your hands. If you wish to reclaim her, come join our camp."

"I'll not say it again. Release the woman." Daniel materialized out of the forest, and strode calmly into view. He looked more Indian than before. Aimee had never seen him with the bow he held almost carelessly in his hand. Pierre raised his rifle and took aim.

"No!" Aimee screamed.

With imperceptible speed, Daniel raised his bow and an arrow lodged itself in Pierre's heart before he fired off his shot.

153

The force of the impact sent him backwards a few paces before he collapsed face down into the fire.

"*Merde!*" Françoise darted for Aimee. He grabbed her around the waist, and pulled her roughly in front of him to shield himself from Daniel's arrows. He pulled his knife and held it to her throat.

"I will kill her, Daniel," he called. "Don't come any closer."

"Let her go, and I might let you live." Daniel's voice was eerily calm. For a few seconds, no one moved. Aimee leaned her body forcibly backwards against Françoise, which caused him to shift his balance from the unexpected move. At the same time she raised her foot and brought her heel down hard on one of his feet. The Frenchman loosened his hold around her waist. Aimee wheeled around and brought her knee up into his groin. Françoise cursed again. Enraged with pain, he backhanded her, knocking her to the ground.

* * *

Daniel wasted no time and sprinted across the camp. With a vicious roar, he lunged at Françoise, just as Aimee hit the ground. His body collided with the Frenchman. The impact sent them both to the ground. They rolled in the dirt, and Françoise frantically struggled to gain the upper hand. Daniel threw his full weight against the Frenchman. He straddled the man's hips. Francoise stabbed wildly in the air with his knife.

"No man touches her and lives," Daniel snarled. Françoise's eyes widened in terror. His knife made contact with Daniel's upper arm. Daniel grabbed hold of the man's wrist and squeezed. The Frenchman's sweat-soaked face turned red from strain. His arm trembled. Turning Francoise's wrist so that the knife now pointed downward, Daniel pushed the man's arm until the sharp weapon plunged deep into Francoise's chest. The Frenchman looked up in surprise for a split second before his face froze. His body went limp.

Daniel pushed himself up off the ground, and caught his breath for a moment, hands on his knees. He swiped his arm across his forehead, then looked around to where Aimee had been thrown to the ground. She had pulled herself to a sitting position and watched with wide, fearful eyes. He approached her slowly. Had he been too late? His beautiful, brave little wildcat had once again amazed him with her quick thinking and actions.

"Aimee," he said softly. He dropped to his knees in front of her. She wordlessly held out her hands to show him her bound wrists. Cursing, he pulled his knife from its sheath, and with one quick move, sliced through the leather ropes binding her hands. Like a coiled spring that had been released, she threw herself at Daniel and wound her arms tightly around his neck. The impact almost knocked him off balance. With an anguished sigh, he wrapped his arms around her, and crushed her against his chest.

Her body shook in his embrace, and she sobbed into his chest. Silently, he held her while she cried. He gently stroked her back, and combed his fingers through her loose hair. His mind reeled from one emotion to the next. Anger, fear, joy, love.

He wanted to kill those two bastards over and over again for what they had done to her. He reveled in the joy of holding her close to him, knowing she trusted him. He feared what might have already happened before he found her. Consumed by a burning love for this woman he held in his arms, he suddenly realized he couldn't let her go. The thought of losing her today had tested his strength and endurance to the limit. Daniel knew he would do it all over again if he had to.

Chapter Sixteen

After what seemed like hours, Aimee stirred in his arms. She sniffed and wiped her nose and face on her sleeve, and raised her head from his shoulder. He cradled her dirty, tear-streaked face in his hands while his thumbs caressed her cheeks. His eyes devoured her.

"You came for me." Her voice was a mere whisper.

"I would follow you to the ends of the world if I had to," Daniel said in a sultry tone.

Aimee smiled weakly and touched a trembling hand to his cheek.

Daniel cleared his throat, and slowly rose to his feet. "I'm afraid my legs are numb from kneeling so long," he said with a tentative smile. He held out his hand to help her up. She placed her small hand in his, her eyes on his face. He pulled her to her feet, and she cried out. Her knees gave out, and she sank back to the ground. Startled, he reacted purely by reflex. With one arm under her knees and the other at her waist, he scooped her up and held her close.

"What is it?" He searched her face for answers. What had those animals done to her?

"My legs are so sore, I can barely stand," she answered with a weak smile.

"Did those bastards . . ." he hissed, unable to finish his question, dreading her answer. Aimee shook her head.

"No, they didn't . . . not in that way." Her words alleviated his fear. His tense muscles relaxed. "I haven't ridden on a horse in years, and muscles that I didn't know existed are protesting." Aimee gave him a reassuring smile.

Daniel set her feet on the ground gently, but held her at the waist. She sucked in a deep breath, and her hands reached out to hold on to his shoulders for support. His gaze locked intently with hers.

"No man will ever touch you again." Then, in a whisper, he added, "No man but me."

His hand reached up to gently cup the side of her face. His thumb stroked her satiny cheek, tracing where a bruise appeared from being struck by the Frenchmen.

"Daniel . . ." She breathed his name.

Slowly, he lowered his face to hers. He hesitated for a moment. Searching her face, he waited for her to tell him to stop, waited for her to stiffen. When she did neither, his lips brushed hers gently, and Aimee let out a soft moan. Her arms crept up around his neck, and she leaned into him. His heart pounded in his chest.

Daniel deepened the kiss, and wrapped one arm around her waist to draw her closer to him. His fingers caressed her cheek, her eyelids, her forehead, and finally entwined in her hair, then he cradled the back of her head. He groaned as Aimee returned his kiss with equal passion. The hunger for her that had been building in him for weeks threatened to overtake him again, but he remained in control of his emotions this time.

He savored her mouth, nipping, tasting, cherishing. When he could bear no more, he pulled back. He was not going to take advantage of her. And he would be taking advantage. The way she clung to him and kissed him back was almost more than he could stand. He trailed a few more light kisses along the side of her mouth, her cheek, and down her neck before pulling his face several inches from hers.

How often had he dreamed of holding her, kissing her, making love to her? He cursed himself for the timing. He released his hold at her waist, and took a step back. With a heavy sigh, he said, "We should get away from here. I know where we can make camp and you can rest for the night."

Aimee grabbed his upper arm. "Daniel." Her eyes turned large and round, the deep blue pools shimmering with need. "Daniel . . . I . . . I want to be with you."

157

Adrenaline surged through him. Had he understood correctly? He stepped close to her once more, and cradled her face in his hands, tilting her head upwards to search for answers in her eyes.

"You've been through hell today, Aimee. I have dreamed of hearing you say those words, but . . . not here . . . not now. Not like this." This was not how he wanted to make her his, with her mind and body battered and bruised. He wrapped her in his arms and whispered in her ear. "I have done everything to try and get you out of my mind. I thought sending you away would be the solution, but I realized today that . . . by God, I can't let you go." His voice was husky with want.

* * *

The strong front that Aimee had mustered all day crumbled completely. She was exhausted, both mentally and physically, and her entire body screamed out in pain. She cried into Daniel's shoulder like she hadn't cried since the death of her parents. She clung to the one person who represented safety and security. This man, who had become her whole life over the course of the last six weeks, had once again, selflessly, come to her rescue.

What she asked was going to cause her more pain than she could imagine later on, but she couldn't bear the thought of leaving this place and time without giving in to her desires for him. After today's ordeal, she couldn't deny her love for him any longer. It didn't matter anymore what happened in a couple of months. She needed him now, in this time, and she would be able to carry that memory back to her time. It would have to be enough.

She wrapped her arms around his middle and buried her face in his chest, inhaling deeply of his woodsy scent that she'd come to associate completely with him. Being held in Daniel's arms was pure heaven. Nothing would harm her here, and she never wanted him to let go. With a deep shuddering sigh, his words were a stark reminder that she only had a few short weeks left, and then both needed to live their lives in their own time again. She raised her head to stare up into his smoldering dark eyes. Desire and something else reflected back at her.

Aimee wrapped her hand around his neck, and pulled his

face back down to hers. She kissed him desperately. Daniel groaned as he responded, and she molded herself to his rock solid form.

"We need to leave this place," Daniel panted, and pulled his head back. His hands spanned her waist and held her away from him. "I'll get the horses ready."

"I can't ride anymore today," she protested.

"You don't have to. We can walk, and I will lead the horses, but you'll be glad to be able to ride tomorrow. It's a long way back to the cabin."

Aimee sighed wearily, but Daniel was right. They needed to get away from here and find a different campsite. Hesitantly she glanced at the two bodies on the ground. Pierre's body had put the fire out when he fell on top of it, and Aimee shuddered to think what he looked like. The heat would surely have burned him. Francoise still had the knife in his chest. Aimee looked at them with a mixture of pity and disgust.

"Come away from here, Aimee," Daniel called from where he stood with the horses.

"Are we just going to leave them like that?"

"Yeah." There was not a hint of remorse in his tone. "The wolves and bears can have them."

"You wouldn't want to bury them?" She wasn't sure how she felt about leaving the bodies for predators to find.

Daniel walked over to her, and gently took hold of her elbow to lead her away.

"After what they did, and wanted to do to you, you want to bury them?" he asked, disbelief in his voice.

"They're human beings," Aimee argued weakly.

"Hardly," Daniel scoffed. "They will serve as a warning to all others that I protect what is mine," he said fiercely. "Come."

She stared at him for a moment. His words were a harsh reminder of the differences between their worlds, and she finally nodded in acceptance. She was too tired to ponder the full meaning of his words.

She turned away from the camp, and followed Daniel without further question. Setting one foot in front of the other was pure agony. Her inner thigh muscles seemed to have lost all their elasticity, and she couldn't possibly sit astride a horse at the moment. The sun had set fully, and a near-full moon illuminated their way.

"We'll only walk a few miles. I think I know of a spot you'll like," Daniel said gently. "But walking is good. If you don't use the muscles, they'll only hurt more."

"I know that, that's why I'm not protesting," she said between gritted teeth.

Daniel led her through the darkness for about an hour when he finally stopped. "This is a good place to camp for the night," he announced. She couldn't make out much of the landscape, but a stream trickled nearby.

Daniel unsaddled the horses and hobbled their front feet so they couldn't wander off too far.

"There were a couple of blankets tied to the saddles. They must not have gotten much use, because they don't reek like those bastards back there." Daniel's voice was still full of venom. "I'll start a fire. It shouldn't be too cold tonight."

"Well, I do have my own personal heat blanket," Aimee said wearily. "You radiate so much heat, there's no way I could possibly get cold."

Daniel didn't respond. He quickly made camp. He unrolled the two blankets, and had a fire started in no time. She drifted in and out of awareness while standing up until Daniel scooped her in his arms and carried her away from camp.

"Where are we going," she asked sleepily.

"There's a reason I chose this spot." His deep, husky voice close to her ear sent shivers down her spine. "There are several hot water pools here, and I believe it would do your aching body some good to soak in one of them."

Aimee tensed, her mind instantly alert.

"Hot springs?" she asked in alarm. "But Daniel, that's ill . . ." She stopped herself before finishing the word *illegal*. Bathing in the hot springs was definitely illegal in modern times, but this was 1810.

"Ill? You won't get sick, I promise."

"I meant to say ill advised." She quickly amended her original word. "How do you know which ones are safe, and which ones are too hot? Surely people have boiled to death in these pools."

"Do you trust me?"

"Yes, I trust you," she said without hesitation. There was not another person on earth she trusted more.

"Then just relax."

Daniel set her down, and she strained her eyes, trying to focus on something in the dim light. They stood near the edge of a hot spring. The slight smell of sulfur permeated the air.

"This one should be just about right." Daniel bent down to feel the water. Aimee did the same.

"Oh, that feels great!" The combination of over a month without a hot shower and her aching muscles was enough for her not to hesitate about what she was about to do. She had never imagined she'd ever be "hot-potting" in Yellowstone!

Without any reservation, she pulled her t-shirt off over her head, and unzipped her pants and wriggled out of them. She didn't care that Daniel stared at her. She stood unashamed in front of him in the moonlight, clad in only her bra and panties. She smiled tentatively up at him.

"Are you going to join me, or am I on my own?" Aimee asked.

"I believe it would be best if I gave you some privacy."

She waded into the steaming pool. "Aaaaaahhhhh, this feels sooooo good," she sighed as she sank down into the water.

"I'll be back with a blanket for you to dry off." Daniel turned to head back the way he came. "I'll see if I can find us something to eat, too. Call out if you need anything."

She smiled as she watched his quickly retreating silhouette. She should be terrified after today's events, but once Daniel had shown up, her world was put right again. She felt completely safe when he was near. He had proven over and over again that he was her protector, provider, and teacher. And now, would he also be her lover? The look in his eyes earlier, and the way he kissed her, told her without question that he wanted her.

She sank up to her chin in the water, and closed her eyes. It was just about as hot as she could stand it. Her skin tingled, and her pulse quickened. The hot water soothed her aching muscles, and she relaxed.

Aimee didn't know whether to laugh for joy, or cry in despair. What was she going to do? She loved Daniel more than she thought possible. Today was a turning point in their relationship. There was no doubt in her mind that he had feelings for her, too. Everything about him felt so right. Making love with him was the right thing to do. She would take what she could get now, and live every moment with him to the fullest. The weeks she had left in this time would have to last her for a lifetime. Her only regret was that she would hurt him when she disappeared from his life. Was she being selfish? Absolutely. Was there a way to stop what was happening between them? Absolutely not.

* * *

Daniel returned with a blanket a short while later. Aimee sat in the water at the edge of the pool. Her eyes were closed. He came up behind her, and gently put a hand on top of her head. She whirled around, and Daniel regretted his move. He hadn't meant to startle her.

"How do you do that?" she asked, expelling a breath of relief.

"What?"

"Not make a sound when you walk."

He simply smiled at her, and held out his hand. "Come, I have some food for you. You must be hungry."

She sighed, then stood and reached for his hand, and he pulled her from the water. He immediately wrapped the blanket around her. There was a definite chill in the air, and he didn't want to stare at her nakedness.

"Feeling better?" he asked. He bent to pick up her clothes, and tossed them over his shoulder. With one arm behind her knees, and the other around her waist, he scooped her up in his arms.

"Much better." Aimee wriggled her arms loose from the blanket and wrapped them around his neck. Daniel clenched his jaw and ignored the rising heat in his body.

He carried her the short distance back to camp, and set her down close to the fire, making sure the blanket stayed wrapped around her. He pulled the skewer of meat off the fire and tore off a piece for her. When she didn't reach for it, he nudged her arm gently. A slow smile formed on his face. After today, he couldn't blame her for her exhaustion, but she needed to eat.

She sighed and reached for the skewer he offered, mumbling a quiet "thanks." He eased himself to the ground next to her, and they ate in silence. She leaned her head on his shoulder, and he wrapped an arm around her.

"I feel so safe with you, Daniel," Aimee said softly.

He looked down at the top of her head, and smiled. What a fool he had been. How could he have ever thought to take her to St. Louis? The thought of her surviving in these mountains nagged at him. Was he being selfish to want her with him and not return her to the city? Of course he was. He wanted exactly what his father had warned him about his entire life. But he couldn't help it. It took almost losing her to make him realize how important she had become to him. His arm tightened around her shoulder. She was almost asleep again. Daniel nudged her one more time.

"You need to put your clothes on," he said softly in her ear. He banked the fire while she dressed, then sat behind her on the blanket, and pulled her up against him. He wrapped the other blanket around them. Aimee sighed and leaned back into his chest. His arms tightened around her middle, and he rested his chin on top of her head. They sat like this for a moment, until he gently eased her to lie down, and wrapped his body around hers to keep her warm. She didn't make a sound, her breaths steady and even. Daniel smiled to himself as he held this precious woman in his arms. A sense of peace and contentment that he hadn't felt before washed over him. It was as if he finally found something he'd been missing all his life.

* * *

Aimee awoke the next morning to the sounds of loud bird chirping. Her mind cleared gradually, waking from one of the best nights' sleep she remembered in a while. She was warm and secure. She rested against a solid form, her head cradled by a strong arm. She slowly opened her eyes as memories of the previous day came flooding back. Daniel was lying on his side next to her, and looked down at her intently. Aimee smiled leisurely and stretched. Her stiff muscles ached dully through the stretch.

"Did I sleep too long?" she asked groggily.

"You could lie here all day and I wouldn't mind," Daniel whispered. "Those two grizzlies over there, though," he gestured with his head in the direction of the woods, "aren't too happy with our presence here."

Startled by his words, she bolted to a sitting position, and her eyes darted around nervously. Daniel's arm pulled her back down.

"Daniel," she protested. Why was he so relaxed with two bears so close?

"Shhhh." He grinned broadly. "They're young. Their mother probably cast them out just recently. They won't bother us."

"Okay." She hesitated, then relaxed again. She wriggled to turn and face him, and entwined her arms around his neck. Daniel bent over her, closer to her face.

"Good morning." He smiled, and kissed her on the forehead.

"You're going to have to do better than that," Aimee scoffed with faked indignation. She pulled his face to her and kissed him soundly on the lips, enjoying the rough feel of his day-old growth of stubble against her skin. He apparently needed no further encouragement. He wrapped his arms around her and kissed her deeply, one hand on her hip, pulling her closer to him. Her body responded instantly. Delicious chills spread through her, and she clung to him with wild abandon, pressing her body to his wherever she could. God, how was it that he sent her mind and body spinning out of control like that? She had been kissed plenty of times, but this was a totally new experience. His hand at her waist stroked and kneaded, pulling her against his growing arousal, which sent new waves of desire through her.

Daniel pulled away abruptly. "It's a long way back to the cabin," he said in a sultry tone. He pushed himself up off the ground. Leaning over her, he kissed her once more, then whispered, "Not here," with a hint of regret in his voice.

"Are you still planning to take me to St. Louis?"

Daniel stared hard into her eyes. "For selfish reasons, I think

I may not be able to." He stood and ran a hand through his hair, then turned and headed for the horses grazing a short distance away.

Aimee sat up, admiring his backside as he walked off. Why was he holding back? It was obvious that he wanted her, so why did he pull away? Daniel wasn't taking her to St. Louis. That was one problem solved. Her other problem seemed to be much worse, though. He had said for selfish reasons he wouldn't take her away from here. Her heart sped up at the implication of those words. She had to stop thinking about what would happen at the end of her three months when Zach returned, and just enjoy the time she had left with Daniel.

With a long sigh, she left her warm spot, and walked on stiff legs to the creek to splash water on her face. The hot water the night before had definitely helped soothe the tightness in her muscles. She could walk the last of the stiffness out of her legs on the way back to the cabin.

* * *

Daniel found the horses grazing a short distance away from camp. He threw a saddle over the back of the first horse, and reached under the animal's belly for the cinch. He replayed the events of the last few days in his mind. He had been ready to take Aimee back to the city for her own sake, and now, in the course of one day, that had all changed. A month ago, it would have been easy to simply take her to his bed. It was different now. He finally admitted that he wanted her for his wife, not merely as a woman to share his blanket. He would protect her and keep her safe. She was much stronger than his mother had been. She could survive here. She didn't want to go back to the city. He wouldn't even consider the man she was supposed to marry. He had not come for her.

How might he claim her as his wife properly? She had no family he could go to. In the Shoshoni tradition, he would offer furs and meat to prove his ability as a provider to her kin. In the white man's world, he knew it was customary to ask the woman's father for her hand in marriage.

He finished saddling the horses. There was only one way. He had to abandon all tradition and simply take her as his wife, as Elk

165

Runner had suggested all along.

"Are we ready to go?" Aimee's question pulled Daniel out of his thoughts. He turned and smiled warmly.

* * *

Daniel chose a different, more direct route back to the Madison Valley. He stopped often to let Aimee off her horse and walk so her muscles wouldn't tighten up again. By late afternoon, the cabin came into view.

"Now that's a sight for sore eyes." She smiled at him.

As the horses splashed through the Gibbon River, she glanced longingly at the inlet of the Firehole. A bath would be great. She was covered in grime and trail dust. Turning her head, a wicked grin spread across Daniel's face. He guided his horse along the banks of the Madison until he reached the spot where he had tossed her in the river so many weeks ago.

"Why are we stopping here?" She raised her eyebrows, and Daniel dismounted his horse. He walked around to her side and wordlessly pulled her out of the saddle.

"Daniel, what . . .?" She couldn't finish her sentence. He strode a few feet into the river, and tossed her out into deeper water.

When her head emerged again, she shouted "Do you take some perverse pleasure in throwing me into this river?"

Daniel had already unbuckled the belt at his waist and was pulling his shirt off over his head. He quickly removed his moccasins and leggings, and dove in after her. When his head popped up in front of her, he snaked his arms around her waist.

"I have some unfinished business here." His voice had gone husky.

"Oh?" her heart began beating faster. She shivered in anticipation.

"Unfortunately, you're about to make a dishonest man out of me."

"What do you mean?" she frowned. Her hands slid up his chest and around his neck.

"The last time we were in this river together, I told you afterwards that I would not repeat my actions. Do you remember?"

166

"Yes." Aimee smiled. The day he nearly kissed her in the river. It seemed so long ago now. Where would this relationship be now if she hadn't told him to stop that day?

"Well, here we are again, and I wish to finish what I started then."

Daniel lowered his face to hers, and this time she didn't stiffen up, or tell him to stop. She buried her fingers in his hair, and met his hungry kiss with a moan.

The current carried them lazily while they were wrapped in each other's arms. When Daniel pulled back, she panted breathlessly. "How come you get to undress first, but I'm in my clothes?" she managed to whisper.

"Because I like the way your wet clothes cling to your body when you get out of the water." He flashed her a purely mischievous grin.

"Daniel, you are a . . ."

"Pig, I know," he finished her sentence for her. He kissed her again before maneuvering them to shore.

She climbed out of the water, and wrapped her arms around her waist. Her body shivered uncontrollably in the late afternoon breeze. The smoldering look in Daniel's eyes as he hoisted himself onto the riverbank was worth the cold.

"You better get to the cabin and warm up," he whispered, and wrapped his arms around her.

"What about you?" she asked between chattering teeth.

"I need to tend to the horses. I'll be along shortly." His hand cradled her cheek, and he kissed her gently one more time.

Aimee turned and ran for the cabin. She quickly stripped out of her wet clothes and wrapped herself in a blanket. She piled kindling in the hearth and set fire to it with her flint. After adding wood, a warm flame grew quickly, and she sat for a moment to absorb the fire's warmth. She rummaged through her pack for her last pair of clean underwear and bra. A set of her clothes was lying around outside somewhere. Hopefully they were still there from where she had dropped them two days ago when she ran from those trappers. She would have to look for them in the morning. The sun had already gone down.

With no clean shirt available, she slipped into one of

Daniel's homespun cotton shirts that hung on a peg on the wall. She rolled up the sleeves several times to free her hands. The shirt fell almost to her knees. Her eyes darted around the dark room, and lingered on her bed. With trembling hands, she lit the lantern on the table. She sliced some bread and meat, and set these on a plate. The cabin door creaked, and she spun around.

Chapter Seventeen

Aimee stood by the table. Daniel quietly opened the door and walked in. He hadn't dressed, and wore only his breechcloth. Her fingers dug into the wood. He hadn't yet looked her way. Silently, he tossed his shirt and leggings on his bunk, propped his bow and arrows by the door, and hung his pouches on the wall. Her heart stopped when he slowly turned. His heated gaze scanned her from top to bottom. Their eyes finally met. The dancing flames in the hearth reflected in Daniel's eyes, and the cabin grew much too warm all of a sudden. His silence, and his penetrating stare made her mouth go dry. She slowly walked toward him on rubbery legs. *I feel like a nervous bride on my wedding night.*

"Are you hungry?" she asked tentatively, and pointed at the food she had set out.

Daniel's hands framed her face, and he drew her to him. He claimed her mouth with possessive urgency. The intensity of his kiss stunned her. When he broke away seconds later, they both gasped for breath.

"Yes." Daniel's eyes locked onto hers, and he pulled her into his arms.

Yes, what?

She couldn't remember what she'd asked him. Did she even ask something? She placed her palms on his chest, feeling the strong beating of his heart, the warmth of his skin, and inhaled his masculine woodsy scent. She slid her hands up and around his neck, and Daniel's mouth found hers again. While the kiss a moment ago had been full of hunger, he now kissed her with agonizing slowness and deliberation, coaxing her lips apart as their

169

tongues met. Her head spun dizzily as shockwaves of desire reached each and every one of her nerve endings. She would have collapsed from pure pleasure if Daniel hadn't wrapped his arm around her waist. No one had ever made her feel this way before, nor had she ever been kissed like this. Her body had certainly never reacted this heatedly to anyone's kisses.

After several tantalizing minutes of exploring her mouth, Daniel trailed his lips all over her face and down her neck. His hands slowly moved up and down her back, caressing her tenderly, almost reverently. She shuddered under his touch. Goose bumps erupted all over her skin.

His exploring hands slid under the shirt, and she lifted her arms to help him slip the garment over her head. He let it fall to the ground. Her hands traced the contours of his chest, exploring his firm skin over taut, solid muscle. She inched her arms around his waist, her fingers exploring their way along his chiseled back, arms, and shoulders with feather light touches. He shuddered. How could a man this big and strong, who was able to kill another man at a moment's notice, be so tender at the same time?

"My body burns for you," Daniel said huskily against her lips. "I have dreamed of this moment since I first laid eyes on you." His kisses down her neck and his hands on her bare skin sent renewed ripples of desire through her.

"You have?"

His hand moved across her flat stomach and up her ribcage, and finally covered one of her breasts, his fingers stroking gently.

"How does this come off?" he whispered, and slipped his thumb under the shoulder strap on her bra. Aimee smiled seductively, and reached her hands behind her back to undo the hooks. Unashamed she slid the bra off her shoulders.

Daniel devoured her with his eyes, and groaned. "You're so beautiful." His voice was raspy.

"Daniel . . ." she whispered slowly.

"Hmm?" he asked absently, and stroked his thumbs across the top of her breasts. She found it harder and harder to breathe while his thumbs teased her nipples into hardened peaks, but she needed to say something.

"Daniel, I . . . I just want you to know that I'm not . . . oh

170

God." She squeezed her eyes shut at the sensations he awakened in her body. What she wanted to say became more difficult as his hands and mouth made every nerve ending on her skin come alive.

"Daniel, you're not the first man I've been with," she finally blurted out. "I just thought you should know."

He scooped her up in his arms and carried her to her bed, where he lay her down gently and covered her with his own body, bracing his weight with his elbows on either side of her. He kissed her again, long and gently, while slowly getting to know her body with his hands. His thumbs brushed across her nipples repeatedly, and Aimee moaned. She arched her back to his touch. His tender caresses left scorch marks on her skin. Nothing and no one had ever made her feel this good. With Brad, it had always been hurried. Daniel was in no rush as he slowly explored every inch of her with his large and capable hands.

"I will make you forget any other man you've been with," Daniel growled softly in her ear.

"You already have," she barely managed to respond. Daniel continued to kiss her neck and moved lower, kissing her shoulders, then the top of her breast.

She almost protested when his weight slid off her body, until she realized he was removing his breechcloth. He drew her into his arms an instant later and kissed her so deeply and with such hunger, it took her breath away, and sent her mind spinning into a dizzying vortex. She wound her arms tightly around his neck, and one leg around his lower back wanting to hold him to her forever.

He hesitated when he made contact with her bikini briefs. She slid her fingers down the elastic band and pushed them down. Daniel's hand was on hers as he followed her motion, helping her remove the offending underwear. His hand abandoned hers to slide slowly and torturously up her inner thigh. He drew her right nipple in his mouth and made gently circling motions with his tongue, while at the same time his fingers found her most intimate place. Aimee thought she was going to burst. She opened her legs to him, and met him with her hips.

"Daniel," she panted as his relentless, torturous exploration continued. "Please . . ."

Daniel moved on top of her again, and entered her slowly. Aimee couldn't take the slow sweet torture any longer. She was standing on the edge of something she couldn't define, and she wanted to let herself fall.

She wrapped her legs around his waist to draw him fully inside her. She gasped at the sensation of him filling her. Her body began to convulse almost instantly, and she fell over the edge as her senses exploded in a million brilliant stars.

Daniel moved slowly and rhythmically within her, his momentum building until he plunged deeply inside her. She arched her hips to meet each one of his thrusts. His mouth crushed down on hers when she felt his body shudder and he spent himself inside her.

"I have never known a woman like you."

Daniel lay on top of her, breathing hard, and nuzzled her neck. Her hands moved lazily up and down his sweat-dampened back, her eyes glazed over in wonder at what had just happened.

"I've never . . . you're amazing," she whispered in awe.

Daniel was still inside her, and Aimee kept her legs wrapped tightly around his middle, loving the feel of him there. When she moved her hip slightly, Daniel growled and in one quick movement rolled onto his back and pulled her on top of him.

She let out a playful cry, then sat up and straddled him, and moved seductively on top of him. To her surprised delight, he grew hard again inside her. He reached up and cupped both her breasts and squeezed and kneaded gently, as his hips began to thrust upward. She arched her back, leaning into his hands as she rode him thrust for thrust. Soon, she could feel the waves of another orgasm overtake her as Daniel took her over the edge once more.

Aimee collapsed on top of him.

"You are the most incredible man." She rolled off and snuggled herself against him, her head resting on his chest. As impossible as it seemed, she shuddered with renewed desire when she inhaled deeply of his woodsy scent that mingled with the musky odor of their lovemaking. Daniel glanced down at her, a thoroughly satisfied grin on his face.

"I am not good with words, but you make my heart sing,

Aimee." He kissed her forehead, and caressed her face. "I swore I would never have feelings like this for a white woman, but I was lost to you the moment I first saw you."

"Did you feel this way about . . . her?" she asked. This was probably not a good time to bring up the woman who hurt him, but the words were out before she could hold them back.

His body tensed.

"I thought I was in love with her," he finally said after a prolonged silence. "I was young and foolish. I had never been further east than St. Louis when my father took me to Philadelphia to meet his sister. It was a world I didn't even know existed. I was there for almost a year when I first met Emma." He smiled warmly at her and kissed her forehead repeatedly.

"Emma," she repeated the name.

"She was the daughter of one of the wealthier merchants in the city. I had never seen a more beautiful woman, but then my contact with white women was very limited." Daniel gave a short laugh. His eyes roamed over her face, and his hand moved to gently caress her shoulder and arm. "And now I found you. Emma hasn't entered my thoughts in weeks. My mind is consumed only by you. I don't even have words to describe what I feel for you." She raised her eyes to gaze into his. The warm glow she saw told her everything she needed to know, even without the words.

"I wish to tell you about her." Daniel held her gaze.

She shook her head slowly. "You don't have to do that." Her hand came up to touch his face. He covered it with his own.

"Yes, I do. I want you to know. I have never spoken to anyone about it. My father and Elk Runner know I thought myself in love and nothing came of it. They don't know the reason."

Aimee waited patiently while Daniel seemed to gather his thoughts.

"We met through a mutual acquaintance at a social gathering. She seemed as smitten with me as I was with her, and I called on her a few times. As I said, I had no experience in the ways of eastern ladies, and I chose to turn a blind eye to her delicate and frail ways. Growing up, my father has often told me of the gentle nature of a white woman raised in the city, and warned me not to

173

fall in love with one unless I planned to abandon my life in the mountains. He blames himself for my mother's death because he brought her here, but that's another story altogether." He took a deep breath.

I already know that story.

Aimee ran her hand down his jaw and along his neck, curling some strands of his hair around her fingers.

He continued. "I didn't listen to his advice. I was so taken with Emma, I became blind to everything else. I had visions of bringing her here, about how she would fall in love with the mountains." He scoffed. "I never saw that she couldn't stand to even get her shoes dusty. One day, I went to her home unannounced. A servant told me that she had gone to the stables. When I sought her out, she was there . . ." Daniel's voice hardened. His muscles tightened.

Aimee caressed his shoulder and kissed his chest. His fingers entwined in her hair as he held her tightly to him. "I called her name when I didn't see her at first. At the far end of the barn, in one of the empty horse stalls I saw her, clutching her dress to her body. She was obviously quite surprised to see me." Daniel let out another short disgusted laugh. "She asked me what I was doing here. That's when I saw him. William . . . something, I don't even recall his last name. By the looks of him he had just gotten dressed himself. I was overcome with rage, and ready to lunge at him, when she yelled at me to stop.

"I asked her how she could do such a thing, that I thought she loved me. She just laughed at me. She told me she could never love a heathen, that I was nothing but a filthy savage. She mocked me by saying she was merely using me to get the attention of William, and even thanked me that her plan had obviously worked. She started to scream. She called for help, yelling to anyone who would hear that I had attacked her. That I had . . . attacked her and intended to rape her, and William came to her rescue."

"Daniel," Aimee gasped. The savage look on his face reminded her of that first day, when he had looked at her with such hatred. Anger welled up inside her, at the thought of it. She wanted to give that little twit a piece of her mind.

"Wasn't it obvious what really happened?" she asked. It was a simple matter to resolve, she reasoned. *Yes, but not in this time.* There was no such thing as DNA testing and forensic evidence.

Daniel snorted. "My word against hers? No one would believe me. So I ran," Daniel continued, as if speaking to himself. "I've never run from anything before or since, but that day I ran. I didn't stop to bid my aunt farewell. I ran straight back here, and I've never looked back."

"I see why that would leave you bitter toward white women," Aimee said simply. "I was really shocked those first few days after you found me, when you seemed to absolutely hate me."

"The only thing you and she have in common is your fair skin," Daniel reassured her. "I wanted to hate you simply for that – that you are a white woman. I had all but forgotten Emma, but seeing you brought all those unpleasant memories back. And I was angry with myself because I had these powerful feelings for you right from the start. It left me confused, and I lashed out in anger. I swore I would never be fooled by the lying, deceptive ways of a white woman again."

It was her turn to stiffen. Wasn't that exactly what she was doing? Everything about her was a lie. How would Daniel react if he ever found out the truth about her? A shiver ran down her spine.

Daniel bent his head and kissed her, a languid gentle kiss that melted her from the inside out.

"I know now that my infatuation with Emma was only that. It wasn't love. And I didn't love Morning Fawn. I was fond of her, but my mind and body didn't burn for her the way I burn for you. I have fought my affection for you all these weeks. I can't fight it anymore. You are my heart song," he whispered.

"I love you, Daniel," she said simply, a sad note in her voice.

"You are a mystery I can't explain, and I will wait until you enlighten me. You are the bravest, strongest, and most beautiful woman I have ever known. It is selfish of me to ask you to stay here in the mountains with me."

Aimee tried to keep the tears from flowing, but it was no use. In a little over a month she would be leaving, never to return again. She wasn't free to tell him this, though. She'd made a

175

promise. What was she going to do? She was happier than she had ever been in her life, and at the same time she was miserable for the secret she carried with her. Daniel lifted her chin with gentle fingers, and wiped the tears from her eyes.

"If you don't wish to stay in the mountains, I'll go to the city with you" he said soberly.

"You would do that for me?"

"I would."

"I could never ask you to do that." She shook her head. "You are a part of these mountains, and they are a part of you."

"You are part of me. You belong to me now," Daniel said softly, stroking her cheek.

"Let's not talk about this, okay?" She took a deep breath, and tried to smile. "Can we just live in the moment, and not think about what might happen tomorrow. We're together right now, and that's what matters to me, not what might be in the future."

Daniel forehead wrinkled, and his brows drew together.

"Aimee." He inhaled slowly. "The man you are promised to, he is not coming for you."

"I told you that a long time ago." *Why is he bringing that up?*

"I wish to be your man . . . your husband. I want you for my wife." He gazed intently at her. His eyes spoke of hope and expectation.

Her own eyes widened in surprise.

"You want what?" She exhaled incredulously. Her heart pounded in her chest, and her mind raced so fast, she couldn't hold on to one coherent thought.

"I am a good provider, and I will protect you with my life," Daniel stated passionately. He raised himself up on one elbow, and leaned toward her. "I was also wrong to think you could not survive here. You have proven repeatedly that you can."

His hand cradled her cheek and he kissed her again.

Aimee squeezed her eyes shut to hold back the tears. This was killing her. Her heart screamed to tell him yes, she would love nothing more than to be his wife. Her mind told her this was insanity. How could she say she'd be his wife and then disappear? Why was fate so cruel?

"There are so many things about me that you don't know,"

she whispered. *Should I tell him?* God, this was torture.

"All I know is that I can't give you up. You belong with me." He rolled on top of her and claimed her mouth possessively. This time there was no slow and sensuous lovemaking as he pushed her legs apart, and entered her with one swift thrust. With this joining she felt branded, and Aimee surrendered herself completely as silent tears streamed down her face.

Chapter Eighteen

Aimee had never been more happy and miserable all at the same time in her entire life. She accompanied Daniel wherever he went. They would scout rivers and tributaries for beaver habitat in the morning, or go on hunting forays. He insisted on teaching her how to load and shoot the rifle, and how to use a knife and tomahawk to defend herself. She surprised him with some self-defense moves of her own. He started teaching her the language of the Shoshoni, showed her how to tan hides and make arrowheads from obsidian. After supper they would sit together outside the cabin, or walk the riverbank until the sun went down, and often made love late into the night.

One evening after they'd eaten and walked down to the banks of the Madison, Daniel stopped abruptly. With his hands on her upper arms, he turned her to face him. His eyes roamed over her face for a few moments, as if he was searching intently for something.

"What?" She shrugged her shoulders when he didn't say anything.

"Are you with child?" he blurted out.

"Am I what?" she asked, taken aback at the unexpected question. Then she laughed. "Good God, no I'm not pregnant. Why would you think that?"

"Elk Runner has often complained that during the months Little Bird carries a child, she is always weepy and absent-minded. And you haven't bled."

"You think I'm weepy and absent-minded?"

"You have been." Daniel nodded. "If you are carrying my

child, I will take you to the city. I will not let you birth a baby here in the wilderness."

From the serious look in his eyes, there was no doubt that he was thinking about his mother.

"Daniel." Aimee rested her hands on his chest, and met his stare. "First of all, you can relax. I'm not pregnant, I swear." *The convenience of modern contraceptives.* Her preferred choice of birth control was the injectable kind. She found this form easier to manage, and it had the added convenience of no monthly flows. She hated going backpacking and being on her period.

"And second," she continued, "I thought you were over your hang-up about the dangers of the wilderness to me. You said yourself I've proven myself to you. And I am as healthy as a horse."

"Then why have you not had your woman's time?" he prodded. "I have shared your bed for many weeks, and it's something I would have noticed."

"I can't explain that to you right now. Maybe some other time." She sadly lowered her gaze. What else could she say?

"It's all right, Aimee," Daniel said softly. He held the side of her face in one hand, and stroked her cheek with his thumb. "I don't care if you are unable to conceive children. I love you no matter what."

Aimee avoided his gaze. Well, maybe that was a convenient way to end this topic.

"I love you, too, Daniel." She leaned up to kiss him. *Why couldn't I have met you 200 years from now?*

Daniel took her hand and they continued their stroll along the riverbank.

"My father will be back any day now." He squeezed her hand. "I will explain to him that you're my wife."

Aimee stared across the river. Her body stiffened. Her time here was coming to an end, but hearing Daniel confirm it made it more real.

"He will accept you," he added quickly.

She kept quiet and chewed on her lower lip. *I already know your father. And when he returns, my world will end.*

"I also plan to start building our own cabin before winter sets

179

in. Next summer I will take you to St. Louis, and we can get married in the white man's way if you wish."

Aimee swallowed back the lump in her throat. *I'm not going to be here come winter, much less next summer!* Her mind screamed.

"Daniel." She stopped and turned to face him fully. "I want you to know that no matter what happens in the future, I will always love you. I've never loved anyone the way I love you. Please don't ever forget that." Tears threatened to spill down her face, and she blinked rapidly.

"Aimee, what's wrong? You talk in riddles. Do you have the power to look into the future?" He chuckled. "Because if you do, could you tell me if it's going to be a good trapping season this winter?"

He was trying so hard to cheer her up that she couldn't help but smile. She sucked in a deep breath, then put her hands to her forehead, and pretended to concentrate hard. "It's going to be the best trapping season you've ever had. The beavers are going to line up outside your door."

He hugged her to him tightly. Just then, a streak of lightning illuminated the sky.

"There's going to be a big storm tonight. We'd better get back to the cabin."

* * *

The next morning the ground outside had turned to mud. Afternoon thunderstorms were a common occurrence, but the rain last night was unrelenting. Daniel announced it would be best if he went out alone that morning to check on some of his traps.

"I'll be back soon." He kissed her on the forehead as he turned to leave. Aimee threw her arms around his neck and held him tight.

"I love you," she said passionately.

He lifted her off the ground and pulled her to him. Aimee clung to him as if he would vanish if she let go. Daniel had to pry her off him. He gave her a perplexed look before he kissed her.

"You are my heart song," he whispered and set her away from him. "I won't be gone long."

Aimee paced the cabin restlessly, too fidgety to focus on any tasks. The storm had played havoc with her nerves. By mid-morning, she couldn't stay in the cabin any longer. A walk would calm her down. She had done a lot of thinking over the last few weeks. Lying awake in the night, listening to the storm, she had finally come to a firm decision. Nothing she had ever experienced in life came close to what she felt when she was with Daniel. How could she possibly give that – him – up to go back to a life she didn't particularly enjoy? Here, in this time and in this place, with this man, she was completely alive. It's where she was meant to be. She did not want to go back to her own time. She had nothing to go back to. She would miss her best friend, Jana, and triple chocolate fudge ice cream. But in her heart she knew that her life was here with Daniel.

Aimee opened the cabin door to head out, only to stagger back in surprise and shock. In the doorway stood Zachariah Osborne.

"Miss Donovan!" he exclaimed. "It is so good to see you. I am so relieved to find you safe and sound. I must say, I've been worried that I made the right decision in sending you here."

"Zach," she said with a half-smile, recovering from her surprise. The day she'd been dreading had arrived. She moved aside so he could enter.

He perused her from top to bottom. "You look well," he remarked. "Maybe a bit thinner than when I last saw you," he added. "How's that son of mine been treating you? I hope he wasn't too gruff with you. I probably didn't tell you enough about Daniel to prepare you, but I hope he took good care of you."

"Yes, very well." She studied the man. His grizzled hair must have been a dark blond or brown at some point. His height and frame was much like Daniel. His face was wrinkled from a lifetime spent outdoors in the sun, but his skin tone was lighter than his son's. She figured Daniel must have gotten his olive complexion and black hair from his French mother.

"He doesn't know anything, I hope? You were able to keep the secret?"

"He doesn't know anything," she confirmed. "It's been hard because my appearance here is something I couldn't quite explain, and he's wondering about it, but to his credit he hasn't

181

been pushy to find out."

"Well good, I want to keep it that way." Zach smiled. "Go gather your belongings and I'll send you home now, before he comes back."

Zach pulled something from the leather pouch around his neck. She recognized the shriveled-up ugly snakehead with the beady red eyes – the object she had scoffed and laughed at three months ago when he'd first shown it to her. It was the device that allowed him to time travel. How was it even possible to time travel? It was something that could probably never be explained. All she could do was accept it.

"How will you explain my sudden disappearance?" she asked while she kept a wary eye on the snakehead. All she had to do was touch the right eye of the snake, and she would be transported back to her own time.

"Won't have to," Zach waved a dismissive hand in front of his face. "I'm leaving here as soon as I send you back, and won't show up again for another day or two. That way there's no connection between us."

"Zach," she said slowly, tentatively. "I have something to tell you."

"What is it? Come on girl, we don't have much time."

"I don't want to go back to my time," Aimee blurted out.

"What?" Zach boomed in disbelief. "What the hell are you talking about?"

"I love Daniel, and I love it here. I don't want to leave him, or this time and place."

"You can't stay here, Miss Donovan," Zach said firmly, a hard look on his face. "I've told you before that this is no permanent place for a woman. And I know for a fact that Daniel would wholeheartedly agree with me. You two may have . . . ahhh . . . developed a certain fondness for each other." He rubbed his chin as if considering this possibility. "But Daniel would not want you to stay here. I was happy to make your wish come true to experience the wilderness for a while, but now you need to get back to your own time."

"Please, Zach. I've proven I can survive here. Daniel and I love each other." Her voice sounded desperate.

"I . . . I can't." Zach hesitated for a moment. "I can't put my boy through the same pain I went through when I lost his mother."

"I'm not like your wife!" Her voice went shrill out of desperation. "Don't you see that if you send me back, you will be hurting your son?"

Zach seemed to consider this. "Daniel swore he would never bring a woman to live here. He knows better. I'm sorry my son may have used you, Miss Donovan."

"He didn't use me! Ask him yourself," she pleaded, tears of frustration streaming down her face.

"I can't ask him without him finding out about the time travel device. I'm not passing this thing on to him when I die. It ends here with me."

"Why won't you be honest with him? Why can't he know about this?"

"He doesn't need to know about it now, at this point in his life. I wanted to tell him over the years, but it was never the right time. Now he may not ever forgive me if I tell him." Zach looked almost panicked.

"What are you afraid of?" Aimee pressed.

"How is he going to react if I tell him he was born in the year 1985? He believes he is part of these mountains, and that his mother died here, giving birth to him. He won't accept it."

"He is part of these mountains. Telling him the circumstances of his birth won't change that. He's stronger than you think," she argued. "He deserves to know the truth."

"Daniel has been happy here all his life. Why would I want to shatter his world now?"

"You may have already done that," she said. "By sending me here. He has questions, and I couldn't give him any answers. If I suddenly disappear again, how will he react to that? Have you even thought about that?"

"I never imagined there would be feelings between the two of you," Zach conceded. "He was in love with a white girl once. He hasn't told me much, but he came back from Philadelphia abruptly, and swore off all white women. So you see, I never thought much about you and him."

183

"Please, Zach," she pleaded again. "You can't do this. It's my choice to want to stay here."

Zach quickly scanned the cabin for her things. Gathering up what he could find, he stuffed it in her backpack.

"It's time." He thrust the pack in her arms. "I made my mistake with Marie by bringing her here. I will not have you on my conscience, as well. I promised you three months in the wilderness. I gave you that. Now you need to return to the safety of your own time. We stick to our original agreement." He held the snake out to her. "Touch the right eye."

Aimee darted past him toward the cabin door. Zack grabbed her arm. "I'm sorry you're not making this easy." Holding her arm firmly, Zach touched his own finger to the snake's right eye. Instantly, the world went black.

Chapter Nineteen

Aimee slowly opened her eyes. The loud noise of cars and machinery penetrated her consciousness, making her head throb and ears ring. She coughed when she inhaled the foul smell of engine exhaust. With a groan, she raised herself to a sitting position, and realized she was in a parking garage. The echoing sounds of screeching tires, engines rumbling, and blasting car horns all around her were deafening. She held a hand to the side of her head and sat up fully, the concrete beneath her hard and cold. The foul smell burned her throat and lungs, and her eyes stung. Her backpack rested against her feet. A piece of paper protruded from the opening. She reached for it and read the simple words. *This is for the best. I hope you understand.*

She crumpled up the paper and threw it in frustration.

"No," she yelled, her voice reverberating off the walls in the parking structure. Tears streamed down her face. "No, no, no . . . oh God. Daniel!" The distant sound of a jackhammer resonated like gunshots through her breaking heart.

A man in blue scrubs ran to her.

"Miss, are you ok?" he asked, looking down at her sitting on the dirty concrete floor. "Aimee?" His eyes widened in recognition.

She raised her head and recognized him as one of the ward nurses at the hospital.

"Are you all right?" he asked. He knelt in front of her to inspect her more closely. Concern filled his eyes.

"Where are we?" she asked. She struggled to stand on her feet, and fought the dizziness in her head.

"The parking garage at the hospital," he answered, a perplexed frown on his face. His eyebrows narrowed. "Can I do something for you, call someone?"

"No," she said quickly. "I just need to get home," she whispered.

"Do you need a lift?"

"Yeah . . . yeah, that would be great," she answered vaguely. After three months, she didn't expect to find her car here anymore. "Thanks, Eric."

"Sure, don't mention it." He kept giving her odd sideways looks.

She robotically followed him to his car, gave him quick directions to her condo in Yorba Linda, and then simply stared unseeing out the window in a daze for the entire twenty minute ride home. The sounds of everyday modern life seemed foreign to her. The hurried pace of throngs of cars on the freeway and roads left her feeling exhausted. Life shouldn't move at such speeds.

"Are you sure you'll be all right?" Eric called to her once more as he pulled into a parking spot in the condominium complex. She opened the passenger door of his blue sedan and climbed out wordlessly.

"I'll be fine. Thanks for bringing me home. Please don't tell anyone you saw me." She fought hard to keep her voice from cracking.

Eric gave her one more confused look, and simply nodded before backing his car out of the parking space.

Aimee inhaled a deep breath, and walked up the narrow cement walkway to her condo that she shared with Jana. The summer annuals they had planted a few weeks before she had left were in full bloom, looking as nice as the day they went into the ground. This was rather odd. After three months in the summer heat, it was usually time to replace them again.

She felt under the fake landscape rock just outside the front door for the spare key she and Jana always kept there. She had no idea what to expect as she turned the key in the lock.

Everything appeared the same as she remembered. Solemnly, she walked into the bright living room. The beige carpet had recently been vacuumed, and the pillows on the plush off-white sectional couch were fluffed up invitingly. Several copies of *Backpacker* magazine were laid out on the glass-covered coffee table. The air conditioner hummed to life.

Aimee dropped her backpack by the door and listlessly sank onto the couch. She pushed her worn and dirty hiking boots off her feet, and tucked her legs up under her. Grabbing one of the pillows, she hugged it tightly to her chest and began to sob. Her gaze drifted to the Thomas Moran painting of the Grand Canyon of the Yellowstone that hung over the gas fireplace mantle. She stared at it until her vision blurred. Tears pooled in her eyes. They spilled onto her cheek and flowed freely down her face. She sobbed Daniel's name.

She woke with a start when the front door clicked open and slammed shut. It took a few seconds for reality to set in as the events of the day flooded back into her mind. A new wave of grief rocked her. She blinked her tear-swollen eyes and blinked to see Jana standing there, open-mouthed.

"Ohmygod, Aimee!" Jana screeched, and ran over to sit beside her on the couch. She pulled her into a bear hug. "Where have you been? We've been so worried."

Aimee's body remained limp in her friend's fierce embrace. Jana drew away and stared. Her eyes widened and swept over her, taking in her appearance with a concerned look on her face.

"What day is it?" Aimee's face was blank, her eyes unfocused.

"It's Monday," Jana said in confusion. "Where have you been the last two weeks? Brad filed a missing person's report and everything. We thought you'd been kidnapped or something."

"Two weeks?" Aimee whispered absently.

"What happened to you? You look like hell." Jana remarked. Her hands flew to her face. "Oh my God! You were kidnapped, weren't you?"

Aimee shook her head in slow motion. "I . . . I just had to get away for a while."

Jana paused. "Without a word to anyone? No notice at work or anything? What were you thinking?" She wore an uneasy smile. "Aimee, what is going on? You look like someone died."

Aimee didn't respond. Her gritty eyes stayed unfocused on her friend.

"What happened to your hair? It looks longer. And your face is all tanned, and you've lost weight. Where were you?" Jana prodded.

"Yellowstone." Aimee's voice cracked. "I went to Yellowstone."

"But we were going to leave on our trip this week. Couldn't you have waited?"

"I need to get back," she said suddenly, and stared blankly at Jana through swollen, gritty eyes.

Jana shook her head, her eyebrows drawn together. "Get back where?"

"Yellowstone. I need to get back."

"If you still want to go, I haven't cancelled our plane tickets yet," Jana said hesitantly. "The flight is tomorrow morning, remember?"

"Daniel's waiting for me. He's got to be worried where I am," Aimee said as if talking to herself.

Jana picked up one of Aimee's limp hands and squeezed it. "Who is Daniel?"

"My husband . . . Daniel's my husband, and I need to get back to him." Fresh tears rolled down her cheeks.

Jana stared dumbfounded. "Are you going into shock? I think we need to get you to the hospital." She bolted from the couch. "Let me call Brad. He'll be so glad to find you safe."

"No!" Aimee sprang up from her seat to stop Jana from reaching the phone. "I don't want to see him. Please," she pleaded.

Jana looked at her hard. "Okay, I won't call him . . . yet. But, Aimee, you're scaring me. This is not like you."

"You're right. I don't belong here. My life is with Daniel."

"Okay," Jana said slowly. She inhaled deeply. "You look like you could use a shower," she offered. "How about I order a pizza while you get cleaned up, and then we'll talk, all right?"

* * *

Aimee stood in the doorway of her bedroom, and looked around without focusing on anything. Everything appeared as it had been the afternoon she left to see Zach Osborne at the hospital. To her, that had been three months ago. But in this time, according to what Jana said, she had only been gone two weeks. Time seemed to move in slow motion as she walked into the adjoining bathroom and removed her worn and dirty clothes. She stepped into the shower, and stood under the hot water spray. Her tears mixed with the water cascading down her face. Aimee squeezed her eyes shut, and her body began to shudder.

"Daniel!" she screamed his name in anguish. "Nooooo! Why did you do this to me, Zach? Why?" She sobbed, and fell back against the shower wall. She slid down onto the cold tile floor, her knees drawn up to her chest. Burying her face in her hands, she cried loud and hard.

"Are you okay in there?" Jana's muffled voice called from outside the door. "Aimee?"

An icy sensation squeezed her heart, radiating from the center of her body outward into her arms and legs. She struggled to draw a breath. Her heart raced, and her chest tightened. Breathing became painful. She didn't care. Nothing mattered anymore. Everything had been taken from her. Vaguely she heard the shower door open. The water stopped flowing, and someone wrapped a towel around her.

"Aimee, you're scaring the hell out of me." Jana's voice sounded far away. "I'm going to take you to the hospital."

Arms tried to lift her up from her position on the shower floor. They were not the strong arms she yearned for.

"Aimee, please. Should I call 911?" Jana's terrified voice finally prompted Aimee to glance up.

"No. No hospital. Please." Her own voice sounded foreign in her ears.

"Then please get up and out of this shower. Let's get you dried off and dressed."

Trembling, Aimee slowly rose from the ground with Jana's supportive arms around her. She managed to stumble out of the shower. She felt numb all over.

"I'll get some clothes for you." Jana hurried into the bedroom.

Aimee stood before the vanity mirror. She stared blankly at

her reflection. She barely recognized herself. Her face and arms were tanned from hours in the sun. Her hair was definitely longer, and her entire body had a much leaner, toned appearance. Three months of working long days without modern equipment, along with a diet of wholesome natural foods had done to her body what years of going to a gym couldn't do. She let out a bitter half laugh, half sob at the thought.

Jana reappeared with fresh underwear, pajama pants and a tank top, and gave her an encouraging smile. "I'll be right outside if you need me. Get dressed and we'll talk if you're up to it." Aimee nodded solemnly.

She dried herself, the sensation of the plush fabric of the towel foreign on her skin. How often over the last three months had she wished for a soft towel rather than a scratchy blanket to dry herself after washing? *Be careful what you wish for.* She inhaled the fresh laundered smell of the towel, but it was a different scent she ached for.

Please, Zach, I'll gladly give all of this up. Please come back for me. I want to go home to Daniel. Aimee squeezed her eyes shut, but it didn't prevent the tears from escaping down her cheeks. She had to tell Jana the truth. She had to make her believe what had happened. And she had to find a way to get back to Daniel.

"Hey, feeling better?" Jana asked brightly when Aimee came down the stairs and walked into the living room. "The pizza should be here in a few minutes."

Aimee's face remained stoic.

"Sit down, Jana. I have a long story to tell you, and I just need you to listen, no matter how unbelievable it sounds, okay?"

"Umm . . . sure." Jana sat beside her on the couch and stared at her with an uneasy smile.

Aimee started at the beginning with that first night in the ER and meeting Zach. She left nothing out, and concluded with her return a few hours ago to this time. Jana listened, open-mouthed. The pizza delivery boy interrupted them momentarily, but the meal was forgotten while Aimee told her story.

"I don't expect you to believe me," Aimee finished. "I didn't believe any of it either, until it actually happened. But it did." She stared at Jana. "It did happen, and I met the most wonderful man in the world, and . . . and . . . now he's gone forever." The tears flowed again, and her voice cracked.

"Oh, Aimee." Jana hugged her friend close. "I remember when your parents died. It was awful. You were distraught then, too, but," Jana paused as if searching for the right words. "This . . . the way you're shutting down . . . frankly it's scaring the life out of me."

Aimee didn't respond. She sobbed on her friend's shoulder. Her body shuddered violently.

"I can prove to you that Daniel was real." She looked up suddenly with a hiccup and raspy voice. "According to Zach, he was born here in California, I think at Anaheim Memorial. Is there a way to access the medical records archives from twenty-five years ago?"

"This sounds so weird, Aimee." Jana shook her head. "You're saying this guy lived in the past, but was born in the present? Do you realize they'll lock you up in the psych ward if you talk like that?"

"I'm not crazy," Aimee whispered.

"I know that," Jana reassured her. She was silent for a moment. "Listen, I think I know someone who works in the records department at the hospital. Let me make a phone call, and we'll look into this. It's important to you, so it's important to me."

"You're the best friend in the world."

A half hour later, Jana hung up the phone. "I talked to Allison in the HI department. She said it might take some time, but she'll research it. If she can't find anything in the computer, we may have to see if someone can look up an actual file at Anaheim Memorial."

"Thank you."

"It might take her a few days to get back to me. Did you still want to catch that flight tomorrow? If so, I need to pack."

"It won't be the backpacking trip we planned," Aimee said. "But yes, I need to get back there. Only for a few days."

"Okay."

Aimee slept fitfully in her bed that night. She woke

frequently, sobbing. Several times she called out Daniel's name in agony.

The next morning, as Aimee and Jana headed for the airport, Jana asked, "don't you want to call Brad and at least tell him you're okay?"

"No." Aimee shook her head. "I'm not ready to face him." She looked Jana squarely in the eye. "I broke it off with him before I went to see Zach at the hospital, before I ever met . . . Daniel." Fresh tears threatened to spill out of her eyes. "Brad was smothering me, controlling my life. I couldn't take it anymore."

"I know that. I've seen it for a long time. I should have said something to you a long time ago. I never liked the way he treated you. He never mentioned you had broken the engagement."

"I did. I gave him back his ring." She held her face in her hands and cried quietly.

"My God, Aimee, this guy, whoever he is, has really gotten under your skin, hasn't he?" Jana said sympathetically. "I heard you cry out to him last night." She squeezed Aimee's hand. "What will you do if you find him?"

"I'm not going to find him, Jana," Aimee cried. "He's long dead. Don't you understand?" Aimee had really hoped that Jana would believe her.

"Right, the time travel thing."

"You of all people have to believe me," Aimee pleaded. "How do you explain my longer hair, and everything else about me that has changed? That didn't happen in two weeks. Those changes happened over three months, the three months I spent in Yellowstone in 1810 . . . with Daniel."

Jana seemed to think this over for a minute. "Suppose I do believe you," she said tentatively. "What exactly are you hoping to find when we get there?"

"I don't know." Aimee sighed. "Somehow I think it'll make me feel closer to him." She stared out the window of the cab, not really seeing anything at all. She let the tears roll down her face in silence.

* * *

They landed at Jackson airport in Wyoming, rented a car, and drove north to get to the park. Aimee stared silently out the window while Jana drove. The grandeur of the snow-capped Teton mountain range went unnoticed, and there was none of their usual excitement as they entered the park through the south entrance gate. From there, it took them the better part of three hours to get to their destination.

As they approached the Madison Junction area, Aimee said, "Pull into the ranger station parking lot."

Jana barely had the chance to put the car in park before Aimee rushed out the door. She made her way down the gravel walkway and stood next to the log cabin ranger station and bookstore, looking across the Madison Valley. New tears flooded her eyes. Up on the rise of her familiar meadow, Aimee gazed down at the river.

"This is where Daniel's cabin was," she said quietly, distantly. "This is where I've been for the last three months."

She walked toward the river. Gone was the pristine state of the meadow and riverbank. In its stead were several well-worn trails where countless tourists had trampled the grass. Aimee stopped at the river's edge, and gazed longingly into the water. This was where Daniel had forced her out of the river. She smiled slightly at the memory. Back then she thought he didn't like her.

"Oh, Daniel, what became of you," she said quietly. Impossible as she thought it was, she cried again in earnest.

"Can someone dehydrate from crying too much?" Jana asked teasingly.

"It hurts so much," Aimee sobbed. Her voice was raspy, and the tears streamed freely down her face. She sank into the grass and put her face in her hands. Several people strolling the riverbank stared. Jana sank down into the grass and held her tight. Tears trickled down Jana's face as well.

"Is everything okay?" someone asked.

Jana responded quietly, "she lost a friend, and this was their favorite place."

"Oh, I'm sorry," the tourist said, and stared at Aimee with pity before moving on.

"Aimee, we really should get going," Jana finally said. "We can go and get a hotel room in West Yellowstone. It's closer than driving all the way back to Jackson tonight."

"I can't leave." Aimee's voice was barely above a whisper. "I can't." She sniffled and wiped her nose along her shirtsleeve.

"We have to, Aimee. We can't stay here," Jana said gently. "It's time to let go." She stood up and stretched, then gently pulled on Aimee's arm.

Aimee stood slowly, and stared at the peacefulness of the meandering river. Every now and then, a circular ripple appeared on the water's surface as hungry fish bobbed their heads out of the water to snap at one of the countless evening bugs that swarmed the river. Swallows darted up and down over the water to take their share of the insect feast in the dimming light.

"Daniel," she called. "Daniel, I love you . . . you are my heart song." She had no more tears left in her. She was hollow, empty. Something squeezed her heart as if wringing out a sponge, wringing out all the happiness. Reluctantly, she allowed Jana to take her by the arm, and with her head bent toward her chest, she turned and walked back up the slope toward the parking lot.

Chapter Twenty

Three days later, back in California, Jana received a phone call from her friend Allison in the health information department at the hospital.

"Hey Jana, I have some information on that patient you were asking about."

Jana's heart rate sped up in surprise. "Oh? What did you find out?"

"Well, there was nothing in the computer system, so I made a call to someone in HI at Anaheim Memorial. She did me a huge favor and went into their archives." She hesitated, then went on, "Please, if any of this gets out, both her and my jobs are toast, you know that, right?"

"I'm aware we're breaching patient confidentiality, Allison." Jana sighed impatiently. "This is really important, and I swear to you that no one is going to find out."

"Okay." Allison sounded eager to spill the information she had. "Well, this is a really strange case. Twenty-five years ago, on January 20th, 1985, a man named Zachariah Osborne brought his wife Marie Osborne to the emergency room. The woman was in labor. She had a seizure brought on by eclampsia, and the seizure caused a brain aneurysm. They were able to take her baby by C-section before she died. It was a boy. The birth certificate has his name listed as Daniel Osborne."

Jana inhaled sharply. "You're kidding me."

"I thought that was information you wanted."

"I don't know what I was expecting."

"Well, here's the really weird part. The man disappeared not minutes after his wife died," Allison paused for dramatic effect. "And not only him, but his baby and his dead wife disappeared along with him . . . poof . . . not a trace. The little information on his paperwork has a fake address and nothing else."

"Wow, that is weird." *My God, Aimee's story is panning out.*

"Why did you want to know about this case?" Allison asked. "It's like something out of the twilight zone."

"Yeah," Jana said absently. "Look, Allison, I really, really appreciate this. I owe you big time. I need to go." Without further explanation, she hung up. She stared out the kitchen window for a few moments, digesting the information she just received. So, this Daniel Osborne really did exist. But did it mean that he was from a different time? It sure corroborated the story Aimee had told her.

She headed up the stairs to Aimee's bedroom. Since coming home from their very brief visit to Yellowstone, Aimee had pretty much shut herself in her room. She came out only to use the bathroom, and Jana had to almost force her to come to the kitchen for something to eat.

Jana was lost as to what to do about Aimee's depression. Aimee was her best friend, and in all the years growing up, high school and the dramas of teenage breakups, losing her parents, and going to nursing school together, she had always envied Aimee's positive outlook on life. This experience, whatever it was that she had experienced, was killing her. And Jana didn't know what to do about it.

She took a deep breath, and knocked softly on Aimee's bedroom door. She waited but received no answer, so she quietly entered. Aimee lay in a fetal position on her bed. She was dressed in the same pajamas she had worn for the last two days, and hugged her pillow close.

"Aimee?" she called softly. "Are you awake?"

"I'm not hungry," Aimee's muffled voice responded automatically.

"Good, because I didn't bring you any food," Jana said lightly. "I just got off the phone with Allison."

No response.

"Remember?" She prodded, and sat on the bed. "Allison

from HI at the hospital."

No response.

"Aimee, I believe you." She tried a different tactic. "There is a record of a Daniel Osborne born on January 20th, 1985."

Aimee turned her head. Bloodshot eyes blinked up at Jana.

"The mother died due to complications, and then everyone - the father, dead mother, and baby – they all disappeared and haven't been seen or heard from again. Aimee, I believe your story is true." Jana squeezed Aimee's hand.

"You believe me?" Aimee asked tentatively. "Daniel is not a figment of my imagination. He is . . . was . . . real!" Aimee sat up, and looked at her through swollen eyes.

Jana hugged her close. "I believe you that you went back in time and spent three months with him. As crazy and unimaginable as it sounds, I believe everything you've told me."

"Thank you," Aimee said with a relieved sigh. She raised herself to a sitting position. "I just needed you to believe me. I didn't make it up, I didn't make Daniel up, and I didn't make up how wonderful it was being with him."

After a long silence, Jana tentatively asked, "What happens now, Aimee? You can't go on like this. Frankly, you're scaring me to death."

"I don't know," Aimee sighed. "All I do is think about him, what became of him. He was the best thing that has ever happened to me. He was so right. Everything I experienced in that time felt so right. I am so out of place here." Her shoulders slumped.

"Well, it's natural to grieve when you lose someone. But you are still alive, and you have to go on living. What can I do to help you get on with your life?"

"I just need more time." Aimee sounded as if she was trying to convince herself as well as Jana.

"I will do anything for you, you know that, right? I just want the old you back."

"I'll try to be more cheerful."

"Just come back to the land of the living, okay?"

"I'll try."

"Then come down to the kitchen and have something to

eat," Jana coaxed. "I haven't touched that triple fudge chocolate ice cream in the freezer, but I can't hold out much longer. How about we have some of that?"

After a long pause, Aimee sighed and got up off the bed. "Okay," she said slowly. "You've hit on my weak spot."

They headed down the stairs to the kitchen. Jana reached for the container of ice cream in the freezer, and scooped some into two bowls.

"What did you do in Yellowstone for three months without ice cream?" she asked lightly. "You always swore you'd never be able to survive without that for very long."

"I found a new passion," Aimee said quietly. "Something much more delicious than ice cream."

Jana smiled at her.

"Tell me more about him." At least she had Aimee talking. Hopefully asking questions about this Daniel person wouldn't turn the waterworks on again.

Aimee told her in greater detail about Daniel and their budding relationship.

"Sounds like something out of a romance novel," Jana said. "The dark and mysterious hero rescues damsel in distress and sweeps her off her feet." She made a dramatic sweep of her hand through the air.

"Something like that. I never believed in love at first sight, but I was a goner the moment I first saw him. He wasn't too friendly at first, but later I found out it was because he was attracted to me, too, but didn't quite know how to deal with it." Aimee gave a short, sad little laugh. "You know, he asked me the day before Zach showed up if I was pregnant."

Jana's eyes widened.

"Now I wish I was. Then at least I could have a part of him with me."

"Why would he ask you that?" Jana asked. Then understanding dawned on her face. "Oh yeah, right. Depo . . . no periods. I guess he must have wondered about that, huh? How did you explain that one to him?" she grinned.

"I didn't." Aimee sighed. "Like most everything else I ever told him, I either modified and stretched the truths, or avoided the subject. Not once was I ever completely honest with him. Except when I told him I love him."

"So, if he really loves you, why doesn't he just time travel here?"

"I told you, his father never told him about the time travel thing. And Zach told me he was through time traveling, and said it just wasn't the natural order of things. He's always felt uncomfortable with it. He was grateful that it saved his son when he was born, and he's come here to this time periodically to get a heart work-up, but he was done with the whole thing now, and was going to get rid of the time travel device."

* * *

Aimee inhaled deeply to brace herself from tearing up again. Her voice cracked despite all her efforts. "So you see, there is no way he will come back to this time again. I never even got the chance to tell Daniel the truth about me," she added sadly.

"What do you suppose Daniel did when you disappeared?"

"I have no idea." Aimee expelled a long, drawn-out breath. "I'm sure he searched for me for a while. Zach probably talked him out of looking too long and hard. I just hope he got on with his life."

"Just like you need to go on with yours," Jana said meaningfully.

"Yeah," she replied, defeated.

The doorbell rang. They looked at each other before Jana went to answer it.

A familiar voice reached her ears, and Aimee groaned. Why did Brad have to show up here? Why now?

"Hey Jana, I was on my way home from the hospital, and thought I'd . . . oh my God, Aimee?"

Brad swept past Jana from the living room into the kitchen. He grabbed hold of her and pulled her off the barstool at the kitchen counter in a fierce embrace. Unaffected by his touch, she remained limp in his arms.

After a moment, he released her and looked at her face. "Where have you been? We've all been so worried about you, and . . ." He paused and really looked at her while holding her at arm's length. "You look awful. What happened to you?"

199

Anger suddenly replaced Aimee's depressed mood. She was no longer afraid to stand up to Brad. She had faced life and death situations in the last three months. This man no longer made her feel inadequate.

"Thanks for the honest as always assessment of my appearance, Brad." Her tone was icy. "It's nice of you to notice."

"Aimee, what have you been up to?" His eyes narrowed suspiciously. "And why haven't you called? Dear God, we were thinking the worst had happened when you just disappeared."

"Brad, I really don't want to discuss my whereabouts with you at the moment. Last time I checked, I'm still a free person to do as I want. And the last time I talked to you, I broke off our engagement, remember?"

"So you just decided to disappear off the face of the earth for a while?" he asked. His voice rose in anger.

"Yes, maybe that's exactly what I did." She stood squarely in front of him, and didn't waver as she stared up into his face. *He's taller than Daniel, but not as broad.* There was no comparison between the two.

"See, this is the problem, Brad. You think you need to manage my life for me. I can do that just fine on my own. And I need to be able to do the things I want to do without asking your permission first, like some little child." She practically shouted at him now. "Back off, Brad, and give me my space."

Brad stood silent for a moment. He ran his hand along his jaw.

"At least tell me where you've been. You look," he paused, apparently searching for the right words, "different. You've lost weight."

"I'll tell you where I've been," Aimee said in a low tone. Jana stood behind them, still at the door, and shook her head, her eyes wide with panic.

"I went to Yellowstone, just like I told you I would when you pretty much said I couldn't go, remember? I went to Yellowstone on my own, and I survived a wilderness trip on my own. I am capable of living on my own, do you understand? I. Don't. Need. You!"

"So this is it?" Brad asked tersely.

"There is no future between us, Brad. I meant it when I broke our engagement three mo . . . weeks ago," she replied. "We are two different people who want different things in life. I'll never be the wife you want me to be, and I need a partner who is open to the things I enjoy in life. And . . . I am not in love with you."

"Stop acting so ridiculous and melodramatic," Brad said angrily. "I proposed to you, and you accepted. What has gotten into you lately?"

"I woke up," she said simply. "I started to realize that I am not your obedient little puppy, no matter how much you would like me to be. I've grown up, and I see things a lot different now than before. These things became even clearer to me while I was away."

"You think you've grown up?" Brad spat at her. "You're acting more childish than ever. You don't know what it is you want, and it's time for you snap out of it."

She looked at him, dumbstruck. How could she ever have thought herself in love with this man?

"I met someone else, Brad," she said quietly. "I love someone else."

Brad stared, his jaw clenched. "So where is he?" he demanded.

"Back in Montana." She glared at him. She was not about to show that her heart was shattered in pieces.

Brad sniggered. "So you had a quick fling with some – no doubt - backwoodsman from Montana, and you're all caught up in your romantic notions. Well, honey, it's time to come back to the real world. So, how'd he sucker you in? Does he have a cute little cabin in the woods? Did he go out hiking with you? Did you toast marshmallows over the campfire? I'm sure that must be quite romantic to you, but for all your little outdoor games you like to play, you're still a city girl, and you'll get bored real quick playing little house on the prairie. Apparently you already have gotten bored, since you've decided to come back. Or did he get bored with you?"

"Get out," Aimee demanded, and thrust her arm in the direction of the front door. "Get out and leave me alone. You don't have the first idea of what it is I want."

"This isn't over," he finally said. "I'm not giving you up this easily." Brad turned and slammed the door on his way out.

Aimee followed him through the living room on his way out the door, and fell on the couch with a deep sigh. She cradled her head in her hands, her elbows resting on her knees. Grinding her teeth, she willed herself not to cry again.

Finally, taking a deep breath, she said, "Tomorrow I'm going to the hospital to talk with my supervisor, and to see if I still have a job."

Jana grinned brightly. "Thata girl! That's just what you need to snap out of your funk. And there's no way they'll fire you. They are so short staffed, and you're one hell of an ER nurse, they'd be crazy to get rid of you."

Aimee smiled weakly.

"You can't bring him back," Jana said quietly.

"I know that," Aimee snapped heatedly. She punched the pillow beside her, and threw it across the room. "Dammit, I know that."

Chapter Twenty-One

Yellowstone Wilderness, 1810

Zach sat quietly and observed his son rake a frustrated hand through his hair. The look of despair in Daniel's weary eyes tore at his heart. He had met up with Daniel two days after sending Aimee back to her time. Daniel had been searching for her near the falls of the Little Buffalo River. Zach had agreed to join him in the search, hoping Daniel would give up after a few more days. The anguish on his son's face, the feeling of loss was something he knew all too well when his sweet Marie was taken from him. And that had all been his fault as well.

Only, Aimee Donovan wasn't dead. He could make this right for Daniel and take the pain away in an instant. That, however, required him to come clean with the truth that he had kept from his son all his life.

He had never wanted to cause Daniel this pain. Thinking on it now as they sat camped along the *Roche Jaune*, he should have realized that something like this could have happened. Aimee Donovan was a beautiful young woman, full of life. He had recognized her thirst for adventure instantly when he met her during his last trip to the future to have his heart examined by the doctors with their superior knowledge of medicine. Perhaps he should have had his head examined instead for telling her he was a mountain man from the past, and had the means to travel through time. He had never told his secret to anyone. After his first experience with time travel twenty-five years ago, he had buried the snakehead device, and never wanted to use it again.

203

Years later, his health began to fail him, and his heart was weak. He didn't want to leave his young son without a father, although Daniel was doing just fine growing up amongst the Tukudeka clan that resided in the area.

Realizing that he had the means to get himself fixed up, he had used the device again to come to the future and seek medical care. He had learned to pose as a homeless vagrant in order to get care at the hospital emergency rooms. There were so many hospitals in the future, he never had to visit the same one twice. It had been strange and rather frightening the first few times, but as the years went on, he had become more comfortable with the ways of the future. During his last trip, the doctors had told him they would need to cut him open to work on his heart in order to make him better. Medicine alone would no longer work. He had decided then and there that he would not allow that to happen. He had lived a full life, and his son was a grown man. Truth be told, Daniel had taken care of him more over the years than the other way around. He was ready to die and join his wife. He had also decided that the time travel device would die along with him.

That's when he met nurse Aimee Donovan. She loved his stories, and enthusiastically told him that she enjoyed spending time in the wilderness. Apparently, that was something people in the future did for enjoyment. Something compelled him to tell her of his time travels, and he offered to send her to the past. He didn't know what had put that crazy notion in his head, but she'd been so darn likable, and the way she had spoken about her abilities to survive in the wilds had him believing she could do it.

He knew she didn't believe him, but offered her the chance to go back in time to truly live in the wilds for a few months while he took care of his medical needs here in the future, and then attend to his business in St. Louis in this time. He had tried to prepare her as best as he could when he told her he could send her to the past. He figured if she could make it to his cabin, Daniel would keep her safe. He'd told her his story of how he came to be a time traveler, and of Daniel - the same story he would tell his son now.

The thought that Aimee would want to stay in 1810 permanently had never entered his mind, nor that his son would fall in love with her. It was unthinkable to let her stay. She would regret her decision after the adventure wore off. He had seen things in the future. Life was easy. There were no hardships, and once she came to that realization if he had allowed her to stay, she would have resented her choice.

With a heavy sigh, Zach glanced at his son. He cleared his throat. It was time to come clean with the truth. This way, Daniel could end his search, and they could get on with their lives.

Zach cleared his throat. "Daniel, I know where Aimee Donovan is."

Daniel blinked and slowly raised his head from staring blankly at the dancing flames of their campfire. Seconds passed and his eyes narrowed.

"How do you know her name?" Daniel spoke barely above a whisper.

"What?" Zach asked, apprehension in his voice.

"Her name. I never mentioned her surname." Daniel's eyes blazed, the words grinding between his teeth. His body visibly tensed.

"Take it easy, son." Zach held out a hand. "I'll tell you everything you need to know."

* * *

An icy chill washed over Daniel. His father had never been secretive before. Was it too much of a coincidence that he had found Aimee shortly after Zach left for St. Louis, and now she was gone and his father had returned?

"Aimee Donovan is safely back in her time, where she belongs." Zach met his son's hard stare.

"What do you mean, her time?" Daniel shook his head. "Dammit, where the hell is she?" Daniel leapt to his feet, anger and frustration in his voice, and Zach involuntarily shrunk back.

"She's returned to the future. To the year 2010."

Daniel stared. His father's words made no sense. Minutes passed in silence.

"What the hell are you talking about?" Daniel finally roared. His pulse throbbed at his temples. The sounds of the river and evening crickets around him ceased. Stars floated in front of his face as the world spiraled out of control. He clenched one hand into a tight fist, and raked the other through his hair.

"It's as if she dropped out of the sky" . . . *"There are things about me I can't talk to you about."*

The clothing, her strange words, her unconventional behavior, her knowledge of healing people . . . *"She's returned to the future . . . 2010 . . . 2010 . . . 2010 . . ."*

"For you to understand, I need to start at the beginning, son. Something I should have told you a long time ago. I hope you'll find it in you to forgive me." Daniel stared at him blankly, waiting for his father to elaborate.

"It begins in 1785, on the day of your birth." Zach shifted uncomfortably. Daniel settled himself, stone faced, back on the ground, and waited silently for his father to continue.

"It was winter, 1785. Your mother . . . my Marie, was in labor with you."

Daniel nodded. He knew his mother had died in childbirth in the midst of a winter blizzard here in the mountains. His father had been unable to go for help from the nearby Tukudeka clan. How often had he heard his father blame himself over the years for his wife's death, for taking her away from the safety of New Orleans and bringing her to the mountains?

His father cleared his throat again. Each word seemed to cause him pain to speak out loud. "What I didn't tell you before, is that we had a visitor that night."

"A visitor?" Daniel echoed.

"He was old. A Tukudeka elder. He got caught in the snowstorm and found the cabin. He was nearly frozen to death when he managed to pound on the cabin door."

"Continue," Daniel said slowly, when his father paused again.

"I tended to both your mother and the old man throughout the night. She was getting worse, and he was starting to thaw out. That's when he offered me the chance to save your life."

"My life?" Daniel's eyes narrowed.

"He handed me this." His father reached into the pouch around his neck and produced a shriveled up, dried snakehead with eerily unnatural gleaming red eyes. Daniel stared at the object, then back at his father.

"He told me a story of how his grandfather received this

snake from some ancient people who came from the sky."

"The Tukudeka legends are full of stories of the Sky People." Daniel nodded.

"Yeah, well, he said he wanted me to have it for my kindness. He told me the snake had magical powers to send someone 200 years into the future. He explained it couldn't be used to alter one's past, only one's future. It takes the holder 200 years forward in time to the last place the object has been. It can then bring you back to this time, to the same time and place as when you left." Zach let his words sink in for a moment. Daniel said nothing, his expression set in stone.

"I didn't believe him, of course, but I was getting desperate. Your mother was slipping away, and out of desperation I took the snake and followed the old man's instructions. I held onto your mother and touched the right eye of the snake, and we were instantly transported to the year 1985. I was scared to death. The future is unimaginable from what we know here, Daniel." His father's eyes glazed with unshed tears, and he ran his hand over his face. He coughed to clear his throat, and took a long drink of water from his water bag.

"They have carriages that are made of metal and run by themselves without horses. One almost killed us when we arrived. A helpful man showed us the way to a hospital. The healing powers and knowledge of the people in the future is beyond anything you can imagine."

I can save your friend . . .I have treated many wounds like this . . . 'This is what white healers do in the east.' 'Where I come from, we do.'

A little boy, drowning in a river. Aimee hovered over his lifeless body, breathing and pumping life back into him.

"I have seen Aimee use some of these powers," Daniel said quietly, staring into the fire. He raised his head and met his father's eyes. Zach nodded in understanding.

"Your mother went into fits in the hospital. There are words the doctors used to tell me what had happened to her, but I can't remember them. They told me it was a condition that was brought on by being with child. It was too late to save her. If she had had proper care sooner, she would have lived. They were able to take

207

you from her body before she . . . died." Zach quickly wiped his eyes.

"So, you're telling me I was born in the future?" Daniel asked incredulously. This was too much for him to think about.

"You wouldn't have been born at all if not for the miracle of this device." Zach answered, staring at the snakehead still in his hand. "I couldn't stay in that strange and foreign place any longer. I took hold of Marie, and with you in my arms, while no one was looking, I touched the snake's left eye, and it brought us back home, just like the old man said. He was dead in the cabin when I returned with you. The blizzard was over the next morning. We were gone no longer than a day. You were cryin' your bloody head off, and I knew I'd lose you, too, if I didn't find a wet nurse for you. I took you to the closest Tukudeka clan I could find. Gentle Sun had recently given birth to Elk Runner. She was more than happy to take you. I left you with her to tend to my grief. You know the rest of the story. You got to grow up amongst the Indians and with me. I tried my best to do right by you."

After a lengthy silence, Daniel spoke. "You traveled to the future again. Why?"

"I didn't for many years. I buried the snake. You were about seven years old when I got to realizing that my heart was giving me some trouble. It was another year later before I finally decided to get help. I had the snakehead. I could go to the future and they could help me. I was thinking of you, Daniel. I didn't want to die and leave you. I know you had your Indian family and you were happy, but I wasn't ready to go under yet."

"Why did you keep this from me?" he asked solemnly.

"I never found the right time to tell you. I'm sorry, son. I know I should have told you. As time went by, I figured you were happy with your life the way it is, so why burden you with it? I kept the snake for selfish reasons. I don't think it's right to be meddling with things like living in different times. I've decided to destroy the snake. No more time travel. It just ain't natural."

Daniel quickly looked up at him. "What about Aimee? Does she have the ability to travel in time?"

Zach shook his head. "No. Aimee is a nurse at the last hospital I visited three months ago." He continued to tell him how he had met her and ended up sending her to this time.

"People in the future know nothing about time travel, either. She didn't believe me, so I'm sure it must have been quite a shock to her when she actually ended up here. I told her to find you. She knows these mountains from her time. She comes here on what she calls backpacking trips. It's hard to explain, but the lives of people in the future are vastly different from what we know, and they have countless inventions that make life easy for them. To escape their normal lives, people in the future go on trips they call vacations. Aimee enjoys going out into the wilderness, what's left of it in her time, to live a little as we do in this time. I thought to give her the opportunity to experience what it's truly like."

"She knew about me?" Daniel asked. His throat went dry.

His father nodded. "I told her your story, and to find you. I knew you'd keep her safe while she was here."

Daniel's heart sank to his gut. Hadn't he known that Aimee kept things from him? He kept telling himself if he loved her enough, she wouldn't lie to him anymore. She had become the woman of his heart, and he had been sure she loved him, too.

Her words of love, and the way she gave herself to him, made love to him, had been very convincing. Could it have all been a lie? Had she just considered him part of her wilderness experience? He had opened his heart, even told her he had been deceived by a lying white woman once before. And all along, she had known she would be going back to her time. She didn't even have the courage to face him in the end and bid him farewell. How did he let this happen? How could he have allowed himself to be used and deceived by a white woman a second time?

He stood abruptly and kicked dirt onto the fire. There was still daylight left.

"Let's go, father. I wish to return to the cabin. We have a lot of winter preparations left to make." He picked up his Bighorn bow and rifle, and headed out into the forest. He didn't wait to see if his father followed.

* * *

The older man stared after his son. With a twinge of guilt, Zach sighed and heaved himself off the ground. He had left out some important bits of information. This was for the best, he

209

convinced himself. If he told Daniel that Aimee had begged him not to send her back to her time, what would Daniel do? Insist on bringing her back? No, it was best this way. Miss Donovan was safely back in her time, and Daniel would forget about her soon enough.

Chapter Twenty-Two

California, present day

For all outward appearances, Aimee seemed to have resigned herself to her former life. She went to work each day, performed her duties without flaw, and even went out socially with her co-workers as before. Jana knew better, however. Aimee was no longer the fun-loving socialite she had been. She went out, but she was always far away, never quite part of the conversations around her. She would often hear Aimee cry out for Daniel in her sleep, and knew that Aimee cried a lot when she thought she was alone. Jana never brought it up, and hoped that time would heal her friend's wounds. Brad had been polite and unusually friendly. He called and stopped by the condo often. He asked Aimee out on dates almost weekly, but she turned him down each time.

One evening, eight weeks after Aimee returned from her trip into the past, Jana's desk phone rang. She sat at the nurse's station in the surgical recovery unit, charting some long overdue patient information.

"Hey, Jana." Aimee's voice sounded tired. "I'm heading home now, just wanted to let you know."

"Okay," she said. "My shift doesn't end for a couple more hours. Do you want to rent a movie and order some Chinese for when I get home?" she asked hopefully.

"Sure," Aimee responded halfheartedly.

"What's wrong?" Jana didn't like the sad tone in Aimee's voice. Things had been much better lately, or so she thought.

"I'm just tired," Aimee sighed. "Long shift, and Ashwell was in rare form today . . . It'll be two months today," she added in a

211

solemn whisper.

Jana inhaled a deep breath. "Well, go home and get some rest. I'll pick up dinner and a movie. You don't have to."

She stared at her phone for a moment after they'd said their goodbyes. How much longer was Aimee going to grieve? Jana had even thought about talking her into getting a prescription for anti-depressants, but thought better of it. If things didn't change soon, she would reconsider. Her focus returned to her charts. A half hour later, a couple of nurses walked through the recovery area toward the surgical rooms.

"Hey, Jana," one of them greeted.

"I thought all the surgeries were done for the day," Jana called out.

"Yeah, well, ER is sending someone up. I think it's a stabbing victim."

"What surgeon is on call?"

"Dr. Bigsby's been paged."

"Well, hope it doesn't take too long." Jana turned her attention back to her charts. Moments later, her phone rang.

"Recovery," Jana answered.

"Mary in ER," the voice on the other line said. "You're Aimee Donovan's roommate, right?"

"Yeah," Jana answered.

"Do you know if she left for the day, or is she still in the building?"

She's probably soaking in the shower right now. "She's not here anymore. Are you guys short-staffed?"

"As always, but that's beside the point. There's a man here insisting he needs to talk to Aimee, and wants me to tell him where she lives."

"What man?" Jana frowned.

"His name is Zach Osborne."

Jana's heart leapt into her throat.

"I'll be right down," she said and hung up the phone. "I gotta go, Linda," she yelled at her astonished co-worker. She ran down the hall and frantically pushed the down button on the elevator. "Come on, come on," she said between gritted teeth. Her body shook violently from the adrenaline rush of hearing that familiar name. The elevator door opened and she sprang in, pushing the button to the first floor.

Jana was usually a lot more reserved. Bold and assertive definitely did not describe her. However, anger welled up inside her as she thought about everything her best friend had endured in recent months.

Like a bird of prey, she swooped into the crowded emergency room and rushed to the nurse's station. She paid no attention to the chaos around her. Her sole focus rested on the man talking animatedly with the nurse at the desk. She had no doubt who he was. The fringed leather pants gave him away.

"How dare you!" Jana practically shouted at him. Her voice cracked nervously, and she stopped in front of Zach Osborne. He turned to her in surprise. Mary at the desk stared wide-eyed from Jana to the man.

"I beg your pardon?" he asked, a haggard, tired look on his face.

"How dare you come here again and want to speak to Aimee!" Jana shouted. "Haven't you messed up her life enough?" She inhaled a deep breath for courage. Her heart pounded fiercely, and her face flushed hot with anger.

"I never meant to hurt her," Zach said in a quiet voice. "Please, if you know where she is, I need to talk to her. My boy . . ." His voice cracked. Jana stared. He pointed to where all the commotion was coming from. Jana looked to see nurses and Dr. Ashwell working over a patient. Blood was everywhere.

"I thought if he sees her, he'll fight," Zach said.

Jana's eyes darted back to the older man. The worn look of worry and anguish on his face gripped at her heart.

"That's the stabbing victim we're sending up to surgery," Mary chimed in helpfully.

"That's Daniel? Aimee's Daniel?" Jana asked in disbelief. At that moment, the team working on the patient wheeled the bed out of the cubicle and toward the elevators.

"They're headed to the OR," Jana said. "What happened? Aimee told me all about her trip," Jana added in a hushed tone when she noticed him hesitate. She motioned for Zach to follow her to a quiet corner.

213

"He's been looking for Aimee for days," Zach said. "I went after him, and finally talked him into calling off the search. On our way back to our cabin, we were surprised by a party of Blackfoot." The older man wiped a hand over his face.

"Days?" Jana shook her head, trying to understand. "Aimee's been back here for two months."

"Less than a week has passed in our time," Zach said, his voice raspy. "I never meant for any of this to happen."

"Okay. Let me call Aimee," she said. "One of the best surgeons here is working on your son. If anyone can save him, it'll be Dr. Bigsby." She pulled her phone from her back pocket, and pressed the speed dial to Aimee's cell phone.

"Come on, answer," she said impatiently. When the voicemail picked up, Jana hung up and dialed again. This time, someone picked up.

"Get down here now," she ordered before Aimee even had the chance to say hello.

"What? I just got out of the shower," Aimee protested on the other end of the line.

"You need to get down here now," she insisted again. "I'm standing right next to Zach Osborne."

There was silence on the other end, then a loud clanking noise. The phone must have fallen to the ground. "Aimee? Aimee!" Jana yelled.

"I'm . . . here," Aimee's voice sounded weak and shaky. "Daniel?"

Jana took a deep breath. "You need to get down here. He's alive, but it's bad." The call disconnected.

"She's on her way," Jana said.

Zach looked around. "Where did they take my boy?" he asked.

"They took him to surgery. They are no doubt operating on him as we speak," Jana said. She walked back over to Mary at the nurse's station, who raised her eyebrows in a questioning look.

"When Aimee Donovan shows up, tell her to meet us in ICU," Jana said. "Come with me, Mr. Osborne." She turned to Zach. He followed her to the elevator. "You can stay in the waiting area in the ICU. They'll get you when he's out of surgery."

Zach nodded wordlessly.

Jana hurried to the operating suites, grabbed a facial mask, and walked in.

"How bad?" she asked no one in particular.

"Someone butchered this guy," one of the nurses said.

"Dr. Bigsby?" Jana formally addressed Brad, who was focused on tying off a bleeder. Without looking up, Brad said, "He might make it. What's up, Jana?"

"Nothing, I just wondered about the patient."

"We'll be a while," Brad said. "Scrub in if you want to help."

"I think I'll pass on this one," Jana said. She left the operating suite. Anxiously, she waited for Aimee. She didn't need to wait long. Not fifteen minutes passed when the elevator at the end of the hall dinged, and Aimee flew out the doors. Jana headed her off before she could barge through to the operating rooms.

"Hang on, you can't just charge in," she said, and grabbed a hold of Aimee's arm.

"How is he?" Aimee's work scrub top had soaked up the water from her dripping wet hair.

"Do you want to see Zach?" Jana asked. "He's in the waiting room."

"How's Daniel? Who's operating on him?"

"Brad."

"Oh my God!" Aimee's eyes widened, and her hand flew to her mouth.

"That's what I thought, too. But he's in the best hands. As long as you don't barge in there and Brad figures out the man whose life he's saving is his biggest competition for you." Jana said meaningfully. "His scalpel might slip with that knowledge."

"I see your point," Aimee said. "How long have they been in surgery?"

"Since I called you. Hey, why don't you go sit with Mr. Osborne? He's in the waiting room," Jana suggested. When Aimee looked as though she was about to object, Jana said, "I'll go with you. At least you can get the scoop on what happened."

* * *

Aimee entered the waiting room ahead of Jana. Zach sat on a

215

couch. His elbows rested on his knees, and his head was bent low. The muffled sounds of gunfire and screeching tires from a show that played on a television set that hung on the wall created the only sound in the room. Zach looked up, and scrambled to his feet.

"Aimee, I'm truly sorry for what I've done," Zach said. His face looked haggard, his eyes bloodshot. She stared at him. His appearance was different from the man she'd first met five months ago, and from their last meeting when he sent her home.

"Spare me." Aimee's voice was ice cold as she stared at him. "You forced me to come back here when I begged you to let me stay. I love Daniel, and he loves me, and I told you that, but you wouldn't listen. So why did you come back here? I thought you would have destroyed the device by now."

"I've brought Daniel back to save his life. He would have died. It's all my fault, too. I don't want to lose my son because of my stupidity, the way I lost his mother. That's why I came back."

She kept staring, unflinching. "What happened after I left?" she asked coldly.

"Daniel searched for you when we met up in the woods two days after I sent you home. I offered to help him with the search." Zach paused, his eyes pleading for understanding. Clearing his throat, he continued, "On the fourth day, I couldn't keep up the lie anymore. I told him everything – about you, and about him."

Aimee tried to picture that conversation. What must have gone through Daniel's mind at finally hearing the circumstances of his birth? How did he take the news about her? An icy sensation flowed through her. She'd never been honest with him. Now he knew the truth. Did it matter? Did he still care about her?

"How did he react to what you told him?" she asked almost fearfully.

"He didn't take it too well. He really didn't say much after I finished. He broke camp and headed home."

Aimee drew in a sharp breath. Daniel had to forgive her. She had to make him see that she'd had no choice when she disappeared from his life; that she never wanted to hurt him.

"How did he get injured?" Her words were barely a whisper. Her heart pounded in her ears.

216

"We set up a new camp after dark. Daniel wasn't much in the mood for more talk, and I thought it'd be best if I left him alone with his thoughts. The next morning, he was already gone when I woke. He must have been elsewhere with his mind, otherwise he'd have never let himself fall into an ambush. A party of five Blackfoot surprised him. By the time I caught up with him, he already killed three, but they got him good. I shot one before he could finished Daniel off, and the last one hightailed it into the woods."

Aimee's hand covered her mouth. Her eyes stung with tears at Zach's tale.

"I've become too damned dependent on that snake. I knew if I didn't bring him here, he'd be a goner. I couldn't watch my son die." Zach ran a weary hand over his face.

"So, this all just happened? In 1810, I've only been gone five days?" Aimee shook her head, trying to comprehend the timeline.

"The device doesn't send someone forward in time exactly 200 years. Going back, it's no more than a day or two difference, but going forward ain't always exact. Sometimes weeks or months more, but never less. I think it's so there can never be a repeat of something that's already happened to the person doing the time traveling."

Aimee closed her eyes, and inhaled long and slow. "When Daniel gets out of surgery, he's going to be completely disoriented," she finally said. "He's the only one who doesn't know what's happening. I need to be there when he wakes up." She looked at Jana, who nodded. "I hope he forgives me for all the lies I've told him."

    * * *

Another hour passed before Brad strode into the waiting room. Jana had gone to finish her shift, and Aimee stayed with Zach. Neither one of them spoke, each absorbed in their own thoughts.

Zach sprang up from his seat when Brad called his name. Aimee didn't move. She sat quietly in the corner of the room. She watched and listened. Brad, still wearing surgical scrubs, extended his hand to Zach.

"Well, he made it through surgery. The next 24 hours are going to be critical, and . . ." his voice trailed off when he spotted her. "Aimee? What are you doing here?"

"Waiting to see how your patient is doing," she said.

"Do you know him?" Brad asked.

"Yes," she said while looking straight at Brad. He seemed a bit confused, but turned his attention back to Zach. "No vital organs were badly damaged, but there was a lot of internal bleeding. He's had several blood transfusions, and we need to monitor him close to make sure the bleeding has stopped." His eyes darted to Aimee while he spoke to Zach.

"When can I see him?" Zach asked.

"He'll be in recovery for a while. When we move him to ICU, you can speak to him."

Aimee rushed from the room. Brad called to her, but she ignored him.

"He just went into recovery." Jana emerged from the recovery suite. "He hasn't woken up yet."

"I need to get in there and be with him when he wakes up," Aimee said urgently.

"Follow me."

A nurse stood and adjusted an IV line on Daniel's arm when Aimee and Jana walked in.

"I'll take it from here," Jana said.

"Thanks," the nurse gave Jana a grateful look. "I really need to use the restroom." She hurried off.

For the first time, Aimee stared at the patient in the hospital bed. Her hand went to her mouth, and her eyes filled with tears. She almost didn't recognize him. His hair framed his face in matted strands, and a week-old beard covered his handsome features. A white hospital sheet concealed him from his torso down, the tops of a bandage visible. Spots of betadine and dried blood still splattered his chest.

"Daniel," she whispered softly.

Jana stood by silently as Aimee took hold of Daniel's limp hand and held it gently.

"Daniel, if you can hear me, it's me, Aimee." She bent over him, her head close to his face. Daniel stirred, and his arms reached up defensively to his face.

"Shh, shh," Aimee tried to calm him. "You have to lie still, Daniel. It's okay. I'm right here with you."

Daniel slowly opened his eyes, and squinted against the bright lights.

"Aimee?" His voice was barely audible.

"It's me, Daniel." Silent tears rolled down her cheeks. "Please don't be afraid. I know when you wake up everything will look very strange to you, but you have to trust me. Everything we're doing is to help you live, okay?" She sat on the hospital bed and cradled Daniel's head between her hands. She rested her forehead against his. Daniel's arms lifted, and his hands reached for her face.

"I thought I lost you." His voice sounded weak and hoarse.

"Never," she whispered, her heart beating wildly.

"Aimee? What the hell is this?" A tense, familiar voice barked behind her.

Her head shot up and she straightened.

"Let me guess," Brad finally sneered, glaring at her, then at the patient in the bed. "That's your Montana woodsman."

Jana turned to face him. "Don't make a scene," she whispered to him. "You took a Hippocratic oath, remember?"

"You can't be serious!" Brad glowered at Jana. "I'm not going to hurt my patient, but you'll have to excuse me that I'm not doing the happy dance to see her with another man."

"Leave them be," Jana said softly. "Please."

With a snort, Brad turned and left the recovery room. "Page me if you need something," he called over his shoulder.

"Thank you once again, for coming to my rescue." Aimee breathed a sigh of relief.

"Where the hell am I?" Daniel asked weakly.

"I'll tell you everything, Daniel, but for now just lie still to let your head clear, okay?"

Daniel squirmed and tried to raise his upper body off the bed, but stopped and groaned in obvious pain.

"I told you to lie back," Aimee ordered, and pushed against his shoulders. "You've been stabbed several times, and those wounds are going to split open again if you don't stay still."

219

Daniel complied, and grimaced. "Did you sew me back up?"

"No." Aimee held her breath.

He raised his head to look around, a frown forming on his face. "Where the hell are we?" he asked again.

"We're in a hospital," Aimee answered.

Daniel's forehead wrinkled. "Hospital? How did I get here?"

"Would you just be still? I'll tell you later. Everything is going to look very strange to you, but you have to wake up fully before I can explain everything. Don't freak out at the tubes in your arms and everywhere else."

"Freak out?" Daniel glanced down at his arms and chest.

"It's what you're about to do. And don't pull on that! It's a needle in your arm that is putting fluids in your body."

Daniel stared at his arm, then back at Aimee.

"Your father brought you here when you were trying to commit suicide with those Blackfoot," Aimee offered quietly in the way of an explanation. Her heart pounded in her ears, dreading Daniel's reaction.

* * *

Daniel struggled to clear the fog from his mind. There was something he should remember, but his brain would not function properly. He'd never been this drunk before. His father must have offered him a lot of alcohol to numb the pain.

"Jana, come meet Daniel." Aimee turned briefly to her friend, then faced him again. "Daniel, this is my best friend, Jana Evans. I think I've mentioned her to you before."

"I've heard a lot about you, Daniel," Jana said cordially. "And I have to say, Aimee was not exaggerating one bit."

Daniel stared, cursing his foggy mind. The woman in front of him wore the same type of clothing as Aimee. Her hair was darker than Aimee's and shorter than his own. Where the hell was he?

"What is going on?" he asked. His eyes darted from Jana to Aimee, to his strange and unnatural surroundings.

With a pained look on her face, Aimee said, "No more half-truths, Daniel. Your father and I are going to tell you everything."

"What's my father got to do with this?" His mind was trying to tell him something, but it stayed just beyond his reach, and each time he thought he had a grasp on what he should remember, it vanished again.

"We'll explain everything, and you'll finally know the truth about me, too." Aimee smiled uneasily. Tears shimmered in her lovely eyes.

Daniel focused on her face, and tried to clear his muddled brain. Suddenly it came to him as his bleary eyes took in the strange lights and surroundings. Unfamiliar noises everywhere pounded in his head. Aimee was from the future! Aimee had lied to him. Used him. Deceived him. Comprehension suddenly dawned as to his whereabouts. He closed his eyes again to shut out the reality of his situation. His father must have brought him to the future. Daniel wished he had left him to die.

Chapter Twenty-Three

Strange sounds echoed in his head. Daniel couldn't focus his eyes or ears. His eyelids felt heavy, and his vision blurred when he did manage to keep his eyes open. He just wanted to give himself over to sleep, but his deeply ingrained instinct to be alert at all times prompted him to fight the sensations.

He felt as if someone had beaten him over the head several times while coming out of a drunken stupor all at once. He had never felt this weak before, and his surroundings were surreal. Too many strange noises that he had never heard before pounded in his head, and the bright lights shone in his eyes, nearly blinding him. Perhaps he was already dead. He dismissed that thought immediately. If he were dead, he wouldn't be feeling any pain, and right now his gut was on fire.

Those damn Blackfoot had gotten him good. Five warriors had come out of nowhere. He'd killed two of them immediately with well-aimed arrows. He disposed of another attacker with his knife, but a fourth warrior stabbed him several times. His father had caught up to him at that point and shot one. Daniel couldn't remember anything after that.

He hadn't been able to think straight for a week prior to that incident. He had come back from checking his traps, and Aimee was gone. Her pack and all her belongings were missing as well. Everything except her moccasins, sheepskin coat, and the deerskin dress was gone. She wouldn't leave without letting him know. An icy fear had gripped him. Aimee had been acting out of sorts for weeks, but never had she indicated that she wanted to leave.

His father's tale came back to him full force. The memory of that conversation flooded his mind, the memory of how his world and everything he had believed to be true shattered apart. Traveling through time. Aimee was from the future. She was no different from Emma after all. Another lying white woman had deceived him. Only this time it was worse. He had lost his heart to her.

For a moment, he ceased his struggle to open his eyes. Instead he focused on his pain - the physical pain in his gut, not the pain in his heart. His head pounded as if a herd of bison bore down on him, and dizziness threatened to overtake him. His insides were molten fire. He refused to lie still, however. He needed to find his father, to get away from this place, this time. He needed to get back to the world he knew, even if his entire existence had turned out to be a lie.

* * *

Aimee tensed. At first, Daniel seemed relieved to find her beside him. Now, he acted withdrawn. He needed to fully wake up, but he obviously remembered what had transpired back in his time. Was he thinking about his conversation with his father?

"Daniel?" she asked hesitantly.

"Where's my father?" he rasped.

"He's . . . he's waiting to see you," Aimee stammered. Tears threatened to spill from her eyes. His sudden anger was apparent. It was all her fault. She had lied to him all this time, and his reaction was exactly as she'd feared.

"I wish to see him now." Daniel's voice sounded more forceful. He struggled again to raise his torso off the mattress. Jana quickly moved to his side, and she and Aimee both tried to push him back down.

"You have to lie still, Daniel. It's too soon after your surgery," Aimee pleaded. Daniel fought against the pressure of their hands on his shoulders.

"Get my father," he commanded through gritted teeth, his cold stare piercing Aimee's heart.

"He's going to reinjure himself," Jana said. "How can he even move already?" She shot Aimee a look of amazement. "I've never seen anyone try to move so soon after abdominal surgery."

223

"I have," Aimee said solemnly. "Daniel, you need to lie back and stop fighting," she implored.

"Dammit, woman, go and get my father!"

Daniel's confrontational attitude and shouting brought a few more nurses to his bedside. One of them had a syringe in her hand, and injected its contents into the IV line in his arm.

"Boy, he's a fighter," she commented.

Aimee stepped back and watched in horror. She may have lost him all over again. A crushing sensation grabbed hold in her chest. Daniel threw a final accusing look in her direction before the sedative he'd been given made him slump back against the pillow. She sucked in a breath at the cold stare of betrayal in his eyes. Then they became unfocused again, and his lids drifted shut. His body relaxed against the mattress.

Aimee collapsed onto a nearby stool and buried her face in her hands. She didn't look up when Jana's supportive arms came around her shoulder.

"He'll come around," Jana whispered encouragement. "I can't even imagine what this must be like for him."

"No, you don't understand." Aimee shook her head. "I know what's going through his mind. I lied to him and deceived him. He hates me now."

"The way he looked at you, even barely out of anesthesia, before he realized where he was tells me otherwise. Any woman would kill to have a man look at her that way. He'll come around."

Aimee wasn't convinced. She knew him too well.

* * *

The pain in Daniel's gut woke him sometime in the middle of the night. Or was it daytime? He had lost all sense of time. Too many strange lights shone everywhere, none of them sunlight. He fought to clear his mind. He raised his head and scanned his surroundings. Strange unfamiliar contraptions stood everywhere. He didn't even have words to describe them. He eyed the peculiar smooth thin ropes – were they ropes? – that seemed to be everywhere on his body. Some were grey in color, others were white. They were all attached to his chest, and one transparent rope came out of his arm. The line went to some sort of water bag that hung from a shiny pole. Every time he tried to move, he felt a new rope somewhere on his body.

"What the hell?" Daniel growled. He pulled away the blanket covering him. He wore a shirt that reached just past his privates. Sure enough, there was a tube there as well! This was too much. He had never felt this trapped before. He pulled on the tube, ignoring the sudden burning sensation, until it was out. He was tempted to do the same to the rest of the lines attached to him, but he held off for the moment. He raised himself to a sitting position and slowly pulled his legs over the side of the bed while clutching at the bandage around his middle. White-hot pain shot through his insides, and he clenched his jaw.

He looked around the strange room. Aimee sat curled up in a chair in the corner. Her chest moved up and down rhythmically in sleep. Daniel studied her for a moment. Something squeezed his heart at the sight of her. Her beautiful long hair framed her face, falling in cascades down her shoulders and over her breasts. He wanted to burn the sight of her into his memory, then quickly thought better of it and looked away. She had turned out to be nothing but a deceptive white woman after all. The ache in his heart that came with that knowledge overrode the pain in his gut.

Daniel tried to stand, but a tugging sensation on his chest prevented him from leaving the bed. He reached his hand under the shirt to find where the lines were attached to his skin. He jerked them off impatiently, then stood. The feel of the smooth cold ground beneath his soles was as foreign as everything else. His legs shook and his insides throbbed but he needed to be out of this bed. The shirt he wore only covered his front, while his backside was completely exposed. What a strange world this was.

An instant later, the door to the room burst open, and a woman came barging in.

"What are you doing, sir?" she asked, a horrified look on her face. Daniel scowled. How had she known he'd gotten out of bed? And was the future made up entirely of females? He couldn't recall seeing a single man anywhere. Was that why they all wore britches?

Aimee stirred awake at the sound of the nurse's voice, and scrambled off the chair.

"What are you doing?" She rushed to his side and grabbed hold of his arm.

"I couldn't lie in that bed any longer," Daniel growled.

"He removed his leads," the nurse remarked in an exasperated tone. She moved swiftly to his side to usher him back in the bed. She stepped forward, and glanced down at her feet. "Oh Jesus, he pulled out his urinary catheter as well!"

Daniel scowled, and Aimee giggled. She held her hand over her mouth.

"Mr. Osborne, you need to get back in that bed so I can hook you up again," the nurse said with a stern voice.

"I refuse to have any more of these . . . things attached to my body," he sneered.

"Can I have a few moments with him, Susan?" Aimee asked quietly. "I think the drugs are making him uncooperative, and I'll try and calm him down."

"Okay, Aimee," the woman said with a shake of her head. "I'd best turn off the EKG alarm at the nurse's station. But make him see reason, 'cause I don't need Dr. Bigsby chewing me out in the morning."

"I'll take full responsibility," Aimee assured her. Facing him, she gently took his hand in hers. He flinched as if she'd burned him and pulled away. Aimee set her face determinedly.

"If you don't cooperate and lie back down, they'll give you more drugs to subdue you." Her tone sounded indifferent. "You're a strong man, Daniel, but you can't fight the medicines in this time."

He only glared at her.

"Remember what I told Elk Runner? How he needed to lie still? Well, your injury is much worse, and . . ."

He didn't let her finish. He tugged on her shirt at her waist, and pulled her to him, then brought his mouth roughly down on hers. He couldn't help himself. He had to taste her lips one last time. Daniel abruptly released her again before Aimee had a chance to even respond.

"You have to listen to me right now. You need to get back in that bed." Aimee's voice sounded labored.

Weak and in no state to fight anymore, he complied. He

refused to look at her, and reluctantly sat down and pulled himself into the bed.

"Where's my father?" he asked coldly.

"He's probably sleeping in the ICU family room. I'll go get him." She glanced over her shoulder once more and left the room, quietly closing the door behind her. Daniel sank back against the pillow, clutched his side, and stared at the ceiling.

* * *

"Leave us." Daniel's voice chilled the room when Aimee returned with Zach in tow. Biting back the tears, her eyes darted from Daniel to his father. Zach gave her an apologetic glance, and nodded almost imperceptibly for her to leave the room.

Aimee reached for the door handle, then turned to gaze one more time at the man she loved more than anything. "Please, Daniel, if you'd only let me explain."

"No! I've heard enough lies!" Daniel lunged up from his position on the bed, but stopped short as he clutched his injured side. Grimacing, he groaned and slumped back against the pillow.

Every cell in her body screamed to rush to his side, to implore him to listen to her, beg his forgiveness, but his reaction just now held her back. She didn't want to be the cause of him reinjuring himself.

"I love you, Daniel," she said barely above a whisper, and left the room. Hopefully Zach could talk some sense into him, and she could come back to reattach his leads. Eventually he would have to listen to her and allow her to explain.

Aimee had barely closed the door, when Daniel glared at his father. "Why did you bring me here?" he demanded. "You should have left me to die."

"I couldn't do that, son," his father said quietly.

"Take me back," Daniel ordered. His father's eyes widened in surprise. "Take me back, now."

"Daniel, you don't know what you're saying. Your injuries."

Daniel cut him off. "If I die, it's as it should be. Take me back."

His father's eyes drifted over him, and he finally nodded. His hand reached for the pouch around his neck and he removed the snakehead. "All right," he sighed. "If that's what you really want.

But what about Aimee?"

"What of her? As you said yourself, she is safely back in her time. This is where she belongs."

His father opened his mouth as if to say something, then closed it again, and walked around the bed to the side that held the clear line in Daniel's arm. Pulling quickly, he removed the needle from beneath the skin.

"Put your hand over that so it don't bleed," Zach said gruffly. Then he held firmly to Daniel's arm, and pressed a finger to the snake's left eye.

Chapter Twenty-Four

One month later. Yellowstone Wilderness, 1810

Daniel wrapped the buffalo robe tighter around his shoulders, trying to ward off the chill of the cold October wind. His hair whipped around his face. He gazed out across the gaping expanse of the canyon before him. Sitting on a rocky outcropping, he solemnly watched the brilliant yellow and red colors of the canyon walls change their shimmering hues with each passing moment as the morning sun's rays illuminated the rocks. Off in the distance, the mighty *E-chee-dick-karsh-ah-shay* roared as its turquoise waters plunged loudly several hundred feet deeper into the canyon. He never tired of this awesome spectacle in all the years he had come to this spot. This time, however, it brought no joy to his heart. Everywhere he looked, visions of Aimee materialized before his eyes. The sound of her voice echoed on the wind, sometimes so clearly, Daniel thought he was losing his mind.

"I want you to know that no matter what happens in the future, I will always love you. I've never loved anyone the way I love you. Please don't ever forget that."

Had he been wrong? Had she tried to tell him something that last day? With the way she clung to him the morning he left the cabin? The intensity and passion with which she made love to him the night of the storm, and her words of love couldn't have been acted.

He stiffened at the rustling sound of leaves behind him, but didn't bother to turn around. He had been aware of Elk Runner watching him from the trees for some time already.

229

"Why do you come here, brother?" he finally asked, his eyes still riveted on nature's splendor before him. He had wanted to share this spectacular place with Aimee, but had never gotten the chance.

Elk Runner approached, found a spot next to him, and lowered himself to the ground.

"Your father asked me to seek you out." Elk Runner peered sideways at him. Daniel let out a dismissive snort.

"He is dying, White Wolf. He asked to speak to you before he leaves this world and joins your mother."

Daniel didn't reply. What more could his father have to tell him? If he was asking for forgiveness, Daniel had already granted him that before he left the valley and their cabin three weeks ago. After a week of lying in bed, waiting for his body to heal, he had grown restless. He'd still been weak when he left to set out on his own to try and escape the anguish in his heart and head. Day after day, one fair-haired woman consumed his thoughts.

Aimee. His *gediki*. His heart song. Her scent lingered on the blankets and furs of his bed, tormenting his mind and body. He couldn't remain in the cabin any longer, the place that held such bittersweet memories.

He had told his father he was leaving to find which path he would take from hereon out. Zach had simply nodded in understanding. His parting words had been of forgiveness because he knew it was what his father wanted to hear. Daniel wasn't sure if he truly forgave the man for never telling him the truth about his birth. He had accepted it. What else could he do? He realized it didn't change who he was now. He had no desire to leave the mountains or seek out another way of life.

"He will not live much longer, White Wolf." Elk Runner interrupted his thoughts. "You must go and make peace with him."

"I've already made my peace with him," Daniel said indifferently.

"He has important words to share with you. Perhaps you have made your peace, but he has not. He cannot leave this world until he has truly made peace with you. He is your father," Elk Runner implored.

230

Daniel sighed heavily, and stood from his place on the rocks. He clutched the side of his abdomen. The wounds had healed on the outside, but certain movements still caused some discomfort. It was getting easier every day. He had even managed to remove the stitches himself, recalling how Aimee had removed Elk Runner's.

"Let's go, then," he said without emotion, and turned away from the canyon.

Two days later, Daniel quietly opened the door to the cabin and stepped inside. His father lay on his bunk. Sweat drenched his face and chest. His breathing came in quick and shallow gasps. Daniel barely recognized him. His father's eyes were sunken in his head, and his features were gaunt.

Daniel sat down on the edge of the bunk. "Hello, father," he said quietly. When Zach's eyes flew open, Daniel held a cup of water out to him. Zach took several swallows, then handed the cup back.

"I'm glad you came back, son," Zach said breathlessly, his voice a weak rasp. "It's time I joined your mother, but before I go, I want to do the right thing for once in my life."

Daniel's eyes narrowed. "I don't understand."

"Aimee Donovan," Zach said, then went into a coughing fit. A jolt of adrenaline shot through Daniel at the mention of her name.

"I've done wrong by her, and by you," Zach whispered. "I need to make this right before I go."

"Make what right, Father?" Daniel hissed between clenched teeth.

"I've lied to you all this time, son," Zach implored him with watery eyes. "I've kept the truth from you."

"What truth, Father? You told me about my birth. What more is there?" His voice rose in anger. What more could there possibly be?

Zach reached for the pouch around his neck. With shaking hands, he removed the snakehead, and held it out to Daniel.

"Remember, the right eye takes you to the future, the left eye brings you back," Zach said. "Take it. Go and bring her back. Then destroy this cursed thing."

231

Daniel stared blankly from the snakehead to his father's face. The man was losing his mind. When he didn't reach for the object, Zach sat up with great difficulty, and reached for Daniel's arm.

"Aimee Donovan is the one true path in your life, Daniel. Her intentions were good and honest from the beginning. I . . . I made her swear to me not to reveal my secret to anyone, most of all you. She kept that promise, even at great . . . personal sacrifice to herself and . . . to you. She is an honorable person. The lies and deception are mine." Zach's words came between labored breaths, and his forehead beaded with perspiration.

Daniel tried to absorb what his father told him.

"You falling in love with her never . . . entered my mind when I sent her here. Just as I never expected her . . . to fall in love with you." Zach met his penetrating stare. He took a deep breath, and continued. "She told me of her love for you, and begged me to let her stay here when I came to send her home. I . . . I had to forcibly remove her."

Daniel leapt to his feet from the bunk as if he'd been burned, and his eyes narrowed in anger. His jaw clenched and unclenched. He spun away from his father, and raked his hand through his hair. Aimee truly loved him? It wasn't a lie? His father forced her to leave.

"I've made wrong decisions all my life . . . hurting the people I care about. First . . . with your mother. She never wanted to leave New Orleans . . . and come into the wilderness with me. That was my dream. If she'd had a midwife . . . in the city, she might not have died. Then I've kept the truth from you . . . all this time . . ." Zach paused. His head fell back against the furs on the bunk, and he closed his eyes. "And finally Aimee," he continued. "I didn't think letting her stay here was for the best. Seeing her again when I brought you to the future . . . I should have brought her back with us then, but you . . . were so fightin' mad and didn't want to listen to anyone, and I was afraid you'd do yourself more harm."

Daniel slowly turned to face his father again. Zach raised himself up with great effort, and held out his arm, urging him to take the snake.

"Go and bring her back, Daniel. It's what you both want."
Zach sank back down into the furs right before another coughing
fit overtook him. Daniel sat down next to him and offered him
more water, but Zach waved it off.

"How will I find her?" Daniel asked quietly. A tiny shimmer
of hope dispersed the dark cloud hovering over his heart. Would
she take him back, forgive him, after the way he had treated her?
"I know nothing about the future."

Zach let out a bark-like laugh. "You've never had trouble
tracking anything in your life, son. Just remember, don't. . . don't
take any weapons with you when you go. It's a lesson I had to
learn. The hospital where I met her is called . . . argghhh." Zach
suddenly lurched forward and clutched his chest. His eyes opened
wide, and he gasped for air. Daniel grabbed his father's arm just as
the old man's body went limp. His eyes took on a glazed, lifeless
look, staring into nothing. Daniel eased him back into the furs.
His father's image became a blur as his own eyes grew moist.

"Go in peace, Father," he said quietly, and swiped a hand
across the old man's face to lower his eyelids. Countless minutes
passed before Daniel picked up the snakehead that had fallen to
the ground. He stared at it for a long time before stowing it safely
in the pouch around his neck.

* * *

Daniel blinked, and opened his eyes with a start at the loud
noises that came at him from all directions. He quickly pushed
himself off the hard ground, fighting off the dizziness that swept
over him. The belt around his waist felt too light without his knife
and tomahawk.

"What the hell, man! Get outta the street!" Someone
shouted, and Daniel found himself staring at the metal objects that
moved on their own that his father told him about.

Glancing quickly around, he noticed a number of people
several paces to the side of him scurrying about, and he darted in
their direction. No wonder his father had almost been killed by
one of these monsters. They moved at incredible speeds.

Daniel surveyed the unfamiliar scenes around him. His eyes
scanned the large structures that rose in a line beside him. This
must be the city, but nothing even vaguely resembled the world he

was used to. The air was hot and thick with foul odors he could not identify. Strange trees with long bare poles and fan-like large leaves in their canopies rose in an unnatural straight line in front of the buildings. He had never seen trees like these before.

He studied his surroundings. The horseless carriages moved endlessly up and down what must be a street, and he observed their movements for some time. They were everywhere. Even in Philadelphia, he had never seen such hustle and bustle. He had to find Aimee quickly. Staring at the moving monsters rushing by, his search might prove to be impossible. He had no idea how to track her in this unknown world.

"You lost, mister?"

Daniel whirled around to stare down at a young boy sitting astride a bright red contraption with two wheels at either end.

"Cool pants!" the boy said, when he didn't respond.

"Which direction is the hospital?" Daniel finally found his voice again.

"Which one?"

Daniel frowned. "I'm not sure."

"The closest one is Anaheim Memorial."

"Can you lead me to it?" he asked hopefully.

"Umm . . . sure. It's only a few blocks."

His spirits renewed, Daniel followed the boy through a labyrinth of streets until they stood before a huge building with the words *Anaheim Memorial Hospital* in large red letters at the entrance.

"Thank you for your help." He reached into the small pouch around his neck and pulled out a large curved claw, and handed it to the boy.

"Grizzly bear claw," Daniel said with a smile. The boy stared with his eyebrows drawn together. A Tukudeka boy would have reacted with sheer joy at such a gift.

"For real?"

"I killed the bear myself, and have the scars to prove it."

"You're just pulling my leg, mister. But thanks anyway." The boy stuffed the claw in a pocket in his britches, mounted the strange contraption, and took off. Daniel shook his head. He stared at the large letters on the building again, and headed for the wide transparent doors into the building, as he had seen several other people do. He shrank back momentarily when the doors opened on their own before he had even reached them.

Daniel was determined not to let anything in this strange world deter him from finding Aimee. His father had told him how unimaginable everything was in the future, and he certainly had been correct. He stood in a large hall, unsure of where to go. People moved past him, and everyone seemed to be in a hurry. He caught a few curious stares from several who passed by him. On the wall to his right, large white letters spelled out the word *Information.* Squaring his shoulders, he walked up to the huge curved desk, and noticed a dark-haired woman sitting on the other side. Her unnaturally long fingernails were painted a bright red. They were in constant motion, quickly moving over some tiny square pegs on a black shiny board on her desk.

"Can I help you?" The woman peered up at him from under her spectacles. Her eyes widened for a brief moment.

"I require information. I am searching for someone," Daniel said, and leaned forward.

"A patient?" The woman asked.

"No." He hesitated. "Her name is Aimee Donovan. She is a nurse."

"She works here?"

"I don't know." Daniel took a deep breath, noting the woman's contemplative look.

"I'm afraid I can't be of much help. There are hundreds of nurses employed here.

"Hundreds?" Daniel echoed. His shoulders sagged in defeat. This search might truly be impossible. How was he supposed to track someone who didn't leave any tracks in the traditional sense? How did one person search for another here in this time?

The woman must have seen the downtrodden look on his face. "Can you tell me anything else? What department does she work in?"

Daniel searched his memory for any information Aimee might have divulged about herself that could be useful to him now.

"I know she lives with a woman named Jana Evans." It was

all he could come up with.

"Jana Evans?" Someone behind him echoed the name. Daniel turned his head to find a heavyset Negro woman approach him. She wore clothing similar to what Aimee wore that day when his father brought him to this time for his injuries. The day he shunned her.

"Do you know her?" he asked hopefully, and gave her his full attention.

"I did a surgical internship a little over a year ago with a Jana Evans over at Orange County General," the woman said. Daniel understood nothing of what this woman had just told him, except that she seemed to know of Jana Evans. It was a start.

"How can I find her?" he asked eagerly.

The woman eyed him from top to bottom. "Who wants to know?"

"I do." Daniel's eyebrows furrowed.

"And who might you be?" She held her hand to her hips and leaned forward.

Daniel groaned inwardly. She wasn't going to make this easy.

"My name is Daniel Osborne. I'm searching for my wife. All I know is that she lives with a woman named Jana Evans."

"Your wife, huh?" Her eyebrows rose in such a way that left no doubt that she didn't believe a word he said.

Daniel inhaled another deep breath, and met the woman's hard stare unflinching. He couldn't afford to lose his temper now.

"Please, if you can help me find her."

The woman reached into her loose blue pants and pulled out a small black device, which she unfolded. Fascinated, Daniel watched as the unfolded part illuminated, and the woman prodded at it repeatedly with her fingers.

"Yeah, I still got her cellphone number. Do you want me to call her?"

"Call to her? Will she hear you?"

The woman's eyebrows shot up again and she shot him a skeptical look. Apparently he had said the wrong thing.

"Yes, please . . . call on her." Daniel groaned inwardly. He hated being at this woman's mercy, and that communicating with her had to be so difficult. The woman shot him one final piercing stare, then poked at the little device in her hand again, and held it to the side of her face. Daniel stood by, observing and listening, completely perplexed.

"Jana? Yeah, hi, this is Felicia Harding. I don't know if you remember me, but we interned together a year ago . . . Yeah, that's right! . . . They offered you a job? . . . Hey, that's great . . . No, no, I'm doing fine. I'm in peds at Anaheim Memorial . . . Hey, this is kinda weird, but I got some," – she gave Daniel a perusing once over – "Davy Crocket wannabe here. He says he knows you. Hang on." Looking at Daniel, she asked him, "whatcha say your name was again?"

Daniel gave it to her.

"He says his name's Daniel Osborne, and he thinks his wife is living with you." For some minutes, the woman merely grunted words of acknowledgement. Finally, she said, "Okay, Jana. Will do. Nice talking to ya." She folded the black device in half again, then turned her attention on him. "She says she's on her way, and I should tell you to stay put."

"What about Aimee?" He was almost afraid to ask.

"Didn't say nothing about her," Felicia shook her head and shrugged. "You can go wait over there." She waved in the direction of a row of peculiar-looking chairs lined up against the wall. "Jana should be here in twenty minutes or so."

"Thank you for your help," Daniel said sincerely, and strode over to take his place in one of the oddly shaped chairs. He discretely watched the people sitting around, while several openly stared at him. His heart rate increased. At least he had found Aimee's roommate.

Daniel didn't have long to wait when a slim woman with short brown hair, who looked vaguely familiar to him, walked through the glass doors. She wore blue form-fitting britches and a green shirt held up by a thin strap over each shoulder. The shoes on her feet could barely be called shoes. They were merely soles with the tops missing, and only a small band wrapped around one toe and the top of her feet. A black pouch was strapped over one shoulder.

Daniel bolted from the chair, and rushed over to meet her before she was barely in the building.

"Jana Evans?" he asked hopefully. The last time he had seen her, his mind had been foggy. The woman glared at him.

"Daniel," she addressed him coldly.

"You remember me?"

"Oh, yeah, I remember you," she said, not too friendly. Her eyes narrowed. "You're the guy who broke Aimee's heart."

He ran a hand through his hair, and inhaled deeply before he spoke. "I have come for her. I have no words to correct my mistake, only that I am sorry for the way I treated her."

"How do I know you're not going to hurt her again?" Jana asked, her voice icy.

"She is my heart song," Daniel said simply.

She watched him for a few intense moments. It was evident on her face that she was trying to come to a decision. Slowly, she nodded. "If you hurt her again, I'll kill you."

Daniel's eyebrows shot up in surprise at her words, sizing her up. Then his face lit up in a wide smile. "If I hurt her again, I won't stop you."

Chapter Twenty-Five

Aimee adjusted the flow rate on Mrs. Jenkin's fluids that fed into the old woman's arm. She raised her head to look across the expanse of the emergency room, unsure what had prompted her to do so. Just inside the double door that led to the waiting room stood a wide-chested man with shoulder-length black hair, dressed in tan buckskin britches and an off-white, loosely fitted cotton shirt. The string that held it together at the chest was tied in a loose knot. A wide leather belt encircled his waist, and a small leather pouch dangled around his neck. The moccasins he wore were a shade darker than his britches, and looked well worn.

Aimee inhaled sharply, and her hand flew to her mouth. "Daniel!" The name escaped her lips in a whispered gasp. Her other hand grabbed the safety rail of Mrs. Jenkin's hospital bed. Adrenaline flooded her system, and her knees turned to rubber.

"Are you all right, dear?" the elderly woman asked. Her eyes followed the line of Aimee's gaze. "Oh, my!" she exclaimed. "Isn't he a handsome fellow?"

Several nurses stopped what they were doing. Some whispered to each other while others stared openly.

"Ex . . . Excuse me for a moment," Aimee said softly to her patient after her breath returned. Her heart pounded so fiercely, she thought her ribs might crack. Time stood still, and everything moved in slow motion. Aimee couldn't focus on anything except the man waiting at the entrance doors. He stared back at her, his intense dark eyes drawing an invisible rope around her, beckoning her to him.

She didn't know how she'd moved across the room and stood before him now, her eyes glazed with unshed tears of disbelief. She still couldn't believe he was real and actually standing in front of her. Weeks ago, she had finally conceded that she'd never see him again. But three months of dreaming about Daniel after he vanished from her life hadn't erased the pain of her loss. What was he doing here now? His eyes, those intense eyes she knew so well, were locked onto her, smoldering dark with unspoken yearning. They seemed to devour her as she stood there. She didn't dare to move.

Her voice was shaky and weak when she finally spoke. "Daniel, what are you doing here? I thought you'd have destroyed the snake by now. Is it your father? Is he all right?"

"My father has joined my mother," he answered quietly.

"I'm . . . so sorry." Aimee raised her hand as if to touch him, hesitated, and curled her fingers around the stethoscope draped around her neck instead.

"Then why are you here?" she managed to ask. Seeing him now, after all these months, brought back all the feelings she had tried so desperately to overcome.

Daniel continued to stare at her. His eyes seemed to drink her up. Aimee's gaze didn't waver. It was as if they were the only two people in the world. No one else existed. The noise from the many heart monitors in the room faded, and people's voices became muffled in the background.

"I left something behind," he finally spoke, his voice soft and deep.

Aimee's eyebrows drew together. Part of her wanted to react in anger. Why would he do this to her? Why would he come back, to tear her apart all over again? She had hurt him deeply, and he hated her for her lies and deception. She blamed herself for his rejection of her three months ago, after his surgery.

"I didn't come across anything of yours, except your destroyed clothes, after you left. What is so important that you would feel the need to travel all this . . . time . . . to retrieve?"

"My heart song." There was no hesitation in his husky answer.

Aimee blinked. "Your . . . what? What are you saying?" Her heart pounded in her chest, and the tears spilled from her eyes.

"My life has been empty these past weeks. It holds no

meaning anymore without you. I came here to ask for your forgiveness."

Aimee didn't need to hear any more. She threw herself at him, and wrapped her arms around his waist. She inhaled his wonderful woodsy scent that was his alone, and spilled her tears onto his chest. His arms crushed her to him, and a long sigh escaped his lungs.

"I once said that I would follow you to the ends of the world." Aimee felt rather than heard his words. "I now know that I would follow you across the expanse of time as well."

Aimee raised her head, and blinked away the tears to get a clearer view of his face. His eyes were dark and warm, reflecting the love in his heart. Cupping her face in his hands, Daniel tilted her head up as he bent down and claimed her lips in an agonizingly slow kiss.

Several whistles and good-natured catcalls from her coworkers brought her back to her senses. She cleared her throat and stepped away from Daniel, smiling brightly.

"We've never had an audience before," she whispered.

Daniel's wide unabashed smile melted her heart.

She reluctantly took a step back, afraid he would disappear again if she let go. She ushered him out the double door behind him into the empty waiting room.

"How did you find me?" She barely spoke the words when Daniel pulled her into a fierce embrace that sucked the air out of her lungs, and lifted her off the ground.

"I am a good tracker." He breathed into her hair.

Someone cleared their throat loudly behind them, and Aimee pulled herself out of Daniel's arms. Jana stood in the corner, a wide smile on her face.

"I haven't seen you light up like this in five months," Jana commented. "It's good to have the old you back."

"You knew?" Aimee asked, her eyes darting from her to Daniel. "You brought him here!"

"Long story." Jana waved her off. "He found me, actually. I'll tell you later. Right now I think you should get Daniel Boone out of here."

Aimee touched Daniel's face, and ran her hands down his

arms just to make sure he was real, terrified she'd wake up any moment now to a dream.

"I was just about to do change-of-shift rounds," she said. "You'd better be here when I get back." She looked up into the deep brown eyes that followed her into her dreams each night.

"I'm not going anywhere without you," he promised.

"We'll wait here. I'll make sure he stays put," Jana assured her.

Aimee clasped his face between her hands and kissed him one more time, then headed back into the ER. She returned half an hour later, ready to go. Jana held her back. "Um, drive slow, okay."

Aimee's forehead wrinkled at her friend's words.

"Your hero here is terrified of cars, especially riding in one," Jana whispered. "You should have seen his face on our drive over here from Anaheim Memorial." She grinned. Aimee nodded in understanding. She turned to a silently waiting Daniel, when Jana called to her. "I'll see you at home?"

Aimee understood what she was really asking. She nodded in reassurance. "Yes. I won't leave without a proper good-bye this time."

* * *

Aimee pulled into her designated parking spot at the condominium complex and put the car in park. She glanced over at the passenger side again for the millionth time since the drive home from the hospital. Daniel had suggested walking when she led him to her car. It took some coaxing for her to finally get him to agree to get into the vehicle. The entire drive home, he had sat silently, his hands in his lap, curled into tight fists that made his knuckles turn white.

"Payback, Daniel," Aimee said with a mischievous grin, and helped him undo the seatbelt. He looked up at her, his face ashen. "Payback?"

"I was scared to death on that travois when you practically walked us through a herd of bison that first day," Aimee explained. The color slowly returned to Daniel's face after he extracted himself from the car.

"This is your home?" Daniel asked, and followed her

through the front door into the living room of her condo. His eyes roamed the bright interior of the room, lingering on the painting over the fireplace.

"This was my home up until five months ago," Aimee said. She turned to face him, and reached up to touch his face. "My home has been with you since the day I went back in time," she whispered.

Daniel covered her hand with his. His gaze bore into hers. "You are sure you want to leave your life, everything you know behind, and live with me?"

"I've never been more sure of anything. I missed you so much." Her voice was raw with emotion, and the tears streamed down her cheeks. "There were days I wanted to die, thinking then I might be with you again."

"Shhh," Daniel whispered. He put a finger to her lips. "Don't ever wish that." He ran his hands through her hair, then cupped her face and tilting her head back. He claimed her mouth in a slow kiss that made her go weak in the knees.

"I never wanted to lie to you, Daniel. I hope you can forgive me. You have no idea how much I wanted to tell you everything, and now I feel like a great weight has been lifted off my shoulders, because I can finally be completely honest with you."

Daniel stroked her hair and held her to him. "My father told me you were bound by a promise to him. I should never have doubted you. I'm sorry for my behavior when he brought me here."

She looked up and searched his face for several moments. "Are you okay with everything he's told you?"

Daniel inhaled deeply before he answered. He shrugged. "It doesn't change who I am. It's been a difficult thing to understand, but it doesn't really matter, does it? All I know is that this . . . device brought you to me, and that's all that's important."

Aimee led him into the kitchen. "Jana should be home soon," she said as she turned to face him again. "I want to say goodbye, and then we can leave."

Daniel nodded. His eyes roamed around the kitchen. He ran his hand across the smooth granite countertop, the oak cabinets, the black cooktop. Aimee enjoyed watching him, captivated. It was like watching the wonderment on a child's face making a first discovery. She jumped when the door opened and closed, and Jana stormed in. The urgent look on her face startled Aimee.

"Brad's on his way. Apparently he saw you leave the hospital with Daniel."

Aimee groaned loudly. All this time, Brad had still not given up. Daniel's expression darkened.

"The man you were promised to?"

"He has no hold on me," Aimee assured him.

"I always knew I'd have to face him some day," Daniel said.

Aimee shot him a worried look. "Oh, no you don't," she said, shaking her head adamantly. They all turned their heads at the loud knock on the door.

"Should I let him in?" Jana asked apprehensively.

"Let's get it over with," Aimee sighed. She walked to the door and opened it slowly.

"Can I come in?" Brad asked gruffly. He didn't wait for an answer, and elbowed his way past her.

"What do you want?" Aimee asked. His eyes fixated on something behind her.

"What the hell is he doing back?" Brad roared angrily, and pushed further into the room.

The two men sized each other up. Brad was actually several inches taller, but Daniel was broader, with more muscle mass from a lifetime of hard physical activity. He took a step in front of Aimee to put himself between her and Brad. His stare was unwavering.

"I have returned for my wife," he said in a low tone.

Brad stared, dumfounded. "Your wife?" he bellowed. He shot a disbelieving look at Aimee. "What the hell is going on, Aimee?"

When Daniel moved a half step closer to Brad, she put a hand on his arm.

"Please, can we all just calm down," she pleaded. "Brad, you shouldn't be here. You and I have been over for a long time. I keep telling you that. When are you going to understand that you can't have everything you want? Including me."

"Dammit, I'm going to have my say," he shouted. He

stepped around Daniel and advanced on her. "He's nowhere near good enough for you, don't you see? You're used to the finer things in life, not some backwoods existence. Don't you dare tell me you're going to go off with him again." Brad grabbed hold of her arm and continued to shout. "You are supposed to marry me!"

"Unhand her now." Daniel's voice was deathly calm as he spoke. Aimee recognized that tone as the same one he had used moments before he killed the two French trappers.

"You ruined everything for me." Brad wheeled to face Daniel. "Ever since she came back from that trip where she met you. What kind of crazy notions did you fill her head with? She was supposed to marry me. I can give her anything she wants. She can have a life of luxury and comfort. You look like you're nothing but a vagrant. What can you possibly offer her?" The look in his eyes was one of pure contempt. With a furious roar he took a swing at Daniel, his fist balled up tight. Daniel ducked easily, and Brad's momentum sent him stumbling forward. With a lightning fast move, Daniel grabbed Brad's arm. He twisted it behind his opponent's back and stepped around him. At the same time he put a chokehold on him with his other arm.

"Daniel, no!" Aimee cried. "Don't hurt him, please."

Daniel's eyes blazed with fury, his jaw clenched, and he stared at Aimee. He didn't lighten his hold on Brad, who gasped for air, unable to move.

"Daniel," Aimee pleaded. Seconds passed before his body relaxed. The fire in his eyes still simmered, but he brought his arm away from Brad's neck, and pushed him away. Brad stumbled across the room, and leaned forward, one hand on his neck. He coughed and gasped for breath.

"No man touches my wife and lives," Daniel said in the same low, calm tone he'd used before. He seemed completely at ease, as if he was merely passing the time with someone. "You are fortunate that she is a kind-hearted woman." He grabbed the back of Brad's shirt and slammed him into the front door. Pulling him back, he yanked the door open and shoved him out, then gave the door a kick to shut it behind him.

Daniel slowly turned to face her. Jana stood in the small

hallway that separated the kitchen from the living room, her hands on her mouth.

"I've never seen anything like it," Jana finally said, and moved to stand by Aimee. She gave Daniel a wide berth. "He could have killed Brad without even blinking."

"Yes, he could have. But he's not a violent man," Aimee reassured her friend.

"He's positively hot," Jana whispered. "He would absolutely kill to protect you. Brad got what he deserved. He needed to have his ass kicked a long time ago." She smiled as Aimee stared at her, then the two women giggled.

"Your very own superman," Jana finally commented, appreciation in her eyes as she glanced at Daniel, who still stood at the door, a solemn look on his face. Her eyes darted from Aimee to Daniel. "Um, I have something I need to do upstairs," she said abruptly, then rushed off.

Aimee walked up to him. What was going through her mountain man's mind now? She didn't like the somber set of his face.

"He's right," Daniel said, taking hold of Aimee's hand. She shook her head slightly, puzzled by his words. "I have nothing to offer you. Nothing but a life full of danger and hardship."

Aimee inhaled sharply. "A life I gladly accept and want, as long as I can be with you," she choked out. She threw her arms around him, pulling his head down to kiss him in desperation. He was not changing his mind now about taking her with him, was he? Daniel wrapped her in his arms, melting into her kiss. He pulled away to kiss her nose and eyes, her mouth again, then her neck. He cradled her head in his hands, and Aimee opened her eyes.

"If you are sure you want to spend the rest of your life with me . . . in my world," Daniel whispered against her lips.

"We should get going," Aimee said hastily, and pulled away. "I just want to get my journal."

"Nothing else?" Daniel asked. His hands moved to her shoulders.

"No." She shook her head. "This has to be a clean break. We can't keep living in two worlds, just like your father said. I want to be with you, in your world. That means I have to leave everything modern behind. The snake head has to be destroyed when we return to your time."

Daniel nodded in understanding.

Aimee retrieved her journal from her bedroom. She glanced around one last time, fingering the photographs of her parents on her dresser. Making a hasty decision, she pulled one of the pictures out of its frame, along with the one of her and Jana at their college graduation.

"I guess this is good bye, then." Aimee turned to see Jana standing in the doorway. Aimee rushed to her, and the two women hugged and cried.

"I have to do this," Aimee whispered.

"I know," Jana sniffed. "I know. The two of you were meant to be together." She smiled sadly. "It's as plain as day when I see you together. Who knows?" She sniffed again, and wiped at her eyes. "Maybe that was the grand plan all along with this time travel thing. You and Daniel are two people who are meant to be together, but some glitch in time prevented it from happening. Maybe he was never supposed to go back to his time when he was born," she added hopefully.

"I can't ask him to live here." Aimee shook her head. "He'd never fit in."

"No, I understand that."

Daniel reached out to shake Jana's hand when she followed Aimee down the stairs. Instead, she gave him a friendly hug. Aimee giggled at the surprised look on his face.

"Keep her safe, and yourself as well," Jana said.

"I will protect her with my life," Daniel said, smiling at Aimee.

Jana nodded. "I have no doubt you will."

Jana and Aimee embraced again, the tears flowing freely.

"I'll write to you, whenever I get homesick," Aimee whispered in a raspy voice.

At Jana's baffled look, she elaborated. "Remember that hike we did last year down by Hellroaring Creek?" Jana nodded. "That funny rock formation that reminded us of Mickey Mouse? I will leave my journal somewhere under those rocks. I'll mark the spot somehow so it won't be obvious, but you'll be able to recognize it. Go and find my journal, okay?"

"Okay." Jana wiped her nose on a tissue she pulled from her jeans pocket. "But couldn't you pick an easier hike?" she laughed. "That one was murder."

Daniel removed the snakehead from its leather pouch around his neck, and handed it to Aimee. He nodded a farewell to Jana, and pulled Aimee into his arms. The two gazed intently into each other's eyes, deep brown meeting sparkling blue.

"My heart song," Daniel whispered, and claimed her mouth, just as she put a finger to the snake's left eye.

Epilogue

Jana Evans wiped the tears from her eyes and sniffed. She closed the old, leather-bound journal, and smiled despite the tears. It had been seven months since Aimee and Daniel time traveled back in time to 1810. Jana had wasted no time to head to Yellowstone when the trails were accessible again after winter to find Aimee's journal. She found it exactly where Aimee said it would be. It was preserved well, bound and wrapped in layers of oiled leather. The pages looked worn and old, but they were completely intact and undamaged.

Jana sat in the busy lobby of the historic Old Faithful Inn, and opened the journal, carefully turning the pages to re-read several passages.

October, 1810

It's so good to be back! I am excited to start my new life in this wonderful land with my wonderful husband by my side.

We got rid of the time travel device, just as Zach had wanted. It turned out to be indestructible – fire doesn't damage it, and Daniel couldn't get an ax through it, either. So we disposed of it. I won't say how or where, but I am confident that it will never be found again.

December 25th, 1810

Our first Christmas, and we are completely snowed in! I'm so glad I made Daniel drag a Christmas tree into the cabin several days ago, otherwise it would be Christmas without one. This is his

249

first Christmas tree, and it took a little explaining. He couldn't understand the point of chopping down a tree to bring into the cabin unless it was for firewood, but I think he enjoyed helping me decorate it. Later today I have to give him his Christmas present. I'm just not quite sure how that's going to go over. I wonder how he's going to react when I tell him that we are expecting a baby by summer. No doubt he's going to want to usher me straight out of the mountains when I tell him the news.

July 20th, 1811

Daniel and I became parents today. Twin boys. We named them Zachariah and Matthew, after our fathers. My pregnancy was fairly easy, except for Daniel tormenting me. I felt like a complete invalid. The man wouldn't allow me to carry so much as a bucket of water since Christmas. And of course he wanted to take me to Philadelphia or somewhere back east. He even said he was going to try and retrieve the time travel device (no chance of that happening!) so I could come to the future to give birth in a modern hospital. In the end, Elk Runner and Little Bird convinced him that I would be fine to give birth here. Little Bird and Daniel's foster mother Gentle Sun came and stayed with us for weeks before the birth, at Daniel's insistence, of course. Gentle Sun was a great midwife, and the babies are both healthy and strong. Daniel is a very proud papa.

Jana turned the pages gingerly. Aimee and Daniel had two more children over the years, another boy, and a girl. As more and more fur trappers traveled through the region, Daniel and Aimee had set up a trading post. Aimee told of how she had met Jim Bridger, Jedediah Smith, and some other famous mountain men - except at the time, they weren't all that famous yet. When Jana turned to the last page, more than fifteen years had passed.

September 5th, 1828

Well, I guess this is my last entry. Jana, if you are reading this, I want you to know that I don't regret my decision for a second. I can't imagine my life any other way. This is where I was destined to be. Daniel is the love of my life, and our children get *to grow up in Wonderland! I only wish for you to find the same happiness that I have found. You are, and always will be, my best friend.*

Love, Aimee Osborne, aka Dosa haiwi

Jana closed the journal just as a cold breeze hit her. The front doors of the parlor opened, and a group of jovial hikers led by a ranger walked in. Jana blew her nose and wiped new tears from her eyes.

"Now what would cause such a lovely woman to cry on such a beautiful day here in Yellowstone?"

Jana looked up, startled by the ranger who had sat down next to her on the couch she occupied. A split second passed, and Jana shrunk back in shock.

"Daniel?" she asked, staring incredulously at the man sitting next to her.

"Yeah, my name's Daniel," he said, smiling and pointing to the name badge on his uniform. "But most everyone just calls me Dan."

Jana stared at the name badge, and back at the man's face. The badge clearly read "Daniel Osborne".

"How? What?" she stammered. She continued to stare at the man's handsome face. There were some subtle differences from what she remembered of Daniel's features, but the resemblance was remarkable. The black hair was cropped short in a modern military style, and the intense dark stare that she remembered was absent. This Daniel's chocolate eyes sparkled brightly.

"You look like you've seen a ghost." The ranger flashed her a radiant smile. "Are you okay?"

"Yeah, I'm fine," Jana replied slowly. "You remind me of someone."

"Well, I hope that's a good thing." He grinned. "So, you didn't answer my question."

"Huh?"

"What is a lovely lady doing in this grand park, crying. There is no such thing as a bad day in Yellowstone."

"I was reading." Jana shrugged, and fingered the leather bound journal in her hands.

"Tell you what." Dan patted her on the knee. "I just got back from a six hour hike, and I'm real hungry and thirsty. Would you care to join me for dinner and a drink? I'm off duty as of now."

"Sure, I'd love to." She was still staring at him, disbelief on her face. "Can I ask you something?" she asked tentatively.

"Sure."

"Has your family lived in this area long?" Jana realized what an odd question that was, but she had to find out if her suspicions were true.

Dan laughed. "My family has roots here since time began. I think my great, great, great, great, something great-grandfather was one of the first fur trappers in this region. I was named after him. Legend has it he fell head over heels in love with a woman who appeared out of nowhere in the Yellowstone wilderness, and they lived happily ever after. What a weird question to ask, though."

"Well, Dan." Jana stood up. "It's about to get a lot weirder."

He rose from his seat and led her toward the lodge's restaurant. "Okay, now I'm mighty curious."

Jana assessed him quickly as they walked. Even the height and body type matched the original Daniel.

"Not only are you named after your ancestor, but you could be his twin brother." Jana smiled at the perplexed look on his face. She didn't give him a chance to react further to her statement. She held up Aimee's journal, and continued, "I hope they serve something pretty stiff to drink here, because you're going to need it after I'm done with the story I'm about to tell you."

THE END

Dear Reader

If you enjoyed Yellowstone Heart Song, please help others discover the book, and consider leaving a short review on Amazon.

The adventure continues with Book 2 in the Yellowstone Romance Series, <u>Yellowstone Redemption</u>. Currently, there are five full-length novels, three novellas, and a short story in this series. There are three more full-length novels planned (first of those to be released late summer/fall 2015)

Many of my readers have asked for a timeline for both the Yellowstone series as well as the Teton series, since the two are somewhat related (by setting and time period) and characters from one series make cameo appearances in the other.

A prologue and three first chapters did not make it into the final version of Yellowstone Heart Song. To read about Aimee's encounter with Zach before she time traveled, and to check out the timeline, please visit my blog: <u>www.peggylhenderson.com</u>

I hope you enjoyed Yellowstone Heart Song, the first installment in the Yellowstone Romance Series. I love Yellowstone National Park, and my family and I visit the park every summer for two weeks. Over the years, I've enjoyed learning about the history of the park and its surroundings.

I took the liberty to exercise literary license with some dates and events of the area, but my descriptions of the landscape are as true as I can make it, from memory, photographs, as well as having visited and seen the places I describe in the novel.

The Lewis and Clark expedition of 1804-06 didn't come through the park, having travelled a route further to the north. So, they missed out on seeing the great natural wonders of the area. They did name the Madison River in 1805 for James Madison,

Secretary of State under President Thomas Jefferson. Its origin is in the Madison Valley as described in the book, where the Gibbon River and Firehole River join together, and it flows well outside the park boundaries.

The first white man credited with seeing the area was John Colter, a member of the Lewis and Clark Expedition. Supposedly, he came through the area in 1806 after leaving the expedition. The area was termed "Colter's Hell" after he described some hot springs. It is now believed that he never actually saw the Yellowstone geothermal features, but some hot springs to the south.

No white men lived in the area during the time of this story. When the era of the trappers and mountain men started in the early 1820's, more and more white men travelled through the area, but none built permanent homes. The winters on the Yellowstone Plateau were too harsh for year-round living. The only permanent, year round human residents were the Sheepeater Shoshone.

I want to thank my wonderful critique partner and friend, Carol Spradling, for her wealth of comments, insights, and infinite patience with me while working on this book. Without her constant nudging and prodding, this story would not be where it is today, and would be collecting dust in a dark corner of my computer hard drive. Thank you, Carol, for believing in me, and giving me the courage to send my baby out into the world.

My editor, Barbara Ouradnik, for encouraging me each and every day. Thank you for your friendship and support, and for believing in this story.

Also, thanks to my husband, Richard, for introducing me to the Great Outdoor so many years ago. I may not be at the point where I go backpacking, but you've got me hiking in the wilderness and actually enjoying it. And thank you for doing the laundry so I could write.

~Peggy

Also by Peggy L Henderson

Excerpt from *Yellowstone Redemption*

"I have to talk to your mother, Sarah." Chase couldn't believe what Sarah had revealed. She was clueless, but to him it was as obvious as day and night. No one could make up stories as accurate as what Sarah described. If her mother had time traveled, perhaps she knew how it was possible, and it would get him home. But why did she stay in this time? A sinking feeling came over him. What if it was a one-way ticket? Had she been stuck here, too? Without any other recourse, had she married Sarah's father out of necessity. Chase frowned. As difficult as it was for him to be here, he couldn't imagine what it must have been like for a modern woman, stranded in the past. Marriage to a man from this time was probably her best option. Chase had to have some answers.

"Can you take me to this rendezvous place?"

Sarah's eyes widened. "No, that's not possible."

"Why not?"

"Because I am not allowed to travel there on my own." Chase frowned. "I'm going with you. You wouldn't be alone."

"The way leads straight through Blackfoot country. Any white man, especially one traveling alone, will put his life in danger. The Blackfoot are a hostile tribe."

He shook his head, his eyebrows drawing together. He didn't get it. "But your parents are white," he argued.

Sarah laughed. "My father trades with them as well as all other tribes in this region. My mother is a skilled healer. If anything happens to them, the wrath of many other nations will descend on the Blackfoot, and they know it. They would not harm my parents."

Chase sat on the hard ground, the chill of the earth seeping up into his body. The fire crackled loudly. Sarah's features danced in the shadows, illuminated by the flames. He held his head between his hands.

One month.

Somehow he had to convince Sarah to take him to her parents sooner. He didn't want to be here that long. He needed some answers now. He glanced at her. She sat quietly, stroking her dog's neck. Her fingers moved slowly through the mutt's fur. Chase pictured her hand in his hair, stroking him . . . Irrational jealousy swept over him. *You're insane, Russell. Jealous of a dog?*

These feelings for her confused, and scared, the hell out of him. All the more reason he needed to get home.

"All right. I'll go back to Madison with you," he blurted out. "I hope your mother can give me some answers."

Made in the USA
San Bernardino, CA
06 December 2016